Girl in Red Velvet

Margaret James

Where heroes are like chocolate – irresistible!

Published 2018 by Choc Lit Limited
Penrose House, Crawley Drive, Camberley, Surrey GU15 2AB, UK
www.choc-lit.com

A CIP catalogue record for this book is available
from the British Library

ISBN: 978-1-78189-426-2

Printed and bound in Great Britain by Clays Ltd, Elcograf S.p.A.

Acknowledgements

As always, a huge thank you to the brilliant
team at Choc Lit whose members have all
worked so hard on this novel with me.

Thank you to my designer who created the beautiful
cover, and thank you also to the lovely ladies on
the Choc Lit Tasting Panel who liked this story
enough to recommend publication: Betty, Zeynep,
Isobel J, Alicia B, Stephanie H, Els, Hilary B, Sigi,
Sally C, Kim L, Stacey R, Jenny K and Cathy G.

The Denham Family Tree – Charton Minster Series

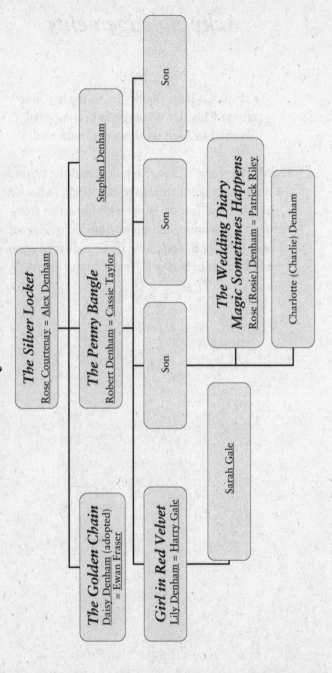

The Silver Locket
Rose Courtenay = Alex Denham

The Golden Chain
Daisy Denham (adopted)
= Ewan Fraser

The Penny Bangle
Robert Denham = Cassie Taylor

Stephen Denham

Son

Son

Son

Girl in Red Velvet
Lily Denham = Harry Gale

Sarah Gale

The Wedding Diary
Magic Sometimes Happens
Rose (Rosie) Denham = Patrick Riley

Charlotte (Charlie) Denham

Prologue

April 1970

You can't do this, you fool, thought Lily Denham.

But she went on walking and, as she made her anxious way between the rows of guests towards the registrar, she saw them standing on the right – the groom's side – at the front.

Their practically-identical dark heads were much too close together.

What could they be saying?

Harry and Max: her two best friends: the men she loved with all her heart, with all her soul, albeit in different ways ...

One was a rock, a shield, a comforter: a man who'd always be a good provider, a perfect father for their perfect children. He was everything a woman with any sense could ever want or need.

The other was wild, exciting, challenging: his children would be brave and double-daring, and with him her life would always be one big adventure.

She'd never dreamed she'd need to make this choice. So did she have the courage to make it now?

Perhaps.

It's not too late, she thought. I could drop this bunch of flowers, tear off this veil, hitch up my skirt and run, be out of here.

She glanced up at her father who was walking by her side. Dad, do something, she beseeched him silently. Somebody do something – anything?

The music stopped, and so did Lily, and her father went to sit beside her mother on the left. The registrar smiled at the happy couple and welcomed everybody to the ceremony on this lovely day.

The room was overheated and the scent of hothouse flowers was overpowering. Lily felt the perspiration trickling down her spine and beading on her forehead. The bodice of her dress was far too tight. She felt light-headed and wondered if she'd faint.

'I'm sorry, but I need some air,' she gasped. She turned to dash straight back the way she'd come, leaving everybody open-mouthed.

Part 1

October 1966
–October 1969

Chapter One

Lily Denham gazed all round her beautiful white-painted study-bedroom with its elegant sash windows overlooking formal gardens, and she felt a surge of satisfaction. She'd actually arrived.

She'd done everything the hard way, too – through the state school system. She had also won a scholarship. So Lily's academic gown was a calf-length scholar's, with long, wide sweeping sleeves, not a commoner's hip-length sleeveless thing with silly streamers.

Now, her mum and dad were no doubt heading home to Dorset. She'd turned down all their offers of an early lunch, of helping her unpack her stuff, of going for a stroll around the town. She wanted them to leave. She wanted more than anything to be grown up at last.

She unlocked her trunk, took out her precious Singer sewing machine and put it on her desk. Books in the bookcase next – what a novelty, to have a bookcase of her own! Clothes in the wardrobe, too – her mum would be so shocked and ask her if she had a temperature because at home her clothes lived on her bedroom floor.

She placed the box of PG Tips, the couple of mugs, the jar of Nescafé and the shiny new electric kettle next to the sewing machine. Very student-like, she told herself, and very cosmopolitan. After all, back home in Dorset, teabags lived in caddies, not on desks, and jars of instant coffee lived in cupboards. But now she was an undergraduate, and her new room was looking exactly like an undergraduate's should.

After twenty minutes of arranging family photographs, however, and after colour-coding, then straightening, the spines of all her Penguin paperbacks, she was getting bored. She went on to the landing, looked around. There was no sign of any other students. They must be coming later.

She glanced out of the window. It was a gorgeous autumn afternoon, all gold and glowing. She had an invitation to meet her personal tutor at two o'clock, but she still had several hours to fill.

She decided she would walk down Norham Gardens, take a better look at all the grand Victorian Gothic houses she'd noticed when she'd come to Oxford for her interview, imagining how amazing it must be to live in one.

Or how amazing it had been a hundred years ago, for these days the enormous redbrick mansions, with their turrets, curlicues and gargoyles, were probably divided into student flats. They'd be full of mismatched furniture and overflowing rubbish bins, not to mention stinking socks and toxic trainers if the students happened to be boys. She had three brothers and knew all about the sordid personal non-hygiene of disgusting boys.

She reached a narrow alleyway, found it led into the green oasis of the University Parks, and that was when she saw them – a couple of teenage boys in jeans and rugby shirts. They were pushing and shoving one another, play-fighting and laughing.

They stopped to stare at Lily, who was wearing her new black leather jacket, her favourite scarlet dress that was her own creation – a velvet smock with tiny silver bells sewn all around the hemline and elaborate beading on the bodice – and lots of ethnic jewellery: bangles by the dozen and a cornelian pendant the colour of her dress.

'It's the Red Queen,' said one of the play-fighters.

'It's Tweedledum and Tweedledee,' said Lily.

'Or maybe you're an Amazon?' said Tweedledum, twisting over sideways and shielding his eyes in a pantomime of being overawed as he gazed up at Lily. 'You're extremely tall.'

'But not *too* tall,' said Tweedledee, whose manners were clearly better than his friend's.

'Debatable, I think,' said Tweedledum, who Lily noticed wore a golden earring; just the one. It made him look like an apprentice pirate.

'It's my heels,' she told them, kicking off her crimson platform shoes, the ones she'd saved for weeks to buy from Stead and Simpson, and which had got her stared at in the streets of Dorchester, and commented on as well:

Did you see that maid?

The girl looks like a lampshade in a brothel.

You know her father is a headmaster?

I'm surprised her mother lets her out dressed up like that.

You know what they say about red shoes.

She'll go to the bad, you mark my words.

'Look, I'm pretty average,' she continued, standing on the grass in stockinged feet. 'Oh, all right. I'm average-on-the-tall-side, I suppose; taller than you, at any rate. You two are hobbits. I'm an elf.'

'We stand reproved,' said Hobbit One, the pirate.

'Did you just come up?' asked Hobbit Two.

'Come up?' Lily frowned.

'Did you arrive today?'

'Oh, yes – an hour or two ago.'

'So you're a student?'

'Yes.'

'What college?'

'Lady Margaret Hall.'

'You mean LMH. Only a tourist would say Lady Margaret Hall. You've had lunch?'

'Not yet.'

'You must be hungry, then?'

'A bit,' admitted Lily.

'We're absolutely starving, so—'

'—do you fancy coming with us to Fuller's?'

'What is Fuller's?'

'What is Fuller's?' Both the hobbits mimed astonishment. 'It's the most famous café in the world. Or in Oxford, anyway. Its walnut cake is legendary.'

'So if you would not object to being seen with hobbits?'

'Or maybe you consort only with elves?'

'I could fancy walnut cake,' said Lily, laughing.

'Great, let's go,' said Hobbit One.

Lily had always realised she would grow up to be tall, and she had never been self-conscious. Or not about her height, at any rate. Most women in her family were tall and proud of it. They never slouched. They stood up straight and wore high heels that made them even taller. She did, too.

As for her hair, however – she'd always hated it. Blue-black and wildly curling, it massed around her head like a great halo in a photographic negative, and she longed for naturally smooth and silky tresses like Twiggy's or Jean Shrimpton's.

She did her best to imitate their looks, conditioning her crazy mane religiously. She ironed it as smooth as it would go, much to the amusement of her brothers when they caught her practically lying on the ironing board. She streaked it blonde with hydrogen peroxide from the bathroom cabinet. When the weather wasn't damp, it sometimes looked all right, but she knew it would always be a trial.

Glancing at the hobbits, she supposed they stood about five-eight to her five-ten. Dark-haired, dark-eyed and solid-looking, a practised double act, they were so similar in looks, speech and behaviour that she guessed they were related.

'So, hobbits: are you brothers, cousins, twins?' she asked as they made their way down Keble Road and then along St Giles into town.

'No, just friends,' said Hobbit Two.

'But joined at the proverbial hip,' said Hobbit One.

'That must be very awkward for you when one needs a bath? Or maybe you don't bother?'

'We stand out in the rain,' said Hobbit Two.

'Do you have a name, Red Queen?' asked Hobbit One.

'I'm Lily – Lily Denham. What about you hobbits? Do you have names and are you students, too?'

'I'm Harry Gale,' said Hobbit Two.

'I'm Max Farley and we're both at Christ Church.'

'We came up yesterday.'

'So you're exploring, too?'

'Yes, I suppose we must be.'

The Fuller's walnut cake was excellent, and Lily soon felt comfortably full.

The beer at The Golden Cross in Cornmarket was excellent, as well; too excellent, in fact.

When Max had suggested going for a pint or two, she didn't want to tell the hobbits that she didn't know if she liked beer. Or if she liked alcohol at all. She wasn't yet eighteen and she had never been inside a pub.

But when they went into The Golden Cross, a gloomy

rabbit warren of a place, black-panelled and so full of smoke that she could hardly see where she was going, she suddenly felt so lost and so confused that she owned up.

'You've never been inside a pub?' repeated Harry, opening his mouth as wide as it would go.

'I'm not eighteen until next month,' said Lily. 'So it's against the law. You look like the village idiot when you do that, you know.'

'That's because he *is* the village idiot,' said Max. 'So – pints of best all round, then?'

'Obviously, idiot yourself,' said Harry.

Lily and Harry sat down at a table. Max brought the drinks and Lily took a wary, nervous sip. But then she took a less reluctant sip, and then a rounded mouthful, and then a greedy gulp. Yes, this beer is very nice, she thought. It's quite refreshing, too. She drank some more.

'You're doing well for someone who's a novice,' Harry said five minutes later, looking at Lily's almost-empty glass. 'You're a natural, aren't you?'

'Yes, well done, Red Queen,' said Max as he passed his own empty glass to Harry. 'Gale, it's your round.'

'Now we've bought you drinks, you have to tell us all your secrets,' Harry said as he put another golden pint in front of Lily.

She was suddenly feeling rather drowsy. But this morning she'd got up quite early, so it was not surprising. 'What do you want to know?' she asked.

'Do you have any sisters?'

'Do they look like you?'

'Or are they pretty?'

'Do you horrid boys have any brothers?' Lily picked up her glass and drank down half her beer in seconds. 'Do they look, speak and behave like you? Or are they handsome, intellectual and charming?'

'We should get this girl a pie,' said Harry.

'Yes, soak up the alcohol a bit.' Max shot a glance at Lily, dark eyes narrowed. 'Do you need a pie, Red Queen?'

'Yes, she does, and I'll have steak and kidney,' Harry told him, handing Max some coins.

'I'll have minsh and onion, if they've got it,' Lily slurred. 'Otherwishe, I'll have shteak and kidney, too.'

Max stood up and went to order pies.

Lily watched him go and realised there were two of him. She must be really tired, she decided, to be seeing double. Or was she dehydrated?

She was also hungry. She must have had that walnut cake at least an hour ago, and hunger made you feel light-headed, didn't it, and perhaps it gave you double vision, too?

She must drink more beer and eat her pie.

Chapter Two

The afternoon took on a mellow glow.

Lily mellowed, too.

Max and Harry told her jokes and clowned around and made her laugh a lot. She thought: these boys aren't horrid, after all. They're kind and generous. They're amusing, too. What more could you ask of boys – of anyone, in fact?

But now she wondered if she'd had enough to drink? How much beer did you need to drink to make you drunk? Maybe she could manage one last pint, but then she should go back to LMH, get changed and go to meet her tutor.

She glanced down at her watch. She saw that it was half past two. But how could it be? 'Oh, God!' she cried, alarmed. 'I was supposed to meet my pershonal tutor at two o'clock!'

'You're in trouble, then,' said Harry calmly.

'On your first day, too,' said Max.

'Theresh no need to sound so pleased about it!' Lily grabbed her scarlet leather bag, rose unsteadily to her feet and fell against the table. 'Do you think I'm drunk?'

'You're rat-arsed,' Max replied.

'You're absolutely schnockered,' added Harry.

'Who's your tutor?'

'She'sh – hang on, I have her letter shomewhere.' Lily scrabbled in her bag. She found the letter crumpled at the bottom of it, underneath some crumbling squares of Aero. 'Dr Minerva Rushman,' she enunciated carefully. 'Do real people have namesh like Minerva?'

'Dr Rushman, eh?' Max grinned. 'Dear me, that's most unfortunate for you.'

'W-what do you mean?'

'She's a typical Oxford spinster, middle-aged and virginal. She strongly disapproves of girls who drink. She's always dressed in cashmere twin-sets, grey tweed skirts and hideous shoes, and she expects her girls to wear the same,' continued Harry.

'No leather jackets, bells or beads or clanking bangles like you're wearing, anyway,' added Max.

'Do you have your gown with you?'

'No – why?'

'You'll need to pick it up and put it on. So don't forget. Minerva has been known to get an undergraduate sent down for failing to be properly attired or being late for meetings and you're both.'

'You'd better go and grovel, hadn't you? Or your first day at Oxford is going to be your last.'

'Mush do I owe you?' Lily tried to get her purse to open, but she failed.

'We'll settle up another time,' said Max.

'When you're not drunk,' said Harry. 'Off you go, and don't forget to cringe and fawn as if your life depends on it, because in fact it does.'

'On your marks ...'

'Get set ...'

The mocking laughter of the hobbits followed Lily as she ran out of The Golden Cross. She charged down Cornmarket, went hurtling along St Giles, got lost and had to double back along the Banbury Road to get to Norham Gardens.

She ran up to her room and grabbed her gown. There wasn't time to change into the tweeds she didn't have in any case, so she shrugged the gown over her scarlet dress, relieved most of the beads and bells would now be covered up.

She finally arrived at Dr Rushman's house well after half past three, desperate for the loo and sick with fright.

Tweedledum and Tweedledee had lied.

When Lily rang the bell of the small terraced house off Little Clarendon Street, a girl who must have been about her own age opened the front door. As she stumbled down the narrow hallway, she realised nobody was wearing gowns, and that no one seemed especially bothered she was nearly two hours late, was out of breath, dishevelled and embarrassingly aware she must smell strongly of The Golden Cross.

When she almost fell into her tutor's sitting room, at first she thought she'd come to the wrong place. Or that Dr Rushman wasn't there? At any rate, there was no one in a cashmere twin-set, middle-aged and disapproving-looking.

'Dr Rushman, here's the other new girl!'

A sturdy Viking blonde – a hockey player, Lily guessed, she had a hockey player's calves and thighs – met Lily's fuddled gaze, her own eyes bright and curious.

'It looks to me like she's been on the beer,' the hockey player added in a sharply piercing voice that skewered Lily's neurons and made her wince in pain.

As the other fifteen to twenty people in the room turned round to stare, Lily felt her face grow even redder than her dress.

'I g-got losht,' she stammered.

'But you managed to find us in the end.' The auburn-haired young woman, whom the hockey player had addressed as Dr Rushman, wore a rather posher velvet dress than Lily's home-made effort and some gorgeous, green suede knee-boots Lily coveted at once.

Minerva Rushman smiled. 'You must be Miss Denham,' she continued. 'You've been busy drinking in the whole of Oxford, have you?'

Chapter Three

'Dr Rushman is your personal tutor,' said the hockey player, tossing back her flaxen Nordic locks, fixing Lily with her glass-green gaze and wrinkling her nose. 'So—'

Yes, I know I stink today, thought Lily.

'—she's the one you'll need to see about your personal problems.'

'I do use deodorant,' said Lily. 'But I've been in The Golden—'

'I mean if you have boyfriend trouble, if you get behind with work, if things are difficult at home or any other private stuff like that.'

'She doesn't teach me, then?'

'It will depend on what you're reading.'

'English.'

'Oh,' the hockey player said. 'Well, that's Dr Rushman's subject too, and so she might. I think you need some coffee.' She ushered Lily to a cafetière, poured and handed her a mug. Lily shakily accepted it. 'I'm Molly Yardley, by the way.'

'I'm Lily Denham.'

'You look very hot. Why don't you take your gown off? You could hang it in the hall and then you won't forget it when you leave.'

So Lily shrugged out of her gown and Molly gave the scarlet smock her critical attention. 'Did you make that dress yourself?' she asked.

'Yes, and Dr Rushman's—'

'Dr Rushman's is admittedly quite similar. But I think *her* dress is from Biba. Yours is very obviously home-made.

You've rather overdone the decoration, haven't you? I wouldn't have sewn those bells around the hem or quite so many beads across the bodice. I don't mean to be rude, but the whole effect is rather like a Christmas tree.'

Lily glanced at Molly's tartan miniskirt and thought: if I had navvy's legs like yours, I'd keep them covered up.

'What were your favourite sports at school?' asked Molly. 'Mine were netball and lacrosse. I played lacrosse for Sussex when I was fifteen.'

'When we had games, I hid inside the shower block or smoked behind the bike shed with all the other skivers.'

'Smoking's very bad for you,' said Molly. 'It's a nasty, dirty habit, too.'

'I have lots of nasty, dirty habits,' Lily said. 'I eat spider sandwiches. I bite the heads off bats.' Why did I say that, she asked herself – am I still drunk? Or is it because this girl must be the most annoying person I have ever met? 'But most of the time I'm calm and rational,' she added. 'Unless there's a full moon, of course.'

'I see,' said Molly Yardley, looking nervous. 'Well, this is supposed to be a party, so I think we ought to try to circulate, don't you?' Only a few seconds later, Molly was in a huddle with a group of other students, all whispering and laughing.

'Miss Denham?' Dr Rushman beckoned Lily. 'Come and sit by me and tell me all about yourself. Molly, dear?' she called. 'Please will you bring Lily a second mug of coffee?'

The following morning, Lily had what had to be the hangover from hell and there was a letter in her pigeonhole.

We hope you didn't get in too much trouble with your tutor?

We also hope you've not been fined, suspended?

You owe us five bob. We'll see you in University Parks on Saturday at two o'clock to reckon up.

M&H

Lily glared at it then tore it into tiny strips.

All through her first week as an undergraduate, all through half a dozen inaugural addresses from terrifying women who *did* wear brogues and tweeds and cashmere twin-sets, all through lectures and tutorials, Lily planned and plotted. She racked her brains to work out how to get her own back on the hobbits.

Max felt slightly guilty about getting Lily drunk.

She was new and ignorant, after all. He was new as well, of course. But some of Harry's cousins had been at Oxford, so he and Harry knew what to expect, which Lily clearly didn't. She'd gone running from The Golden Cross in a funk of terror, sure she'd be sent down on her first day, which obviously wasn't going to happen.

He hoped it wouldn't happen, anyway.

'What did you think, then?' he'd asked Harry, after the landlord called last orders, and they'd left The Golden Cross and were strolling slowly back to Christ Church, not drunk, not even tight, just nicely, comfortably relaxed – the perfect state of mind for anyone.

They'd spent the summer practising their drinking, working out how much they needed to get tight, get legless and, on one spectacular occasion, get chucking-up-their-guts-and-paralytic-borderline-hospitalised. Max never wanted to feel like that again.

'What did I think of what?'

'The Red Queen, of course.'

'She seemed quite pleasant.' Harry shrugged. 'But I'm not really interested in girls. They're too emotional. They cry a lot. They say one thing but mean another.'

'These whip-smart observations are based on your own vast experience, are they?'

'My sister gives her boyfriends hell,' said Harry. 'It seems to me they're nothing but trouble, girls.'

'You think that because you're queer,' said Max. 'Pretty little choirboys, they're your thing.'

'I'm not queer and I don't go for choirboys. But while I'm here I need to work. I want to get a good degree and then a decent job. I won't have time to mess around with girls.'

'It's the only reason I came up, to mess around with girls.'

Lily went to Woolworth's. She bought some cheap cosmetics, made her face up deathly pale, smudged dark circles underneath her eyes, and lipsticked her red lips anaemic-white.

On Saturday she found the hobbits in the Parks, playing football with a pine cone.

'Hello, Lily,' said one hobbit, neatly passing her the cone. 'The goal's between those bushes. See if you can score.'

She ignored him and his cone.

'You okay, Red Queen?' enquired the other hobbit, the one who wore the earring. 'How do you like your women's prison?'

'Do they lock you in your cells at eight o'clock at night?'

'Does the place have electricity?'

'Or is it lit by feeble, guttering candles?'

'Do they keep you manacled to your desks?'

'You don't look well.'

'The bread and water diet doesn't suit you.'

Lily gave them both a withering look. 'Here's your cash,' she said, holding out a couple of half crowns. 'Come on – one of you take it.'

'You hang on to it,' said Hobbit One. 'You can treat us to a pint or several in The Lamb and Flag tonight.'

'It's in St Giles,' said Hobbit Two.

'Professor Tolkien drinks there now and then. So if he's propping up the bar this evening, we'll point him out to you.'

'I don't have time to buy you hobbits pints. I need to pack my stuff.'

'Why, where are you going?'

'You were right about Minerva Rushman. She reported me for being late and getting drunk. I had to go to see the Principal. She said she was disgusted with me and I've been sent down.'

Oh – perhaps I should be crying now, she thought.

She blinked. She screwed her eyes up tight. She thought of Bambi's mother dying. She played the Disney sequence in her head. She imagined shoeless orphans and/or big-eyed puppies lost and homeless in the snow, and finally some tears began to trickle down her cheeks. 'I'll b-be on the train to Dorchester on Monday morning.'

'But … sent down for being late to meet your tutor? That's ridiculous.' Max shook his head. 'There must be some mistake.'

'I threw up on her Persian carpet, too.'

'Oh, bad luck,' said Harry.

'It cost two thousand pounds, she said, but now she thinks it's worthless.'

'She's probably right.' Max flopped down on the grass. 'My father had an Oriental carpet in his study. When I was six or seven, I dropped a bottle of Parker Quink on it. He thrashed me so damn hard he nearly killed me.'

'So unless I find the money to buy her a replacement, which would be impossible ...'

'Come and sit down, Red Queen.' Max reached up, grabbed Lily's hand and pulled her down on to the grass beside him.

Harry flumped down on her other side.

'Let's have a think,' said Max. 'What shall we do?'

'What if we told your Principal what happened, explained we were to blame?' suggested Harry.

'Yes, if we said *we* got you drunk?' said Max.

'Maybe.' Lily dashed away a tear. 'I don't suppose she'd listen, but—'

'Come on, let's go,' said Max.

'Go where?' demanded Lily, suddenly alarmed.

'To see your Principal, of course – confess.'

'B-but won't you boys get into trouble? You were drinking, too.'

'We're allowed,' said Harry. 'We're eighteen. Men are expected to get drunk from time to time, in any case. It's what men do. It's different for you girls.'

'Why's it different?'

'Men are ravening, brute beasts who can't control their passions. Your duty as a woman is to set us an example.'

'Or not sink to our level, anyway.'

'You could write a letter explaining how it happened?' suggested Lily hopefully. Now she was ashamed of telling such a lot of fibs and found she couldn't look the hobbits in the eye. 'Then I could take it to the Principal?'

She crossed her fingers.

'I suppose we could,' conceded Harry.

'I'd be so very grateful.'

'Let's do it, then,' said Max.

Lily exhaled.

They walked together through the Parks to Christ Church, and went upstairs to Harry's rooms. These were quite amazing, Lily thought: high-ceilinged, mullion-windowed, with elaborate plaster cornicing, fine heraldic friezes and Tudor fireplaces of blackened stone. These weren't rooms for teenage boys. These were chambers for young gentlemen. But she wouldn't have wanted to live in them herself. The doors were badly-fitting and some of the window panes were cracked. It must be very draughty here in winter, she decided. There was no central heating. The whole place smelled of damp. She much preferred her own white-painted, modern room at LMH.

While Lily sat and gazed out of a window across the sweeping gardens, playing with her bangles nervously, Harry went to find the college porter to ask him for some Christ Church headed paper.

Max sat at Harry's desk.

Lily somehow knew that he was staring at her profile. She felt a flush of red creep up her neck. But she didn't dare glance round at him, much less demand to know what he was looking at and if he'd had his pennyworth.

Max and Harry wrote their letter and signed it. Max addressed a thick, white envelope to the Principal of Lady Margaret Hall – no abbreviations, Lily noticed.

She read their letter and she was impressed. She was also touched by their confession, almost to the point of fessing up herself. But no – these hobbits needed to be punished.

'Thank you,' she said primly. 'I'll take it back to LMH and put it in her pigeonhole today.'

'Let's hope it does the trick,' said Max.

'But if it doesn't, let us know,' said Harry.

'We'll think again.'

'Good luck.'

'Be bloody, bold and resolute,' said Max, one eyebrow quirking.

'What?'

'*Macbeth* – you know, the Scottish play? The one about the lying bastard who comes to a bad end?'

'Oh, yes,' said Lily.

'You'd better hurry, hadn't you?' said Harry. 'I mean, if you're to catch the Principal before you need to leave on Monday morning? She'll need a bit of time to change her mind.'

Lily had forgotten she was supposed to leave on Monday morning.

'Off you go,' said Max.

So Lily put the letter in her scarlet bag.

She smiled a secret smile.

Men were such clots, such idiots! She'd always guessed as much, basing her assumptions on the antics of her ghastly little brothers and their gruesome friends, and now she knew for sure.

Those two dolts, they'd been so easily fooled. One of them had been fooled, at any rate. Harry had believed her fibs. But she wasn't absolutely sure if Max had believed her, too. Why had he said that stuff about *Macbeth* and lying bastards? She still had her five bob, in any case. So she was in profit.

'What if we get sent down?' demanded Harry as they watched Lily walking through the gateway of Tom Quad then out into St Aldates, to disappear among the weekend crowds of camera-laden tourists.

'I'll join the Foreign Legion,' Max replied.

But he knew it wouldn't come to that, at least not yet, because the letter would never be delivered. Lily had lied to them – that much was plain. Max had spent a lifetime hearing women lie to him, so he knew all the signs: the nervous fidgeting, the blushing, the reluctance to look people in the eye. She's like all the rest, he told himself. She isn't to be trusted.

'She still owes us a pint,' said Harry.

Chapter Four

On Monday afternoon, the hobbits came to hunt her down.

On her return from a tutorial, she found them in the porter's lodge at LMH, apparently anxious to find out if she'd left Oxford yet, and puzzling the porter with their questions.

'You see, we weren't entirely sure about Miss Denham's movements,' Max was saying. 'We didn't know exactly where she'd be.'

'A young lady's movements are none of your concern, sir,' said the porter. 'Miss, do you want these gentlemen to leave?'

'No, it's fine,' said Lily. 'We ... we had arranged to meet,' she improvised, and felt herself blush scarlet.

'Come and have a coffee with us, then?' suggested Max.

'We know a charming place off Cornmarket,' said Harry. 'It's perfect for young ladies. It has sugar tongs and silver cake forks: every last refinement.'

'It ... it sounds delightful,' stammered Lily.

'So?' said Max.

'So ... so what?' said Lily.

'All sorted out with you-know-who?'

'Oh ... yes, all sorted out.' Lily was aware that she was blushing even redder than before, and that the porter was regarding all of them suspiciously.

As the Michaelmas term gathered momentum, Lily often met the hobbits for a lunchtime drink, an evening at the cinema, an afternoon spent punting – the boys taught her to pole, laughed when she got the pole stuck in the mud or poled the boat into the bank – and Molly Yardley grew more prying and more interfering.

As she sat in Lily's room one afternoon assassinating characters, as she tossed her Viking locks and flashed her glass-green eyes, Lily thought how much she'd suit a Valkyrie-style helmet with a pair of horns, together with a shield and spear, and couldn't help but giggle.

'What's so funny?' Molly asked, making herself at home on Lily's window-seat, cradling a mug of Lily's Nescafé and dunking Lily's Bourbons.

'Oh … nothing,' Lily said. 'Please don't eat all my Bourbons.'

'Those boys you're always meeting,' went on Molly, emptying the packet and scattering the crumbs on Lily's bed. 'You know you've got yourself a reputation?'

'What kind of reputation?'

'As a good-time girl – an easy lay.'

'Who calls me that?'

'Oh, everybody – people talk about you all the time.'

'I don't know why.'

'People see you in the pub with them and drinking beer with them and nice girls don't drink beer.'

'Oh, don't be ridiculous.' Lily wanted Molly to shut up, or – even better – go away. 'Harry, Max and I – we're friends, that's all.'

'But they're boys, and even you must know what boys are like?' said Molly. 'What they want, I mean?'

'Yes, of course I do,' said Lily. 'Boys want bacon sandwiches, fish and chips and lots of roast potatoes on a Sunday.'

'They want lots of other things as well,' said Molly darkly. 'We had a little booklet in our welcome pack for freshers that told us all about it. I think you ought to read it.'

'Maybe, when I've finished reading *Troilus and Criseyde*. Minnie wants an essay on its structure by tomorrow. Molly, don't you have some work to do?'

'I have loads of work.'

'Why don't you go and do it, then?'

'Okay, but just remember, I did warn you,' pouted Molly, flouncing out.

'You mean the one with legs like that big Soviet hammer-thrower?' Max demanded as he and Harry sat on either side of Lily like a pair of bookends in The Lamb and Flag, and Lily muttered crossly about idiots who knew nothing but thought they knew it all.

'The one who sounds as if she's taken elocution lessons from a foghorn?' added Harry.

'Red Queen, if she's upsetting you—'

'She isn't, she's too boring to upset me,' Lily told them, feeling like a traitor to her sex.

'We can't have anyone annoying you, Red Queen,' said Max.

'This Yardley woman – she deserves to feel the force of our displeasure,' added Harry. 'We could lob a stink bomb through her window, if you like?'

'Or send her half a dozen big fat spiders in a box of Dairy Milk?'

'Or a pot of jam that's full of worms?'

'God, you boys are infantile,' said Lily with a sigh. 'How old are you, thirteen? You're not still at school, you know. You leave Molly Yardley be. She's probably very nice and I'm just being over-critical.'

Max and Harry – they had seemed so similar at first, joined at the proverbial hip, as Harry had put it when the three of them met in the Parks that day, finishing each other's sentences, reading each other's minds.

But whereas Harry went to lectures and tutorials, worked hard and got his essays in on time, was always suffering from some trivial complaint and was a martyr to his migraines, sinusitis, and his shin splint injuries, Max was never injured, never ill, and seemed to do no work at all.

Avoiding lectures, hardly ever writing essays, Max missed most of his tutorials. He also made it clear he thought that sickness was a silly affectation in people who had nothing else to do.

After he was through with Oxford, Max was going travelling, exploring – so he said.

'Travelling and exploring,' Harry mocked. 'You mean you're going to be idling round the world with half a million other lazy hippies, hitching lifts on psychedelic buses full of girls in hideous patchwork skirts who never shave their armpits or their legs, and lazing in an ashram smoking dope and going *om*.'

'You're such a boring middle-class provincial, Gale,' sneered Max. 'You've always lived a half-life and I guess you always will.'

Harry was also truthful, sensible and law-abiding and took life seriously. Max had a very on-and-off relationship with truth, was anything but sensible and law-abiding, and he loved to tease authority.

'But, Max, you can't do things like that!' cried Lily, when they met for coffee after her tutorial one morning, and Max mentioned that the previous evening he had hung a pair of lady's knickers from the hour hand of a city clock.

Whose knickers? She'd have loved to know but was determined not to ask.

At serious risk of falling to his death, he'd scrambled

27

up the outside of the tower like a monkey, and when he explained all this to Lily she felt sick.

'Why shouldn't I?' he asked. 'While I was at school, I climbed up towers and out of windows all the time. I'm sure passers-by were entertained, and so what harm—'

'If you'd slipped, you would have made a nasty mess and stickied-up the pavement, that's what harm. People would have had to walk around you or get their shoes all bloodied.'

'Someone would have fetched a broom and bucket, swept me up. Did you hear about the traffic chaos in the Broad this morning?'

'Yes, there was gridlock for three hours or more.' Lily looked at Max suspiciously. 'You're saying that was down to you as well?'

'Well, sort of down to me. As I was walking back to college in the early hours—'

'After going where and doing what, apart from vandalising clocks?'

'Please don't interrupt me all the time, Red Queen. It's a very unappealing habit, especially in a girl. As I was strolling down the High and minding my own business, I noticed lots of temporary road signs with arrows indicating a diversion. I thought, if I turn one of them to face the other way, tomorrow morning's rush hour traffic will go round and round in circles, and—'

'You ought to be locked up.'

'You sound like our industrious friend. You're both middle-aged before your time. Why would anybody lock me up? I didn't lie or cheat or steal or murder anyone. All I did was decorate a clock and move a road sign. I added to the gaiety of nations. Oh, Red Queen – don't look at me like that, don't say you've joined the God Squad?'

'I haven't joined the God Squad. But, Max, don't climb up towers. It's very dangerous. I mean, what if you fell and hurt yourself?'

'Do you think you'd care?'

'I might.'

'A little or a lot?'

'I'd probably care a little tiny bit, but I'd also say it served you right.'

'Red Queen, you disappoint me. You sound like those stuck-up, joyless bitches at St Hughes. Those tedious swots at LMH – I'm starting to suspect you're one of them.'

Those tedious swots at LMH, thought Lily, watching Max walk down St Giles. She hoped she wasn't swottish. She liked to read, to study, and she hoped to get a good degree. All the same, she wasn't swottish – was she?

Maybe she should ask her friends?

But, apart from Molly, who'd apparently decided they were bosom buddies, she wasn't making friends at LMH. Most of the other students had been to independent schools and seemed to think it strange that she had not.

Where did her family live? What did her father do?

She got asked these questions all the time, resented it, and found she couldn't resist embroidering. Or make that downright lying. 'Mum's a gypsy fortune teller, works the fairs,' she said to Molly, who had just dropped in to borrow teabags which Lily knew would never be returned. Then she hung around to eat some biscuits and page through Lily's books, cracking all the spines. 'I have the gift of second sight myself,' she added. 'I know how to put the evil eye on people, too. Perhaps you'd like to see a demonstration? You see, when people are annoying me, I sometimes find that I can't help myself.'

Molly shuddered, scurried out of Lily's room and slammed the door. Lily went back to her essay and thought no more about it. But, as the weeks went by, she realised Molly must have been embroidering even more than Lily had herself, and she was not exactly popular at LMH. Once more or less ignored, but passively, now she was deliberately shunned.

On Saturdays the boys played various outdoor games, most of which involved a lot of shouting and rolling in the mud.

Apart from writing essays – and you could get sick of writing essays – Lily often found herself with nothing else to do, and so she went to watch, which didn't help her reputation.

'I know why you go to see those men play rugby,' muttered Molly, who still seemed determined to be friendless Lily's friend. As an enthusiastic member of the God Squad, she probably thought it was her Christian duty. 'It's because you're over-sexed. You like to watch men's bits wobbling around inside their shorts. It turns you on.'

Lily was so entertained by this assumption that she snorted hugely. The older sister of three brothers, she'd always been familiar with men's bits. She thought they were absurd: badly designed and hideous. One of the many proofs there was no God. Or proof that God had absolutely no aesthetic judgement. Or a warped sense of fun.

So why did she sometimes wonder what it would be like to be in bed with Max or Harry? They were friends. You didn't go to bed with friends.

One sunny winter afternoon, she took her camera to a match to get some Polaroids, more because it gave her something interesting to do, rather than because she wanted photographs of men rolling in mud.

After the match, she asked another roller-in-the-mud to take a snap of her and Max and Harry, who preened and posed and larked around, finally telling the photographer that they were ready for their close-ups now.

'Make sure the lighting flatters me,' cooed Harry, pouting and making rosebud lips.

'What do you think, Red Queen – full face or profile?' Max demanded as he fluffed up his hair.

'Just take the photograph,' said Lily to the student.

'Let me see?' demanded Max as the three of them strolled off the pitch, the boys towards the club house for their showers, and Lily to the café where she would meet them later before going to the pub. 'May I borrow this, Red Queen? I'd like to get some copies made and sign them for my fans.'

'What fans are these?'

'I have quite a following at St Hilda's and St Anne's.'

'Oh, you mean the colleges for the blind.'

Lily didn't much like standing in the cold, but she enjoyed the drinking after matches very much indeed. She developed quite a taste for Henley Brewery's best and soon she learned to put away as much as any man.

'It's very tiresome, surely, running up and down a muddy rugby pitch and yelling?' she suggested, when they were in the pub that Saturday evening, after an extremely muddy game. 'I'll never know why you're so keen on sport.'

'I'm not keen on sport,' said Max.

'I hate sport,' said Harry.

'Then why do you play those silly games?'

'We don't play games, Red Queen.'

'We ritualise our natural aggression.'

'We channel our primaeval urges.'

'What primaeval urges?' Lily asked.

'The ones that make us want to kill each other.'

'You two want to kill each other?'

'All the time,' said Max. 'Harry is the brother I never had. So, of course, I want to shoot him dead.'

'Or disembowel me,' added Harry.

'Or stab him through the heart.'

'Or cut my nuts off, anyway.'

'You're quite disgusting, aren't you, hobbits? I thought brothers were supposed to love each other?'

'Rubbish, brothers always hate each other!'

'Don't you know anything?'

'Cain killed Abel.'

'Romulus killed Remus.'

'Seti killed Osiris.'

'Turkish sultans always killed their brothers,' went on Harry. 'They strangled them with silken cords – *bear like the Turk no brother near the throne* and stuff. So one day I'll kill Max.'

'But only if I fail to kill you first.'

'Stop it, both of you.' Lily looked from Max to Harry. 'You're telling me that you don't care who wins the actual game?'

'What game?'

'We don't play games,' said Max. 'Come on, you two, drink up. It's time to have some fun.'

'What kind of fun?' asked Lily.

'Let's go punting.'

'It's too dark,' said Harry.

'There's a full moon, you cretin, so it's light enough to see.' Max's dark eyes glittered. 'Red Queen, you like punting, don't you?'

'Yes, I love it.' Suddenly Lily felt exhilarated and ready for some fun. 'Yes, let's go punting.'

'All the punts will be locked up in boathouses,' said Harry.

'We'll need to go and liberate one, then,' said Max. 'Come on, you miserable spoilsport. The night is young and you are beautiful …'

'The moon is bright,' said Lily. 'There's magic in the air …'

'Oh, shut up, the pair of you,' said Harry. 'You're both insane, you know.' But he downed his pint, got up and followed them.

As Harry had predicted, the Christ Church boathouse was locked up. There were a few punts outside but these were chained together and to the jetty.

Max jumped down into one. He smashed its padlock so it floated free. 'Come on, you two,' he hissed. 'We need to go before somebody sees.'

'We haven't got a pole,' objected Lily.

'We'll paddle, then – like Gollum.'

'Yes, all right.'

Lily jumped into the punt. It rocked from side to side and threatened to take in water.

'Steady,' murmured Harry. 'You'll capsize it.'

'You can't capsize a punt, you clot,' said Max. 'Gale, get in – we're waiting.'

They paddled down the river with the current, Harry sighing, Lily giggling. Max made Gollum noises and grumbled to himself about his Precious.

'I say, you chaps – isn't this the most enormous fun?' he asked as the boat got caught up in an eddy, swung round and floated dangerously close to a big houseboat, threatening to plough straight into it.

'It's cold and damp and if we're caught we'll be in serious trouble,' muttered Harry. 'I think we should go back, tie up and get off home.'

'Oh, don't be such a killjoy,' growled Max.

'Or such a bore,' said Lily. 'What could be more enjoyable than being on the river in the moonlight?'

'I think we ought to turn this thing around and take it back to where it ought to be.'

'Let's go as far as where the ferry stops, and then we'll turn around and head back home, okay?' said Max.

'Yes, let's do that,' said Lily. 'It'll be all right,' she soothed as Harry went on fretting.

It probably would have been all right if Harry hadn't suddenly stood up to check his pockets because he thought he might have lost his wallet.

Later, he insisted Max had pushed him, which Max of course denied. But, pushed or not, he fell into the river, vanishing beneath the surface of the cold, black water.

Lily gasped in horror. 'Max, do something!'

'Gale can swim,' said Max, who had just lit a cigarette.

'But where is he? Maybe he's been sucked into a whirlpool, got tangled up in weeds. Or he could be underneath the boat. Max, this is serious! We need to find him. We—'

'Okay, if you insist.' Max threw his cigarette into the river, pulled off his overcoat and shoes then jumped in after Harry.

Lily stared into the silent water and willed them both to bob back up again.

'I've g-got the idiot,' choked Max. This must have been less than a minute later but it had seemed more like an hour to Lily. 'Come on, Denham, help me get this plonker back into the boat.'

Lily did her best but, as she tried to pull the weight of Harry into the rocking punt, she overbalanced and fell in too.

Down and down she went. The water filled her mouth, got up her nose. She couldn't breathe. She couldn't see. She knew that she would die …

'What a pair of tossers,' muttered Max, who must have hauled himself into the boat, because now he was pulling Harry and Lily back into it as well. 'I take you on a little evening cruise along the most romantic waterways in all of England, and you turn it into farce. Slow, deep breaths, Red Queen – stop wheezing like a frog with asthma.'

Lily took a slow, deep breath, exhaled, and then breathed in the cold night air again. She started to feel better. 'Max, you were brilliant just now,' she said. 'You're a fool, of course, to have thought of doing this at all. But you were brilliant too, to get us both back in the boat. Harry, are you all right?'

'I hope to live.' Harry spat out bits of waterweed, pulled some fronds of it out of his hair and shook himself, spraying muddy water over Lily. 'Yes, I'll be fine – eventually.'

'Of course you will,' said Max. 'Only the good die young. Red Queen, well done. You didn't panic. You weren't any use, of course. But when this pillock overbalanced, at least you didn't scream and wake the city.'

Lily's teeth were chattering. She was frozen. But somehow she was warm, as well. When Max had said well done …

'Take off your coat,' he added and then he draped his own dry coat round Lily's shaking shoulders. 'Okay, children – that's enough excitement for one day. I suppose it's time to head for home.'

'You're a madman, Farley,' grumbled Harry as they

paddled furiously, then clambered, scrambled and hauled themselves on to the nearest bank. 'We might all have drowned.'

'We didn't, though.' Max glanced at Lily then he winked. 'Red Queen, you enjoyed it, didn't you? It was an adventure, wasn't it? When you thought you might die, you felt alive?'

'What are you going on about?' growled Harry. 'You set this whole thing up. You pushed me in the river. You could have bloody killed me.'

'But I didn't. Maybe I'll have better luck next time.'

'Oh, shut up, you halfwit.' Harry turned to Lily. 'You should get off home,' he said as they stood on dry land and shook themselves and wrung out their wet clothes as best they could. 'Go on, run back to LMH – warm yourself up a bit.'

Lily did as Harry said, running through the streets of Oxford, squelching into LMH and dashing past the porter before he had a chance to notice she was dripping all over the floor.

Safe inside her room again, she stripped off all her clothes and towelled herself, gradually warming up and starting to feel better. But, as she rubbed the towel over her stomach and between her legs, she felt some new sensations, wave on wave.

She saw Max, and saw his eyes were sparkling.

She heard him saying: 'Red Queen, you enjoyed it, didn't you? It was an adventure, wasn't it? When you thought you might die, you felt alive?'

Max had been right, she thought. Or was it Max himself who'd made her feel alive, as if she could do anything?

'You okay now, Gale?' demanded Max, as they slopped and sloshed their way to Christ Church.

'I s-suppose so,' muttered Harry, shivering. 'But if I come down with pleurisy, and if it's the death of me, it will be your fault.'

'Come on, man – cheer up.' Max put one arm round Harry's shoulders. 'You're much too young to die.'

'I almost drowned back there.'

'You didn't almost drown. I got you back into the boat in twenty seconds flat. A mug of Horlicks and an early night and you'll be right as rain again tomorrow.' Max pulled Harry closer. 'You know I wouldn't have let you come to any harm. You're my best friend.'

'Yes, after most of Somerville and the other women's colleges. All you think about these days are girls.'

'But they're just girls. You're Harry. You're the brother I always wanted and you'll always be the most important person in my life.'

'As we know, some brothers kill each other.'

'But most brothers don't. David and Jonathan in the Bible loved each other, didn't they? Listen, Gale – you're part of me, and nothing and no one comes between us, right?'

As he said it, Max knew he was lying. Someone had come between them. She'd driven in a wedge that had cracked their friendship open wide. But he didn't need to act upon his feelings, did he? Or not yet, at any rate?

There were other girls.

Chapter Five

'I hear you have two beaux,' said Minnie Rushman, smirking archly as she glanced through Lily's essay on *Twelfth Night* while scribbling copious notes all over it in venomous green ink.

As Lily watched her tutor's Mont Blanc pen slash through her work, she chewed her lower lip. 'Max and Harry are a pair of idiots and they definitely aren't *my* beaux,' she muttered crossly as Minnie scrawled more comments.

So what were they, then?

Since she'd come to Oxford, she'd done a lot of reading round her subject, expanding her horizons and learning all about men's special friendships, how these were particularly popular with people – okay, men – who'd been at boarding school. How they were practically obligatory, in fact.

Max and Harry, were they queer?

After giving it a lot of thought, she decided this was most unlikely. Or it seemed unlikely Max was queer. At a student party in somebody's house in Cowley Road the previous weekend, Max had snogged a physicist from Somerville.

Or maybe she'd snogged him? She'd dragged him off and pinned him up against a wall, in any case – not that he'd seemed to mind. But watching them across a crowded room of people turning on in various ways, Lily had felt her insides twist with – well, what was it, jealousy?

Did she wish she was the physicist? No, because the girl had great big feet, knock knees and greasy hair. Also Max was very drunk. She thought it was unlikely he could see straight, anyway. But what would it feel like to kiss Max?

Why did even thinking about kissing Max make her start to feel so light and weightless that she could float away?

'She'll get her tongue chewed off if she's not careful,' Harry had muttered. He'd been standing next to Lily watching his best friend. 'You'd think he hadn't had a decent meal for weeks.'

'You would.' Lily had glanced at Harry's almost-empty glass. 'Do you want a refill?'

'No, this beer's some home-brewed rubbish made in plastic dustbins. It's tasteless, warm and flat. I'll be on my way, I think. I need to write an essay.'

'I have one to write as well, so I'll come with you.'

'As you wish,' said Harry.

They'd tugged their coats from underneath an amorous couple who were doing something for which Lily thought they ought to be arrested, unless they were zoologists and this was just a practical.

She and Harry walked up Cowley Road then over Magdalen Bridge. Harry's face was screwed up in a frown, his shoulders hunched, his hands thrust in his pockets.

Harry – perhaps he had a thing for Max? She didn't think she could ask him, not right now in any case, not while he seemed so cross – and jealous, too?

Did he want to keep Max for himself? He didn't seem to want a girlfriend, anyway. Whenever he wasn't in the pub or on a muddy pitch, Harry was in the Bodleian Library or the Radcliffe Camera, where he worked and worked and worked.

Perhaps Max felt neglected?

She'd shared this thought with Harry.

'Of course he doesn't feel neglected,' Harry had growled. 'Jesus, don't be such a girl.'

'I am a girl.'

'You might be biologically a female, but that doesn't mean you need to act as if you've only half a brain, or a rather smaller brain than mine, in any case.'

'So any polar bear or elephant must therefore be much smarter than you will ever be?' huffed Lily, as she told herself it wasn't any of her business if by this stage of the evening Max was on Girl Six, Girl Twenty-Eight, Girl Thirty-Nine.

'How could he feel neglected, anyway, when he has us?' asked Harry, who'd no longer sounded cross, but bleak and desperate now.

Harry, are you in love with Max? she wondered. Does Max kiss girls to make you jealous?

But Lily couldn't bring herself to ask him.

What if he said yes?

This would make her an irrelevance, and she didn't want to be irrelevant. She wanted to be in their lives. She wanted them to be her friends, her co-conspirators. She wanted to sit with them in the pub – between them, preferably. Sometimes she wanted Max. Sometimes she wanted Harry. She dreamed of kissing both of them, of more than kissing ...

'I must go and do some work,' she'd said.

'Yes, so must I.'

But surely there was more to life than work?

As Lily walked up Norham Gardens one November afternoon, she decided that whatever might be going on – or possibly not going on – between the boys, it was time she too got into snogging. After all, it wasn't as if there were no opportunities in a city full of male undergraduates and so few female ones. What about snogging Harry, then, she wondered. But what if he and Max ...

Harry didn't seem very interested in snogging Lily. When

they'd said goodnight that evening, and she'd kissed him on the cheek experimentally, she could have sworn he'd flinched. Or perhaps he'd only been surprised? He hadn't returned the kiss, at any rate.

It seemed very likely Max was overstretched already, probably booked up until at least the following summer. She didn't think she wanted to wait until the summer, so she would need to meet some other boys. This wasn't difficult to arrange. All she had to do, she found, was smirk a bit in lectures or in the libraries. The boys smirked back and soon she had some offers.

But, but, but, but … something wasn't right. When the grabbing, groping stuff – which she'd learned about in Personal Relationships and Hygiene sessions in the sixth form while she was at school – inevitably began, it left her cold.

'You're either frigid or a lesbian,' explained a boy at Balliol, after he had bought them both a Wimpy, and they were in his room in college, and the candles on his mantelpiece were casting a soft, romantic glow, and she'd forced herself to kiss him, and she'd let him undo half the buttons on her dress, but had refused to take her knickers off so he could have a rummage round.

She said she must be going now or else she'd be locked out, and he had looked so disappointed that she considered offering to pay him for her burger.

'Molly Yardley told a friend of mine you sew,' he muttered as he tucked his shirt back in his jeans.

'Yes – do you want something made?' asked Lily, seeing a way to make amends for the non-knickers action. 'Or something altered, mended?'

'No, I don't! I think it's very strange for girls – for educated girls – to want to sew.'

'I like designing clothes and making them,' said Lily. 'What's so wrong with that?'

'The other girls I know buy clothes from Peter Robinson or Biba,' said the boy disdainfully. 'They wouldn't wear anything that looked home-made.'

'You mean like this coat?'

'You made your coat? Why would anybody want to make a coat? The shops are full of coats.'

'I made my dress, as well.'

Lily buttoned up her home-made dress, put on her home-made coat and left. As she trudged back to Nescafé and *Prefaces to Shakespeare* and maybe doing some embroidery on a new velvet waistcoat, she wondered if the boy from Balliol might be right about her being frigid or a lesbian.

But how could she be a lesbian when she knew she definitely didn't fancy women, even glamorous, sexy, clever women, even Minnie Rushman? When she'd never had a crush on any female prefect in her life? How could she be frigid when she sometimes had the most disturbing but exciting dreams?

Lesbian or frigid or ...

'You know something? You're a nymphomaniac,' said Molly, who'd apparently decided Lily did it with both Max and Harry and probably with other men as well. 'Of course, to have one boyfriend – that's natural and normal,' she continued sanctimoniously. 'But I can't imagine how anybody copes with two.'

'One at each end,' said Lily.

'My goodness, you're revolting!' Molly blushed. 'All you ever think about is sex.'

Molly clearly thought about virginity and hanging on to it. She was going steady with a Christian engineer from

Keble who had a lot of spots. She was a member of the God Squad. She'd signed the Pledge of Purity and wore the Christian engineer's ring.

The Christian was a cheapskate. The ring could not be gold or even silver. Maybe it was copper? It soon turned Molly's finger a livid, poisonous green.

'You'll get septicaemia,' warned Lily. 'Look, it's not a proper ring at all. It's just a bit of sawn-off piping. I bet he made it in some lab or workshop. Or got it from a plumber. Or found it in the road.'

'You're only jealous.' Molly smiled a smug, Madonna smile. 'It doesn't matter what it's made of because it's still a symbol of our love.'

Chapter Six

Max was walking back home from St Hilda's sunk in gloom.

That girl he'd spent the evening snogging in a rather sordid pub in Marston Road – had she been Lucy somebody? Or had she been Sally, or maybe Caroline? He'd already forgotten.

Most of the Sallies and the Lucies probably forgot him too, he thought, for Oxford offered countless opportunities for girls who wanted to get snogged or laid.

Very occasionally, girls got clingy. Sometimes Max found scented little notes stuffed in his pigeonhole. He wasn't gratified or flattered. He was just annoyed. But it was very easy to rip these idiotic missives up or say he'd never had them in the first place, and even the most sentimental girls soon got the message and moved on.

Lily – he didn't know why it should be, but he got withdrawal symptoms if they didn't meet at least a couple of times a week. This was odd, because he didn't want to go to bed with Lily.

Well, he did – he often fantasised that he was making love to Lily while he was with Lucy, Sally, Caroline. But he didn't want a drunken snog, a fumble in the passage next to The Lamb and Flag, a desperate groping up against a wall – not with the Red Queen.

When the time came – when he could afford it, which regretfully would not be soon, because his father kept him very short – he and Lily would go somewhere gorgeous and exotic. There'd be crystal waterfalls, romantic castles, and she'd have to fall in love with him.

But, in the meantime …

It was late, but not too late. He went into a callbox, picked up the phone and dialled.

'Hello, Red Queen. I haven't seen you for a while.'

'I dare say that's because you've been so busy, what with all those girls from Somerville to snog, more towers to climb, more traffic signs to rearrange, more punts to steal. Drowned anybody lately, have you?'

'Lily, I've neglected you. I'm sorry.'

'Oh, you think I've missed you?'

'I hope you have – a little?'

'Well, I haven't given you a single thought, so there.'

'Red Queen, don't be cross with me.'

'I'm not cross, but it's quite late and I'm about to go to bed.'

Lily caught the porter's eye and mimed a winding motion, indicating that she would be quick. The porter frowned, as well he might, and Lily knew she'd have to grovel and apologise to him – again.

She'd told Max half a million times the number he was calling was only for emergencies. The phone itself was in the porter's lodge, and so he'd had to leave his cosy little den, his *Oxford Mail* and thermos flask to track her down.

'You can't mean to go to bed just yet,' said Max.

'Well, maybe not for half an hour or so, but I need to finish off an essay on metaphors and other imagery in *Wuthering Heights*.'

'I've managed to prise Gale away from bloody Nietzsche. Come and have a drink with us?'

'Max, I said I have to write my essay, or Minnie's going to have my guts for—'

'No she won't, nobody uses garters any more.' Then

Max argued, spent the next ten, fifteen minutes and a lot of sixpences and shillings trying to talk Lily into coming out to play.

She refused, refused a second, third, fourth time, asked where Harry was all this time they'd been talking and had he gone to the pub without them? Then she said she really had to finish off her essay.

Off went the pips again.

Max told her he'd run out of cash and, if she happened to change her mind, that he would be in Norham Gardens, waiting.

She grovelled to the porter, said it wouldn't happen again. The porter said he hoped not, but he wasn't counting any chickens or putting any eggs in any baskets.

He went back to his copy of the *Oxford Mail*.

The essay – she'd already made the notes. She'd roughed out most of a first draft and, since her room was chilly – the central heating in her part of the building was only in the corridors – she had got her coat on, anyway …

'I knew you'd come,' said Max.

'You're so conceited, aren't you? You think all you need to do is snap your fingers and the whole world must lie down, roll over and beg to have its tummy tickled.'

'You're so acid-tongued, Red Queen – so strict. You make me think of Matron at my boarding school. She had a line in ready wit, as well.'

'So where are we meeting Harry, then?'

'Did I say we were meeting Harry?'

'Yes, you did!'

'I can't think why – he has a migraine.'

'It must have come on suddenly?'

'Yes, very suddenly.'

'Do we need to get him something from the all-night chemist?'

'I don't think so. Gale is always well stocked up with aspirins, ibuprofen, paracetamol. You should see his bathroom. It's like a branch of Boots.'

'You made it up about him coming out.'

'You sound so disappointed.'

'Of course I'm disappointed.' Lily had to hurt him now, to pierce his armour, stick a dagger in his side, although she couldn't have said exactly why. 'Harry's very nice and I enjoy his company.'

'What, more than mine?'

'Of course much more than yours. Harry's witty, generous, kind and charming. All the things you're not.'

'Oh, Red Queen, you cut me to the heart.'

'Rubbish – you don't have a heart.'

They began to walk down Norham Gardens in the moonlight. Lily was determined to be annoyed with Max. But then she found she'd linked her arm through his and pushed her hand into his jacket pocket.

She felt the warmth of him. She drew him close so he was snug against her side. Why didn't she kiss him, then? Why didn't she grab him like that girl from Somerville had grabbed him, push him up against a garden wall and snog his face off? She supposed she was too well brought up to make that sort of move, while Max was – well, perhaps he didn't fancy her at all? Perhaps they were – distressingly – just friends? They walked along in silence for a while.

'Where are we going?' Lily asked. 'I mean, which pub?'

'The pubs will soon be shut. Let's go and have a little adventure, shall we?'

'I'm not up for stealing punts again.'

'Okay, we'll do some recreational climbing.'

'I don't know how to climb.'

'I'll teach you,' promised Max. They turned left into Longwall Street. 'Let's break into Magdalen.'

'How would we break into Magdalen?'

'Go over the wall.'

'You mean climb that?' Lily looked at the battlemented wall that towered grey above them. 'But we don't have any ropes or stuff.'

'We don't need ropes, you baby. We find handholds, footholds – there are plenty – and up we go, like this.' Max went up like a gecko. Soon he was sitting comfortably astride the wall, leaning against a battlement. Lily tried to do as she was told, thinking it was just as well that she was wearing jeans today and not one of her special trademark dresses.

She found a foothold, then a handhold and began to inch her nervous way up the high wall. She didn't dare look down. 'Get a move on, or the bloody bulldogs will catch the pair of us, and we'll both be sent down,' hissed Max as Lily clawed and scrambled, trying to find handholds, footholds. 'Then what would Dr Rushman say?' he added, his mouth now twitching in a wicked grin.

Lily didn't want to think about what Minnie might say if she was caught and hauled before the proctors. She took a gasping breath. She knew she had a choice. Go on climbing, fall and no doubt break her neck, or fall right now and break only her leg ...

'Come on, you girl!' urged Max.

'Shut up ... you ... sadist!'

As she groped her way towards the parapet, Max held out his hand. She grabbed it and he hauled her up. 'You're nothing ... but ... an idiot,' she rasped. 'It's like ... I said. You ought ... to be ... locked up.'

'You're probably right.' Max gazed across its deer park towards the bulk of Magdalen, the spires of which were ghostly in the moonlit gloom.

'Max, are there any brambles at the bottom of this side of the wall?' she asked, staring down into the murk.

'I expect so.'

'Good, because I'm going to give you a big push and hope you fall smack into them.'

'Oh, Red Queen ... be nice?' coaxed Max. 'I bet you're feeling really pleased you managed to do that little climb?'

'I'm feeling cold and stupid and I think you're raving mad.' But, as she sat astride the battlemented wall, looking towards Magdalen, hearing various low grunts and rustlings that must have come from sleeping deer below, Lily did feel rather pleased. She felt energised as well – exhilarated – happy. She felt a grin spread right across her face. Actually, her whole body was one great big grin.

'There, I told you we'd have fun,' said Max.

Then he smiled and Lily thought that now – at last – at long, long last – they'd kiss. But they didn't kiss. Max twisted round and jumped into the darkness and Lily heard him crash into some shrubbery below.

'Jump, Red Queen!' he cried. 'Let yourself fall! I'll catch you!'

She knew that now she didn't have a choice.

She didn't dare – in fact, she couldn't – climb back down the wall. She could hear footsteps, too. Somebody was walking along Longwall Street and very soon this somebody was bound to notice Lily, and unless the somebody should happen to be a student, she was going to find herself in rather serious trouble.

So she too twisted round and sort of jumped and sort

of fell. Max sort of caught her in his arms, they both collapsed on to a heap of branches and Max pulled her up again.

'Okay?' he asked.

'Yes, I suppose I must be. I don't think I've broken anything, at any rate.'

Now, surely, surely she had earned that kiss?

But soon it was evident she had not.

Max stared at her for half a second, dark eyes shining in the silver light of the half moon. 'I'll race you back to LMH,' he said. 'The loser buys the drinks on Saturday. On your marks, get set—'

Max started running. He had said she was a girl. So why didn't he treat her like a girl? Why doesn't he take care of me, she wondered as she ran, as frightened deer loomed up out of the darkness, occasionally bumping into them, then blundering off, alarmed.

Why does he not understand that, as a woman, I need cherishing? I need protecting? He was worse than any of her brothers, who always behaved as if she was a boy as well. Or was it just that she was seriously unattractive?

'You're such a bastard,' she informed him when, after climbing various walls and fences, crossing various roads and running across various water meadows and recreation grounds, they reached the LMH side of the University Parks. 'Getting me to risk breaking my neck climbing up walls, encouraging me to terrify the deer, then running off into the night and leaving me to stumble after you. Do you have any good points?'

'I read the *Guardian* and I'm kind to kittens.'

'You don't have any kittens.'

'But if I did, I would be kind to them.' He linked one arm through Lily's, pulled her close – but only in a brotherly kind of hug. 'Come on, if we hurry we'll make last orders at The Lamb. Let's go and have that drink.'

'I'm going home to finish off my essay.'

Max watched Lily run the last few yards to LMH, her long legs scissoring in the gloom, and wondered why he'd messed up so spectacularly again. When he'd caught her in his arms as she'd jumped off the wall, why hadn't he and Lily kissed? Why had he lost his nerve – again?

'I hope you and your beaux are free on Saturday?' asked Minnie, drawing on a pastel pink Sobranie.

'Why?' asked Lily, hoping that she might be offered one. Sobranies might be cancer sticks like all the rest, but they looked so pretty and sophisticated in their golden box …

'Yes, you can take a fag,' said Minnie, following Lily's hungry gaze. 'I'm having various people round.'

'You mean a party?'

'I mean I'm having various people round. Parties are for tedious, boring people from the lower middle class. So although there will be beer and wine, please don't expect a ghastly buffet – grapefruit hedgehogs, diamond-cut tomatoes or sardine pinwheel sandwiches.'

Minnie handed Lily's latest essay back. 'Actually, this isn't bad, Miss Denham. Only half a dozen clichés this time, not the usual hundred. We might make a scholar of you yet.'

Lily looked at all the green ink scrawls defacing her once pristine pages and was inclined to doubt it.

'Tutors' parties: intellectual chat and British sherry made from boiled raisins,' grumbled Max.

'You don't have to come,' said Lily.

'Oh, I might as well.' Max grinned. 'I rather fancy Minnie.'

'You will behave yourself?' asked Lily anxiously.

'I'll keep an eye on him,' said Harry.

So, the following Saturday evening, Lily, Max and Harry met in town and walked to Minnie's little terraced house in Jericho. This was a suburb of the city where the small Victorian terraced cottages, originally meant for college servants and the labouring poor, were now inhabited by dons and trendies, not by the underclass for whom they had been built.

As soon as they arrived, a lecturer in French from Somerville came up and introduced herself to Max, getting him to light her cigarette then breathing smoke all over him, a process he appeared not to mind one little bit.

Lily and Harry listened to their elders being witty for a while. A bearded history don from Queen's appeared to take a shine to Harry. 'You're reading modern languages, I think our hostess said?'

'Yes, that's right,' Harry said, nodding.

'Any special interests?'

'The poetry of Rimbaud and Verlaine.'

'Then, my boy, we have a lot in common,' said the don and led his quarry to a corner of the kitchen – where there were some interesting cheeses, crackers and big bowls of fruit and, Lily noticed, artistic sprays of vine leaves – his hand on Harry's arm.

'Oh dear, I should have warned you about Alistair: he's a dreadful one for pretty boys,' said Minnie, wafting up to Lily in a cloud of Chanel Number 5. 'Harry isn't queer, is he?'

'I don't think so.'

'I don't think so, either.' Minnie took a drag of her

Sobranie. 'But he does have a certain earnest, puppyish way round older men that could be quite misleading. Well, since your friends have both deserted you, let's find you a man and make them jealous.'

'It's fine ... they're only circulating,' Lily said. She didn't fancy any of the men at Minnie's party. Sorry – at Minnie's having-various-people-round. Apart from two or three attractive boys, who were clearly interested only in each other, they were all too old.

But she was occupied quite happily. She was busy studying what everyone was wearing. The lecturer in French wore a black jersey tube and looked exactly like a model who had just stepped out of *Vogue*. Lily had never seen a British woman half as sexy or as thin. Minnie was dressed in what looked like a cobweb and she looked quite amazing.

Lily resolved to make herself a cobweb, too. She'd need grey gauze, grey silk for lining, black silk thread for some machine embroidery, and some antique lace from Oxford Market or a charity shop in Cowley Road.

The gauze would need to be cut on the bias, and as for the pin-tucks all down the back and bodice – if she went home now, she could make some notes on vital details, and maybe make a paper pattern, too.

She looked around for Max and Harry to tell them she was leaving. Minnie saw her looking. 'What's the matter?' Minnie asked.

'I need to tell my friends I'm going.'

'Oh, darling, please don't run away so soon!' Minnie's green eyes narrowed like a cat's. 'They're quite safe,' she added. 'They're both in the conservatory. You can go and find them in a minute. So, who will you be smuggling into LMH tonight? Or who will be sneaking you into his rooms in Christ Church?'

'It's not like that,' said Lily.

'What's not like what?'

'I don't do that kind of stuff with either of them, Dr Rushman. We're just friends, that's all.'

'What a waste,' purred Minnie. 'What a shame.'

Yes, it is a shame, thought Lily sadly. Harry, Max – most nights she still dreamed and fantasised about them both. She undressed them both, made love to both, and woke up hot and bothered.

She found her coat and slipped off home.

Max had not enjoyed the party.

After Minnie whispered to him Lily had gone home, he said goodbye to Mademoiselle Lucille, who'd been kippering him for the past hour and who had such a pecking, stabbing style of conversation that she made him think of hook-beaked vultures pulling guts out of their prey.

He rescued Harry from the don, who was drunk and Max could see was getting somewhat amorous, although Harry probably hadn't noticed. Harry didn't notice anything. Then he went home to dream of Lily.

These days he dreamed of Lily all the time and woke up hot and sticky. It was as if he was thirteen again. So what was the problem? What was stopping him and Lily being together? All he had to do was get her on her own and tell her that he loved her and the threesome stuff was over. Now it would be just the two of them. But Harry would be devastated, wouldn't he, feel hurt, shut out, and Max didn't want to shut his best friend out.

He didn't think Harry wanted Lily that way. Harry wasn't bothered about any girls, or didn't seem to be – and, despite the choirboy jibes from Max, he clearly had no interest in boys. Harry was desperately in love with Harry and deeply fascinated by Harry's health, or lack of it.

Max, on the other hand, would not be ill. He wouldn't acknowledge illness or infirmity. One school term, he'd hobbled round the rugby field for weeks, refusing to accept he had a broken ankle.

The matron finally noticed he was limping and took him to the local A & E, where they told him off and fixed him up. But when he got tired of being in plaster, he pinched a kitchen knife and Harry helped him hack it off.

Christmas came, then Easter and, apart from the obligatory few days at home, during the vacations they all stayed in Oxford in a third-year student's flat in Iffley Road and looked after his cat.

Lily found vacation jobs in Elliston's, where she worked in Modes, selling Crimplene dresses to Oxford city wives. Harry and Max found casual work in various warehouses and factories.

Harry probably didn't need to work at all, thought Lily – his parents seemed to be well off, and very generous, too. Harry always bought more than his share of pints and pies. But Max was permanently short of cash, and wherever Max went, Harry followed – in the daytime, anyway.

While Harry spent his evenings reading Molière and Schiller and making endless notes, Max got to know some city girls, strengthening the links between the town and gown and sometimes wishing – maybe – that he hadn't bothered.

'So she didn't tell you she already had a boyfriend?' Lily asked as she bathed Max's hand in soapy water and attempted to get the gravel out, then dabbed the wounds with TCP.

'I didn't ask,' said Max.

'What was he like, this boyfriend?'

'Big as a bus and all his mates were clones of him.'

'What did they do to you?'

'Got me on the ground and stamped on me.' Max glanced up at Lily. 'You should be a nurse, Red Queen.'

'Why do you say that?'

'You're gentle, sweet and kind. So, come to think of it, you shouldn't be a nurse. They're brisk and strict and bossy, at least in my experience.'

Max flexed or tried to flex his mangled hand on which the boyfriend and his mates had stamped and ground into the tarmac of the Cowley Road. 'Just keep dabbing here,' he added. 'You've got almost all the grit and gravel out.'

'You ought to see a real nurse,' said Lily.

It was the first time she had ever touched him more than momentarily, and although his hand was such a mess, she found that touching, dabbing, holding part of Max was wonderful, electrifying.

She dabbed more TCP on his poor fingers, on the zig-zag cuts across the back of his poor hand – such nice fingers, such a perfect hand – and wondered how she'd bear to let him go.

But she had to let him go – she knew that – so she did. 'Perhaps we ought to go to A & E and get you X-rayed, see if any bones are broken?' she suggested. 'Harry, don't you think so?'

'Farley, do you want to go to A & E?' asked Harry, barely glancing up from Molière.

'No,' said Max.

'Okay,' said Harry. 'I think I've had enough of analysing social comment in *Le Malade Imaginaire*. Let's all go to the pub – and before you say it, yes, I'm buying.' He screwed the top back on his pen then started tidying up his copious notes.

Lily looked at Max.

Max looked at Lily.

She couldn't read the expression in his eyes, but her body seemed to understand him, and she found she was blushing like a rose. Max held her gaze for maybe a few seconds more. But then he looked away.

'All right,' she said. She went to fetch her coat. 'I fancy going to the pub.'

The summer term began and was a dream of punting on the Cherwell, of lying in the sunshine in the Parks, of outdoor concerts, fêtes and balls, and also of a nightmare of exams, sitting in the Examination Schools or other gloomy halls with rows of desks in them, togged up in formal black and white and scribbling feverishly.

Lily and Harry passed all their exams, and somehow Max passed his as well, although Lily suspected midnight cramming and strong coffee might have had a lot to do with it.

Lily knew she should have been relieved and happy for the three of them, but now she realised with a sinking heart that soon they'd be apart for months.

Unless …

Perhaps the boys would fancy coming to stay in Dorset?

'I'm going hitch-hiking and back-packing through Europe, picking grapes or waiting tables, meeting girls and having lots of sex,' said Max, when she and Harry asked about his summer plans.

He added Harry needed to have lots of sex as well.

'Girls or boys or fat old dons, it doesn't matter, just get on and do it,' he insisted. 'It will clear your sinuses.'

But Harry said he wasn't planning to have sex of any kind with anyone. He was spending all July and August in Surrey with his parents, reading round his subjects, and visiting his sister in New Zealand in September.

Lily said she was going home to Dorset, where she'd help her parents and her brothers run various summer courses for disadvantaged children from the cities.

'Mum and Dad have got this place that used to be a stately home,' she told them. 'Now it's an activity centre and a sort of holiday camp for children up to twelve.'

'Why only up to twelve?'

'We tried up to fifteen. It didn't work. Twelve on up, they're teenagers who want to stay in bed all morning, smoke disgusting roll-ups made of dock leaves, snog each other and sneak off to the pub. Max, why don't you come and spend a month in Dorset and get some good fresh air and exercise?'

'It always rains in Dorset. I want to go to Turkey where it's sunny and I'll get to meet some pretty girls. I'm desperate to meet some pretty girls. All the girls in Oxford look like donkeys.'

'I do not look like a donkey!'

'All the girls apart from you, Red Queen, but you're an honorary bloke. So you don't count.'

So that, apparently, was that. As far as Max and Harry were concerned, she was of no sexual interest whatsoever. She was just an honorary bloke.

But still, but yet ...

A couple of days before the end of term, Lily and Max were sitting in The Lamb and Flag and nursing pints. They'd found themselves a dark and private corner and they were alone.

Harry was at some boring meeting – that third term, he'd got involved in politics, had told Max he was thinking of becoming an MP. Max almost told her then. He almost said: my lovely, my adorable, my beautiful Red Queen, you and I must go away together. We'll discover secret and enchanted places where no one will find us, where we can live happily ever after.

But that would be idiotic, wouldn't it? He had no money to take Lily anywhere. They wouldn't even get as far as Swindon. So he didn't say anything of the sort. When she said she hoped he'd have a lovely time in Turkey, all he said was: you have fun in Dorset.

Chapter Seven

Lily didn't have much fun in Dorset. She missed Harry quite a bit and she missed Max a lot. She didn't know why she missed him. She was not in love with Max. She knew she would be crazy to fall in love with somebody like Max, with someone who would never settle down, but would instead always be roaming off somewhere, and always chasing women.

'I'm having various people round on Saturday,' said Minnie at the end of Lily's first tutorial of her second year. 'You must come and bring those pretty boys.'

'Yes, all right,' said Lily.

'You don't sound very keen.'

'I mean thank you. I should love to come. Of course I'll bring the boys, that's if they're free.'

'Did you have a good vacation, Lily?'

'Yes, it was okay. I spent it teaching children from Birmingham and Liverpool to swim and sail a dinghy.'

'Why weren't you hanging out with hippies in Morocco and smoking interesting substances? Why weren't you culture-vulturing in Italy or Greece? Good heavens, you must have a social conscience, mustn't you? Tell me, have you joined the God Squad yet? Or signed the Pledge of Purity?'

'Do you hobbits want to go?' asked Lily.

'Do you know if she's invited that Lucille from Somerville?' asked Max.

'No, I didn't ask her to submit a guest list and I didn't accept for you in any case. So if you two happen to have previous engagements?'

'Oh, I'll come along,' said Harry. 'What about you, Farley?'

'I suppose I might,' conceded Max. 'But could you ask about Lucille? I got the impression she was rather keen on me.'

'You're so conceited, aren't you? You honestly believe you're irresistible to any woman with a pulse. Anyway, she's twice your age, at least.'

'But older women are much more interesting than teenagers. They've been around the block a couple of times. They know it all, and she's not past it yet.'

The having-people-round was very noisy.

But the noise was very, very strange. It was a blurred cacophony of glooping, bubbling, gurgling. Lily felt like she was under water, like when she fell in the river, except she wasn't wet. Maybe this was down to all the drink?

Whatever; after she'd been at the having-people-round an hour or two, Lily knew she must be slightly drunk. Or even very drunk? She wasn't sure. She wasn't used to vodka and its funny little ways.

Of course, she'd learned how to drink beer. Whenever she was on a drinking-beer night out, she always knew when she was nearly-almost-bordering-on drunk. She could calibrate her personal rat-arse quotient to the nearest quarter pint.

She'd learned to treat beer with respect and – in return – beer was kindly, tolerant and forgiving, even though it tended to make her wee a lot. Beer made her happy, witty, sociable and talkative. Later, like a gentle nurse, beer would lull her to sleep.

But vodka was no gentle nurse. Vodka was a dominatrix wearing lots of lipstick, a scarlet whalebone corset and black fishnet stockings. Vodka looked like someone in a pornographic magazine, the kind she'd found last summer in one brother's bedroom and had devoured voraciously herself, in fascinated shame.

Now vodka poked and prodded Lily. At this stage of any other evening, beer would have been making Lily drowsy. But vodka woke her up. Vodka made all sorts of sly suggestions, one of which was that she should have sex.

She realised vodka was absolutely right. So where was Max? She must have sex with Max! Yes, she must, and afterwards she'd get engaged to Max and tie him down once and for all. She'd waited long enough and now the time was right.

What if he didn't propose to Lily? She'd propose to him. Queen Victoria had proposed to Albert, after all. Perhaps it was a leap year, anyway?

But what about his other women, asked a voice inside her head. They were irrelevant, she told the voice. They were of no account. Max had just been marking time with all those girls from Somerville, St Hilda's and St Hugh's. Max had been waiting patiently while Lily made her mind up – while she worked out that she and Max were meant to be together. It was their destiny.

But where could Max have gone? Perhaps he'd found the knowledgeable Lucille? Oh, please don't let him be seriously attracted to Lucille, the older woman who'd been round the block and knew it all! Lily was very well aware that she knew almost nothing. But she was keen – no, at this very moment, she was absolutely desperate – to learn, and who could be better than Max to introduce her to the delights of love?

Minnie Rushman's people-coming-rounds were probably always crowded, she decided, as she looked for him –

always full of people talking, laughing, shouting, arguing and flirting.

The guests at that first party of the term were a mix of dons, postgraduates and undergraduates, filling Minnie's house in Jericho with shrieks and squawks of female merriment and corresponding deep, satanic rumbling from the men, all of it still sounding as if it was under water.

The vodka flowed and flowed. Somebody had sent a case of genuine Black Label all the way from Russia, where he had been teaching that September, so somebody else revealed to Lily. So, since the room was hot and she was feeling very thirsty, she drank one more glass of it, another, then another ...

Someone offered her a cigarette. It wasn't a sophisticated pink or black Sobranie. It was a rather messy-looking roll-up and she knew somebody else had had a drag already because somebody's lipstick was smeared all over it. She took one drag, two drags and then some more.

The walls began to move around the room, receded then encroached again. But it didn't matter because the walls of Minnie's little house were soft and billowy, made of sponge or rubber. The floor was made of eiderdown. When she tried to walk towards a window to breathe in some night air, she had to wade through clouds of downy feathers and she stumbled clumsily.

Where the hell was Max? She needed Max!

'Do you want a refill?' Harry swam into her line of vision, a bottle in his hand. He topped up Lily's glass. Then, as she was about to take a gulp of this most delicious and refreshing spirit, Harry leaned towards her and kissed her on the mouth.

'Harry!' Lily giggled. 'Why did you do that?'

'I thought you looked as if you needed to be kissed.'

'I see,' said Lily and took another drag of messy roll-up then blew smoke in Harry's face.

He kissed her on the mouth again. 'Do you like it, then?' he asked.

'The taste is rather odd, but it's not nasty,' Lily told him. 'Do you want to try it?'

'I meant the kissing, not that disgusting joint.'

'It's not unpleasant, I suppose.'

'I'll take that as a yes.' Harry kissed her on the mouth a third time, opening her lips with his then flicking his tongue against her teeth, which was arousing, somehow.

Lily felt her face begin to glow and soon some other parts of her began to glow as well. 'Do you need kishing too?' she whispered.

'I thought you'd never ask.' Harry put his drink down on a table, then took Lily's glass out of her hand and kissed her properly.

Now desires and needs that she had long suspected must be there but hadn't wanted to acknowledge came bubbling up like lava and told her this was it.

It wasn't Max she'd wanted, after all. She'd just had a childish crush on Max. It was lovely Harry who was meant to press her buttons, ring her bells.

'Come on,' he whispered, five, ten minutes later.

'Come on where?'

'Let's go and have a coffee, shall we?'

'Coffee would be very boring.'

'We'll find something stronger, then.'

Harry kept on kissing Lily. It was lovely – warm and soft but also hard and urgent, demanding and delightful, all at the same time.

'Lily, you're fantastic,' breathed Harry huskily. 'I always

knew you would be, but you're even more amazing than I'd dreamed. Lily, I need to tell you something.'

'Whassat, then?'

'I like you very much. Well, of course, you know I like you. After all, we're friends. But I respect you, too. I wouldn't want you thinking I was trying to take advantage, to seduce you.'

'What if I want to be seduced?'

'Do you?'

'Yes, I think I do.'

'We could rethink our options, couldn't we?' Harry suddenly looked as if he'd won a Nobel Prize. 'Lily, let's go somewhere that's more private.'

'But we can't leave Max, it would be mean.'

'Max is busy.' Harry glanced across the room and nodded towards Max. He was talking to a don from Corpus, an emaciated, leathery geologist called Giles whom Minnie had introduced to them when they had first arrived.

Giles apparently did lots of work in a range of perilous, insanitary places. He had the scars to show for it, and he had clearly mesmerised their friend, as if he were some kind of denim-shirted Ancient Mariner.

'Max has always said he wants to go on expeditions, go exploring,' added Harry as a girl in purple velvet trousers and an almost non-existent top began exploring Max's chest, sliding her hand inside his shirt, but Max appeared to take no notice. 'He means to see a lot of new-found lands.'

Harry was exploring too, discovering the new-found land of Lily. 'Come on,' he murmured as his hand caressed her bottom. 'Let's get out of here.'

The cold air sobered Lily up a little and the walk to Christ Church got her circulation going. So by the time they got to Harry's rooms, she felt rejuvenated and – oh God – even more up for it. But what was Harry doing, fumbling round in all his pockets?

'I've lost my keys.' He met her gaze apologetically. 'I'm always losing keys. I'll have to go and find the porter now. You'll need to hide. There's a cupboard where the scouts keep brushes, brooms and things along the landing.'

'Perhaps you didn't lock the door?' On this evening made for love, romance – okay, for sex – Lily wasn't keen to hide in cupboards along with brooms and brushes. She grasped the knob of Harry's door and turned it. She gave it an almighty shove. 'Open sesame!' she cried and, obligingly, the door fell open.

'Lily, you're a sorceress,' said Harry, pulling her inside.

The room was chilly and, when Harry flicked on the electric fire, the usual all-pervasive smell of damp was joined by a strong scent of dust and burning rubber. There was no increase in temperature. Or, if there was, by only one or two degrees.

'It's so cold in here,' said Lily, shivering and willing him to hold her in his arms and whisper lovely things and be romantic, like Mr Rochester in *Jane Eyre*.

'It'll soon warm up, so take your coat off,' Harry said romantically. 'Or at least undo the buttons, eh?'

Lily undid two buttons on her coat. Now she was wondering if this was what she wanted, after all.

Yes she did, said half of Lily. Yes, yes, yes!

No she didn't, said the other half. Or not in this cold, damp room in a decrepit crypto-boarding school for the over-privileged and over-educated, anyway.

But then Harry kissed her on the mouth, then on the neck, and soon she wanted him to kiss her everywhere. She kissed him back and ran her fingers through his hair.

She heard him groan and mutter something.

'What was that?' she whispered, her teeth grazing his neck.

'Oh, Lily, Lily, could we ... should we ...'

Yes, she thought, of course they could, of course they should. Why else would she be here?

'Harry, do you want to go to bed with me?' she asked. 'I mean, do you literally want to go to bed? Or do you just want sex? Only I can't help noticing your bed is very small.'

'Small is cosy.' Harry slipped one hand inside the bodice of her dress and stroked one breast. His fingers brushed its nipple and she gasped.

More, more, more, more, more! her body cried.

Touch me, touch me, touch me!

'Small is snug and intimate and private,' added Harry, his fingers busy circling. 'Big beds are for exhibitionists, for people who like having sex in fields. Lily, are you still drunk and stoned?'

'No! Yes ... well, maybe just a little bit.'

'You look quite flushed.'

'You mean you're chickening out?'

'Of course not! Why, are you?'

'No, but before we ... have you done this before?'

'Yes, loads of times.'

'Oh?' Lily looked at him and tried to focus on his face. She almost managed it. 'You've shagged the whole of Shomerville? Screwed everybody at St Anne's including all the dons and all the scouts?'

'Okay,' admitted Harry, frowning. 'I've done it once or twice.'

'Once or twice – which is it?'

'Once.'

'I bet.'

'All right, I've never done it – satisfied?'

'I think shatishaction – satishashon – oh, whatever– must come later.'

Then, suddenly feeling very fond of Harry as well as very anxious to have sex with him, Lily kissed him, stroked his forehead, smoothed away his frown. 'Come on, Harry, don't look like my father when he's about to yell at me for something. I don't want to go to bed with Dad. Lishen, we can work it out together.'

Lily slipped her coat off, pulled her dress over her head, unclipped her bra then threw it on the bed. 'Come on, slowcoach, take your clothes off, too.'

Harry took his shirt off.

Lily ran her hands over his chest.

'You're very nice,' she said.

'Lily, are you on the pill?'

'Why would I be on the pill?'

'I thought all modern girls were on the pill.'

'You shouldn't believe the stuff you read in *New Society*. Do you have some things?'

'What sort of things?'

'Oh, for God's sake, contraceptive things! I thought all modern men kept half a dozen in their wallets?'

'I could go and find someone and ask if he—'

'There's no need.' As they'd been talking, Harry's hands had been massaging Lily's breasts and this was such a lovely, lovely feeling that she didn't want to let him go.

'I'm sure we can work out what to do,' she whispered as his hands moved up, moved down, moved sideways, round and round and round, exploring, colonising Lily, making her his own America.

'You really want to?' whispered Harry as he slid one

hand between her legs and almost made her faint, the shock and pleasure were both so intense.

'Yes,' said Lily. 'Tomorrow morning, I'll go to a lady doctor in the Banbury Road,' she added as he planted little nibbling kisses all along her collarbone. 'Apparently, she doles out morning-after pills like Shmarties.'

Later, Harry wound a lock of Lily's hair around his index finger, then slipped off the curl and slid it on to the third finger of her own left hand.

'What are you doing?' Lily asked him.

'Just affirming our betrothal.'

'Do you mean you're plighting me your troth?' It came out as flighting me your froth, but Harry seemed to understand.

'Yes,' he said, and trailed his other index finger down her chest and then on to her stomach, lower, lower, lower, igniting her again. 'So now you have to flight your froth to me.'

'You're still drunk,' said Lily.

'So are you.'

'If we're both drunk, then, does it count – this froth-flighting, I mean?'

'Of course it does. Lily, let's get married, shall we?'

'What, tomorrow?'

'No, you idiot,' said Harry. 'When we graduate, of course.'

'Okay.'

'Lily, do you love me?'

'Yes, I love you.'

'I love you to distraction, more than anything in the whole world.'

'More than Max?'

'Much more than Max!' Harry took Lily by the shoulders, made her meet his gaze. 'Max is just a friend. You're the centre of my universe.'

'Good ... that's very good.' Lily took his hand and led it where she needed it to go. 'But no more talking now. Let's do what we just did again.'

Chapter Eight

'You did what?' demanded Max, when Harry joined him in the breakfast queue the following morning, looking like the cat who had not only got the cream but had become the dairy's major shareholder as well. 'You and Lily?'

'Yes, I know it's been a long time coming,' admitted Harry happily. 'But of course it's always been inevitable. That first time I saw her in the Parks in her ridiculous red dress, I knew she was the girl for me. So now it's all worked out and we're engaged.'

'Good ... that's very good.' Max didn't know how he'd managed to say good, that's very good, when what he really meant was bad, that's very, hugely, spectacularly bad.

As he tried to force down bacon, eggs and sausages, Max struggled to believe what Harry had just said. But he'd never known his friend to lie. Harry was very many boring things and being unimaginatively truthful was easily the most boring of them all. So Max had no choice but to believe the treacherous bastard, the devious villain, the false friend who had seduced his beautiful Red Queen.

Harry grabbed his exhibitioner's gown and went off to a lecture, bouncing across Tom Quad like Spring Heeled Jack. Max gave up trying to eat his breakfast, spent half an hour in shock, then started to consider various options.

He would murder Harry, obviously, and then jump from the top of Carfax tower to dash his brains out on the paving slabs of Cornmarket. Or might St Mary's steeple be a better bet? It was higher, anyway. He'd liberate some ropes and karabiners from the Mountaineering Club and scramble up ...

Or maybe he should run across to LMH, ask Lily what the hell she had been doing when she slept with Harry, and say she had to marry him today, this very minute? She would laugh and say that it would have to be some other time. She had a tutorial now. Then that girl with whom she sometimes hung around – that bulbous-breasted, hockey-playing Molly Whatserface, with whom he couldn't imagine any non-blind, non-mad person wanting to have any kind of sex – would giggle as she mocked him.

He sloped off to a lecture. He'd come up to read history for when he started travelling and exploring and needed to impress the locals with his knowledge of the places where they lived. He wanted to know more than they did about Genghis Khan, Eva Perón and Josef Stalin. He'd said this at his interview and it had made the interviewers laugh and ask if he should not be studying Modern Languages?

'Any fool can learn a foreign language if he sets his mind to it,' Max had told them. 'I intend to pick up lots of languages en route.'

As the undergraduates filed out of the lecture, he realised he hadn't heard a word of whatever some old bore who had been droning on for the past hour had actually been saying. He hadn't made a single lecture note. It didn't matter. He'd soon be leaving Oxford, the tedious, provincial little dump, full of tedious, provincial people, and his real life could begin.

What did he want with a degree? What use was a degree? He couldn't eat it, wear it, sell it, could he? I must speak to Lily, he decided. So, that evening, he phoned the porter's lodge at LMH.

'I've told you not to use this line,' she snapped, when she realised it was not her father calling after all, to tell her that her grandmother was dead.

'I'm sorry, but I need to see you,' Max said humbly.

'Now?'

'Yes, now – this very minute.'

'I'm meeting Harry in half an hour.'

'I promise I won't keep you long. I'll meet you at the gate into the Parks.'

'Oh, all right,' said Lily, sounding cross.

At least she wasn't blooming with the radiance of love. She still looked hung over. She had a couple of spots, and she had a cold sore coming, too. 'What do you want?' she asked.

'Gale told me the news.'

'What news?'

'Oh, Lily!' Max could feel the tears well up behind his eyes. 'About you and him, of course. About you going to his room, and—'

'What does it have to do with you?'

'Well, nothing, I suppose, but—'

'You're suggesting Harry and I can't do what you do all the time? That you're a model of purity yourself? The blonde girl who was groping you last night—'

'Lily, this is not about that girl, it's about you and me.'

'There is no you and me.' Lily scuffed the pavement with her shoe. 'Yes, we're friends, but Harry and I—'

'You're suddenly more than friends? It hit you like a bolt of lightning, did it, that Harry is your destiny?'

'There's no need to be so horrible.' Lily turned to walk away. 'It's not as if you want me for yourself.'

What stopped him saying: yes, that is exactly what I want? Well, something did.

'What are your plans, then?' Max asked Harry a couple of days later, after he had spent most of an afternoon in tears, and grumbling to himself, and muttering and scowling round the Parks, and torturing himself with Technicolor® images of Harry and Lily having sex.

Or even making love? But they couldn't have been making love. It wasn't possible. Lily didn't belong to Harry. She could not love Harry. She was his Red Queen.

'You mean in the long term?' Harry asked.

'There's going to be a long term?'

'Yes, of course,' said Harry, grinning. These days, he was grinning all the time. He looked deranged, thought Max, as if he should be in some bin. 'We have it all worked out. Although to be quite honest, there was nothing to work out. Lily and I, from that first day we met, we both knew it was meant to be. We'll graduate, we'll marry and then we'll have some children – be happy ever after.'

Harry smiled complacently, the happy-ever-after bastard, smugly unaware – or at least, Max told himself, he must suppose that Harry was completely unaware, otherwise he'd have to kill him, stab the shitface through his treacherous heart, disembowel him there and then – that when he talked of marrying the Red Queen, he hammered white-hot spikes through Max's own poor bleeding heart.

Lily's words came back to haunt him.

'*Harry's very nice and I enjoy his company*,' she'd said. '*Harry's witty, generous, kind and charming. All the things you're not.*'

At the time, he'd thought she must be joking. He had laughed it off. How could he have been so dim, so stupid, so naïve?

The next few days were terrible. Max couldn't eat. He couldn't sleep. He couldn't concentrate on anything. He phoned a girl at Somerville he saw once in a while. She said he should come round for coffee, kept him occupied all night, and then at nine o'clock the following morning she threw him out because she said she had to write an essay.

So now, although he knew he'd need to force it down, he decided it was time he got some food inside him. He would be too late for college breakfast. So he slouched into a café in St Giles, slumped into a big old-fashioned, high-backed wooden settle, and ordered scrambled eggs on toast.

He was starving – ravenous – but found he couldn't eat. Listlessly, he pushed the yellow gunk around his plate. Then he added ketchup, hoping to improve the general look of things and maybe stimulate his appetite. It didn't work. The mess just made him think of blood and vomit.

As he was about to give up on the eggs, he became aware of women's voices. Two other customers had just arrived and they were sitting in the booth behind his own. He didn't mean to eavesdrop, but couldn't help overhearing what they said.

'Yes, I do accept that Harry's safe while Max is trouble,' Minnie drawled, apparently continuing a conversation started some time earlier – today, the previous day? 'But safe is very tedious in a man. Yes, please, coffee would be lovely, thank you. May we also have some toast and marmalade?'

'What's a girl supposed to do, then?' Lily asked.

'You could renounce the pair of them, perhaps – become a nun?'

'You're so funny, Dr Rushman.'

'I'm not being funny, Lily. Sex is nice, but celibacy has its own attractions, as you might discover one fine day.'

'I'm going to marry Harry.'

'Oh, don't be ridiculous. You mustn't marry Harry Gale. He'd be a disaster as a husband.'

'I think he would be perfect. He's good-natured, kind –

hardworking, too. He'll be a great father to our children and a loving spouse to me.'

'He'll also bore you stupid. Although you're not a genius, you're averagely bright, but Harry's bordering on mentally defective.'

'How can you be so horrible?'

'How can you be so obtuse?'

'May I ask you something, Dr Rushman?'

'I suppose so.'

'Why are you not married?'

'I don't see the point.' Minnie sighed theatrically. 'You're such a disappointment, Lily Denham. I thought you were special. When you turned up paralytic on your first day here in Oxford, looking like you'd come from Marrakech by way of Ruritania, I was quite impressed. Yes, here is an original, I told myself, even if she looks as if she's wearing her grandmother's old curtains. Here is someone interesting at last. But I was wrong.'

'Dr Rushman, everyone is special. But, like most other women, I'm almost sure that one day I shall want to be a mother. So perhaps I ought to marry someone?'

'My dear, ever since you came to Oxford, I've encouraged you and nurtured you. But, in view of your declared ambitions, it seems you could have spent your days more profitably reading about cookery and knitting in the cheaper women's magazines. You evidently have no soul, no spirit. You came up to Oxford, the best place in the world to get a liberal education, and you turn out to be a dull, suburban trainee housewife after all.'

'That's not fair! Harry and I – we love each other and we want to spend our lives together. We—'

'What about the other one?' asked Minnie. 'What does he think about it, eh?'

'He ... he's very pleased for us, of course.'

'What are his plans for the future?'

'After Oxford, he'll be going travelling, I expect. He'll get himself mugged, maimed and mutilated in the world's most dangerous and unhygienic places and then write books about it.'

'Why don't you go with him?'

'I can't see the attraction of rowing down the Ganges or up the Orinoco or wherever in some old canoe. Or of eating snakes and slugs and snails and salamanders and other horrid things. Or of getting bashed over the head then fried and eaten by savages myself. It's like I said – I'm going to marry Harry.'

'I'm going to marry Harry,' Minnie mocked. 'Tell me, Lily, how did he propose – down on one knee in moonlight?'

'May we change the subject? About Milton and my next week's essay – do I need to read the whole of *Paradise Regained*?'

'Yes, I think you do,' said Minnie tartly. 'It's time you read the rest of Thomas Hardy and Henry Fielding, too. I dare say your ambition after graduation is to write bestselling semi-pornographic bodice-rippers for the popular press, while simultaneously nursing twins and knitting your own lampshades from wool you've spun yourself. So I feel I must insist you read some actual literature while you're still here in Oxford.'

'D H Lawrence wrote a lot of not-so-semi-pornographic bodice-ripping stuff,' retorted Lily mutinously. 'So why shouldn't I?'

'Do stop being such a silly girl and eat your toast.'

Max packed up his last few books then shoved a change

of clothes into a rucksack. He told the college porter he'd been called away on urgent family business. So could the porter please arrange for Max's trunk to be sent after him?

'You'll be away for how long, sir?' the porter asked.

'Sorry, I don't know,' said Max, and a fiver stopped the porter asking further questions.

He walked out to the ring road where he meant to hitch a ride to London. What had he been doing, wasting all that time in Oxford, when there was a world out there waiting to be explored?

'You want a lift, son?' called the driver of a petrol tanker.

'Thanks!' Max ran towards the lorry, climbed inside then slumped down in the cab.

'You're a student, right? Off home for the weekend to visit Mum and Dad?' The driver winked. 'Yeah, I know you student lads of old. Run out of money, have you, need a sub?'

'Yeah,' Max replied and forced a grin.

So, goodbye, Oxford – won't be seeing you again.

He had never wanted to go there in the first place. As usual, he'd followed Harry's lead, had done what Harry did, and look where it had got him.

But now he was through with Harry Gale and Lily Denham. He would be nobody's fool again.

He supposed he ought to go and see his father, let the old man know that he'd left Oxford. But would his father care? After Max's mother had run off with a gangster when Max was eight years old, Max had been brought up, ignored or cosseted, depending on their various temperaments and inclinations, by a long succession of nannies, so-called aunts and a variety of European au-pairs.

David Farley was the CEO and chairman of a business started by some obscure ancestor back in the eighteenth century, which imported coffee from Brazil, a country Max's father never visited himself. He went to Switzerland in winter for the skiing and to St Tropez in summer. Max meant to see the whole of South America.

This was out of curiosity, not a desire to go where previous Farleys might have gone, to get malaria where they'd got malaria, be bitten by the same breeds of bird-eating spiders that had bitten them. He had no interest in his father's business or his family, which was only fair because his father's family had never shown the slightest bit of interest in him.

When his mother first left home – it had been one April afternoon – he'd asked his father where she'd gone and when she would be coming back?

'She won't be coming back,' said David Farley.

'But she lives here, Daddy.'

'Yes, she used to live here, but she doesn't live here any more.'

Max did not believe his father, and for several months he waited patiently for Mummy to come home. Then, one evening, while his father was upstairs with a new aunt, Max sneaked into David Farley's study. He found his mother's phone number in the addresses section of his father's diary, and her new address.

He phoned. She wasn't there. A woman with a foreign accent told him Mrs Farley was abroad. He didn't believe the foreign-accent woman because abroad meant countries like France or Italy. Mummy wouldn't go abroad without him, would she?

He took some paper, envelopes and stamps from David Farley's study. Over the next few weeks he wrote her half a dozen letters, telling her about his school, his nanny and his hamster Puffball who lived in Nanny's room.

Mummy, I miss you.
Please come home.
I love you.
I'm sorry I was naughty.

He couldn't remember being naughty. But he decided if he said that he was sorry, Mummy might forgive him and come home.

She did not come home. So he resolved to fetch her home. He found her address on the big map of London that was always on the table in the local public library. He was used to catching buses on his own, so now he planned his route.

When at last he found the house he saw that it was wrong. It wasn't nicely painted. There were no window boxes full of flowers. The railings were all rusty. The windows were so dirty you couldn't see inside. The front door was all scarred and there were burns and kick marks on it, too.

Perhaps it was the wrong address and that was why she hadn't answered any of his letters? There must be lots of streets with very similar-sounding names all over London? A flame of hope leapt up inside his heart. When he got home, he'd slip into his father's study, check his diary again. But, since he was here ...

He rang the bell but soon decided it was broken. At any rate, he couldn't hear it echoing through the house. So he used the knocker and, after several minutes, a man opened the door.

'I'm looking for Mrs Farley,' Max announced.

'Who might you be, then?' The man was wearing a lady's scarlet dressing gown and his big feet were bare. Perhaps he'd been asleep in bed, even though it was the middle of the afternoon? Or maybe he was ill?

'I'm Max,' said Max.

'Max who?'

'Max Farley.'

'Who is it, Terry?'

When Max heard his mother's voice, his heart beat faster and he tried to see inside the house, which smelled of stale cooking and like the outside lavatories at school.

'Mummy, it's Max!' he called.

'Max?' Then Dolly Farley came clattering down the hallway, her feet in high-heeled shoes, but otherwise wearing nothing but a bath towel clutched tightly to her chest. She pushed past Scarlet Dressing Gown, who leaned against the doorjamb and stared at both of them. 'Max, whatever are you doing here?'

'I've come to fetch you home,' said Max, who somehow knew that even as he said it she was never coming home. So now he wanted more than anything to cry.

But he refused to cry – instead he looked at Mummy, willing her to change her mind, to say of course she'd come with him …

'I can't come home,' said Dolly. She started chewing on a fingernail, a long nail red with varnish. 'It's … it isn't possible.'

'Why?' asked Max.

'Your father won't allow it.' She wouldn't look at him. 'Darling, let me go and put some clothes on. Then I'll find a taxi for you, get you taken home.'

He gave it one last shot.

'Why can't you come with me?' he demanded. 'Daddy wouldn't mind, you know. He's hardly ever there. I haven't seen him for a week.'

'I don't live with you and Daddy any more – and Max, your father thinks it's best if we don't see each other.' She leaned towards him, kissed him on the cheek. She smelled of cigarettes and scent and also something dirty, like the hamster's cage. 'Come inside while I get dressed and then we'll find that taxi.'

'I don't need a taxi.' Max started walking down the grimy, broken steps. 'I'll catch the bus.'

'Be good for Daddy?' called his mother. 'Max? Please wait a moment? We haven't said goodbye!'

Max continued walking down the steps. Once he was on the pavement, though, the flame of hope flared up again and he looked back.

But Dolly had already turned away, was being shepherded inside by Scarlet Dressing Gown. He had one hand on her bare back and she was giggling like a girl. Scarlet Dressing Gown glanced round, saw Max, mouthed: beat it, kid.

Max beat it, ran along the street, towards the busy road where he would find a bus. As he sat on the bus, he thought: it wasn't possible to be good for Daddy. He'd tried, but everything he did was wrong. 'Max, don't be more ridiculous than you can help,' Daddy had said just a few weeks ago, when Max had finally summoned up the courage to ask him if he would consider playing in the masters'/fathers' cricket match one Saturday. 'You'll soon be going to boarding school, thank God,' he'd added sourly.

Max had read some stories about boarding schools and thought that going to one might be good fun, some of the time, at least. It seemed there would be endless opportunities for climbing out of upstairs windows, slithering down drainpipes, catching burglars trying to pinch the silver cups from the headmaster's study, and having midnight feasts.

As it turned out, his own school almost managed to live up to this fine literary reputation. The masters were all monsters, but they'd been monsters at his day school, too. Masters, monsters – they were interchangeable, all ugly, vicious and unpredictable. They were the enemy, to be avoided.

He soon made friends. He knew how to make friends. All you had to do was share your tuck, know how to punch your way out of a fight, and not snivel when a monster whacked you. Then he made a special friend. 'Who are you?' asked somebody who wasn't in his house, but he had seen in French and Latin.

'Farley,' Max replied.

'You look like me.' This statement sounded like an accusation and it was an accusation. 'Ghastly Gormley grabbed me as I walked along the corridor this morning and the bastard twisted half my ear off. He said he'd seen me slithering down a drainpipe and I was a stupid little bleeder who was going to break my neck and it would damn well serve me right. I said it wasn't me. So was it you?'

'Yes, it was me.'

'You'd better go to see him and own up.'

'All right,' said Max.

He did, and Ghastly Gormley twisted half his ear off too, and also gave him six detentions, and said there'd be a beating if he did anything else as idiotic.

'Good man,' said Harry, when he next saw Max in Latin. 'I mean for fessing up. Do you want to come to lunch at my house this weekend? Gormley will give you an exeat if you say my mother has arranged it and will pick you up.'

Harry was a day boy whose own parents clearly loved their son – adored him, actually. He was the child of their old age, born when his sister was a teenager, and she lived on the far side of the planet nowadays.

Max never quite worked out why he liked Gale, who was a swot, who never lost a house point, and who scooped up merit marks as if they were pebbles on a beach. Max himself was always in detention, always being punished for some crime or misdemeanour.

'You're nothing but a crawler who lives up Gormley's trousers,' Max told Harry when Harry won a house point or got a merit mark.

'You're nothing but a juvenile delinquent who lives down drains and smells like it,' said Harry.

'I hate you, Gale,' said Max. 'I hate you like I hate the stink of Gormley's pipe.'

'I hate you, too,' said Harry. 'I hate you like I hate cold tapioca.'

But they were still best friends. Max went to stay with Harry and his parents most school holidays. Mrs Gale invited him as company for Harry. David Farley always seemed relieved to see him go.

Or so Max thought, because his father never said: goodbye, my boy. Or: here's a couple of ten bob notes for you. Or: let's do something interesting, just you and me, when you come home next time. He merely gave him money for the train.

'You never talk about your mother, Max,' said Mrs Gale.

'My mother's dead,' said Max.

'I thought you said she left you and your father? She went to live with some bad hat,' said Harry. 'Someone who wore a woman's dressing gown?'

'Harry, don't be silly,' said his mother. 'Nice people don't do awful things like that. Max, my dear, I'm sorry about your mother. I suspected she must not be with us any more, but all the same I didn't like to pry. You and your father must miss her dreadfully. By the way, I had a very charming

84

letter from him yesterday. He's happy for you to come to Normandy with us because he'll be away on business all the summer.'

It was just as well that as a child Max had relished all the various challenges of travelling alone. Now he would travel round the world alone, he told himself, as the lorry chuntered down the motorway, and he would go on foot. He liked to walk. He liked to feel he was connecting with his mother earth, a mother who had always been consoling and reliable, unlike his actual mother.

Who needed to rely on engines powered by fossil fuels? Well, perhaps he'd take a bus or two, but nothing more elaborate. There would be no hitching rides in juggernauts or hiring motor vehicles. Maybe a few train rides? Possibly, though anybody could get on a train and watch the scenery flash by ...

There would be no aeroplanes. But he would try container ships, perhaps, if he could join a crew and work his passage. Then he would write about his wanderings.

'Pass us a can of Tizer, son?' the lorry driver said, breaking into Max's thoughts. 'Get one for yourself, as well. What's the matter, lad? You look like you lost a quid and found a penny. You got women trouble?'

I'll get over Lily, he told himself. Although she might have run it through with white-hot blades, she will not break my heart. I will not die for love. I wish her well and happy.

'I'm fine,' said Max and popped his Tizer.

Chapter Nine

'So you're Max?' The blonde who opened the front door to him looked Max first up then down. 'I thought you were a little boy.'

'Why did you think that?'

'Oh, some stuff that David said to me.'

'What stuff?'

'How you are at school and very lazy and will never come to any good.'

'He's out of date about me being still at school, but he's right about me being lazy. Who are you, then?'

'Femke – I'm from Holland.'

'Hello, Femke-I'm-from-Holland. Where's my respected father, do you know?'

'I don't, but it's for sure he isn't here.' Femke smiled engagingly. 'I am about to make some coffee. Do you like some?'

Femke's coffee was delicious licked off Femke's lips. Femke's skin on Femke's waist was smooth and warm and soft. Femke's bed was big and comfortable. This was not surprising because the bed belonged to David Farley and was in his large, imposing bedroom that overlooked a leafy London square. Femke's eyes were green as London leaves, their pupils black and shining.

Femke came with very gratifying, shuddering cries. She had not been faking, Max was certain, even though he understood with women it was hard to know for sure. The girl from Somerville had always shrieked and moaned and writhed and sighed, but Max had wondered if it was an act, or maybe she'd had indigestion? But Femke's cries had had the ring of authenticity.

'You mustn't think I do this all the time,' said Femke, coming back from the en suite wrapped up in towels, then flopping down beside him as he buttoned up his shirt. 'After all, I am your father's friend. I do not go chasing other men.'

'But if they turn up on your doorstep needing coffee?'

'Max, don't mock me. David being so often far away, sometimes I become a little lonely. Also I was curious to find if you are like your father in your private ways.'

'What did you decide?'

'You two are very different. David must have everything exactly as he wishes it. He can be very cold, very unkind. But you were warm and generous with me. You seemed to think about the other person.' Femke walked her fingers down his chest. 'You do not need to leave so soon.'

'I do – I have a train to catch,' lied Max. 'But could you tell my father that I called, and say I'm going travelling for a while, so I won't be in Oxford?'

It had been a pointless gesture, Max decided later, having sex with Femke. When he was a little child, he'd experienced the same blend of guilt and satisfaction by scribbling in his father's books and pissing in his shoes. It had made him feel a little better for a while, but then he would be sad and sorry, wishing there'd been no need to make his point, whatever it might be.

'What do you mean, he's gone?' demanded Lily.

'He's scarpered.' Harry shrugged. 'He's packed up all his stuff. The porter's going to send it to his father's place in London. Now it's just you and me.'

'But don't you care that Max has gone?'

'Oh, he'll be back, don't worry. While we were at school, he'd sometimes disappear for days on end. But he'd eventually turn up again, dirty, tired and hungry, clothes in rags, and if he hadn't been so clever and his father hadn't been so rich, they would have kicked him out.'

Lily couldn't believe that Max had gone. But nobody had seen him, and his room was empty, so she had no choice but to believe. He hadn't even said goodbye.

'Lily, is anything the matter?' Harry asked that evening as they lolled on Harry's narrow bed, Lily lying on her back and Harry on his side. 'I hope you're not still fretting about Max? I've already told you there's no need.'

'I'm not fretting about Max.'

'What is the matter, then?'

Why did he go? she asked herself. What if we never meet again? How could he walk out of my life?

'It's … oh, it's nothing.' She stared up at the ceiling where there was a South-America-shaped patch of damp.

'So just relax?' Harry undid the buttons on the bodice of her dress. He pushed back the material and unclipped the front fastening of her bra, exposing both her breasts. He gave each one a squeeze.

Then he started dabbing at her nipples. Then he was circling them. They stiffened, stood erect, and Lily was still thinking about Max.

Of course, she couldn't say as much. It would be somewhat tactless, wouldn't it, while Harry was – what exactly was he doing now, apart from stroking, squeezing, circling? Evaluating, cataloguing, stocktaking? Why did she keep thinking that he was making lists, and ought to have a clipboard and a pen?

'Please don't squeeze so hard,' she said.

'I wasn't squeezing, but you're very tense.' Harry's other hand slid up her dress. It pushed her knickers down. It peeled them off.

Lily thought of that nice lady doctor at the clinic, the one who'd fitted her new IUD.

What had the doctor said? '*Lie on your back, draw up your knees, open your legs. Let them flop apart, try to relax. It might hurt a bit as I insert it, but it won't take long.*' Why was she thinking about the lady doctor?

Lily sighed. It hadn't been like this the first time she and Harry had made love. It had been romantic, wonderful, like in the books and films. But maybe it had been romantic because she was so sloshed on Minnie's vodka? Whatever – she was stone cold sober now. Harry was making truffling, grunting noises and fumbling around inside his jeans. She thought: I need a drink.

'Why don't we go down the pub?' she asked.

'Sorry?' Harry stopped his fumbling. 'What, you mean go now?'

'Yes, this minute,' Lily told him, pushing him away and sitting up. 'You're right. I'm very tense. I need a drink.'

'Oh … okay, then.' Harry stuffed himself back in his jeans. 'Yes, let's go and have a quick one, shall we? Then we'll come back here and carry on?'

'We'll see,' said Lily, who at this very moment wished that she was in her room at LMH, re-reading through the notes she'd made before she wrote her essay on Spenser's hugely tedious and boring *Faerie Queene*.

Max went to see the man the don from Corpus had suggested. A man who always liked to hear from people who were single, clever and adventurous, apparently, provided that they also had a death wish. Or so Giles, the don from Corpus, said.

The don's own publisher, he turned out to be a wobbling jelly of a man who had an office in a turret of a soot-stained tenement in a narrow street off Leicester Square. 'You'll be perfect, darling,' said the jelly.

'Oh?' said Max. 'You don't know anything about me yet.'

'I spoke to Giles last week. I wasn't expecting you to turn up quite so soon, but now you're here it's obvious he was right. You look the part, in any case. You're dark-haired, dark-eyed. You're not too tall and not too short. So you could pass for almost any nationality: a light-skinned Asian, dark-skinned European, an Arab or a Mexican – and that's what really matters. I was saying to Giles only a couple of months ago: please don't send me any blonds or redheads. They're too conspicuous in foreign parts. But you would be all right.'

The publisher tamped down shreds of brown tobacco in his pipe, then lit it, puffing clouds of acrid smoke. 'So off you go and do some travelling. I suggest you start in South America; that's a nasty, violent, dangerous place. Then come back home and sit down on your arse and write a book.'

Nasty, violent, dangerous, thought Max – South America sounds perfect, and I've always wanted to go there, anyway ...

'What would you pay me?' he asked the publisher. 'I mean, to write this book?'

'We won't pay you anything until you write the thing, deliver it and we accept it.'

'So if you don't pay me, how am I going to get to South America?'

'You could stow away, perhaps?'

'Yes, perhaps,' said Max and thought again of those container ships which must always need crew, and might not be too fussy about paperwork and documents.

'You'll stow away?'

'I'll get there somehow, yes.'

'I'm sure you will.'

'I'll need to sort out various visas, won't I? Maybe I should get some jabs for cholera and stuff?'

'My dear sweet boy, we shall be paying you – that's if we do decide to pay you – to go and be adventurous. So you must have no visas, get no jabs. You're not a tourist, after all. You'll get yourself into these dreadful places, lurk as long as possible, make your way back home to the UK, and – as I've said already – write your book.'

'What if I get arrested, thrown in jail?'

'I'm sure you'll think of something. Dig a tunnel with a teaspoon? Bribe somebody with your lovely body?'

'I won't forget the teaspoon.'

'Mind you don't. Now for a word of warning: if and when you get to South America, don't swim in any rivers. The last young man I sent to Venezuela, he did exactly that and all they found of him was bones.'

'I know about piranhas.'

'They're not the only peril you'll encounter. There's this little fellow who's no bigger than a minnow, but he's covered in barbed spikes. He gets into your bathers and then he burrows right up your old man. It's impossible to get him out, so you die horribly.'

'I won't swim in South American rivers.'

'You mind you don't, my sweet. You're so young and beautiful that if you came to any harm I would destroy myself.'

The man wheezed out a foetid cloud of smoke. 'If you're really desperate for funds, my boy, maybe we could come to some arrangement? I have a bijou place near Covent Garden and on Thursday afternoons—'

'I'll get a job or stow away,' said Max.

A year went by and Lily settled into a very comfortable relationship with Harry, who soon proved to be a perfect boyfriend.

Generous and thoughtful, he was always turning up with unexpected presents like a silver bangle, pretty pendant, a pot plant for her windowsill, tickets for the theatre in London ...

Also, nowadays the sex was great. There were no more sessions with a virtual clipboard, no more checking lists. Lily gradually found her way round Harry's body and her own, Harry did the same, and they had lots of fun in bed.

So what was wrong?

Max not being in Oxford – that was what, for Max and Harry had been a perfect pair, practically inseparable in her heart and mind, and now that Max was missing it was as if a photograph had faded. The image was still there, but it was difficult to make it out, remember what had been there in the first place.

'You still look astonishing in your peculiar clothes, but nowadays your mind is so pedestrian you make me want to howl,' said Minnie, tossing Lily's latest essay back across her desk. 'Next time, why don't you try for an original thought or two? Perhaps you could imagine that nobody has read or seen Macbeth before? You're the Jacobean version of the drama critic for the Sunday Times. What did you make of it? Did you love it, hate it? What about the story – did it entrance you, bore you? What about the characters – did you identify with any of them? Why should other people go to see it? Or not go to see it?'

I don't care, thought Lily. I'm not an academic, after all. I'm here in Oxford under false pretences, and now I've been found out.

A dozen or so postcards came from South America, postcards that were grimy, stained and often near-illegible, covered as they were with purple franks or foreign scribble or sometimes thick, black lines of censorship.

Once in a very infrequent while, a letter came as well. As far as Lily could make out, Max was getting himself arrested rather often, thrown in various prisons and off various trains, which were without exception very filthy, especially in Colombia.

'But travelling by train is very cheap,' he wrote. 'Much cheaper than by bus. So cheap, in fact, that only down-and-outs and aimless foreigners like me travel by train.'

There were armed guards on all the trains, apparently, and these guards were easily angered or upset by Englishmen whose papers didn't seem to be in order. So Max would be arrested and would spend a couple of days in jail, until the British consul – or whoever – came to sort him out, to tell him to go home. Or at least to get over the border and cause trouble somewhere else.

'They certainly don't value my spirit of adventure and my genuine thirst for knowledge, these consul blokes,' he wrote. 'One said that if I meant to scrounge and scavenge my way around the world, I should have started off in Pakistan.

'Asians are more tolerant of my kind of behaviour, so this consul reckoned. They respect the British, too. But here, when people realise I'm British, they think I must be working for the Yanks or KGB, that I must be a spy. So I'll probably get myself assassinated one day soon. I'll wind up in a corned beef factory.'

Lily shuddered. Harry merely laughed and said he wouldn't be buying any more corned beef then, if there was some chance that bits of Farley might be in the tin.

'But don't you ever worry about him?' Lily asked.

'Yes, of course I worry.' Serious now, Harry put his arm round Lily's shoulders and pulled her close to him. 'I've always worried about Farley. But we both know he's a maverick. There's a restlessness about him that will never change. You and I: we love him, don't we? We'll always be here for him? He knows it and from time to time he'll want to see us – need to see us. So try not to fret.'

But Lily couldn't help but fret. When there was an earthquake in El Salvador, she worked herself into a state of near-hysteria, ringing the Foreign Office to find out if any British nationals had been injured or – worse – killed.

'He'll be fine,' soothed Harry, gently stroking Lily's hair. 'He'll soon turn up again.'

'How do you know?'

'Farley's indestructible. You'll see!'

Harry was proved right. Only a few weeks later, they got a letter telling them that Max had made his way to Panama, where he'd joined the crew of a container ship on which he'd worked his passage back to Europe, ending up in Malaga.

Then, after hitchhiking through France and Italy and Greece to Lebanon – the starting point for his new expedition, he explained – he would be travelling round the Middle East.

While he'd been in South American prisons and getting thrown off South American trains, he had somehow managed to write a book as well. *Adventures on the*

Amazon was published, got some flattering reviews, and hardback copies were displayed in Blackwell's. He came back home to the UK, got interviewed by newspapers and magazines. He did some stuff on radio and was also booked for author signings, including one in Oxford.

'So I'll hope to see you both again at last,' he told them, on an ancient sepia postcard of some mosque – a postcard bought in Teheran, it seemed, but postmarked Hammersmith.

Lily walked into the shop with Harry and, as soon as she saw Max, her heart began to bang against her chest and she could feel her colour rise.

Max was talking to a customer and hadn't seen her yet. So she had a chance to study him, to notice he was very thin and very brown, and that the boy she'd known was now a man. She felt as if she'd been electrocuted. It was as if a million volts surged through her body, lit her up like Oxford Street at Christmas. 'Max!' she cried.

He turned to glance her way. 'Hello, Red Queen.'

'Oh, Max!' She ran towards him and gave him a big hug. 'It's wonderful to see you!'

'It's good to see you lovebirds, too,' said Max. He didn't return the hug and, when she kissed him on the cheek, he didn't kiss her back. His stubble merely brushed her face.

Then he shook hands with Harry and Lily had a chance to get a better look at him. The pretty boy was now so very handsome, and he had grown a couple of inches, too. Although he was so thin, on Max his gauntness was attractive. It gave more definition to his cheekbones, and made his hands look strong and capable.

She'd been so looking forward to talking to him, catching up. But soon she was obliged to understand that she was not his only fan. On that sunny Saturday in Oxford, at any given moment he must have had at least a dozen women clustered round his table, cooing, smirking, giggling and simpering at him flirtatiously.

No, he said, he couldn't spare the time to have some dinner with them in Oxford. He must go and catch the train to London as soon as he had finished here in Blackwell's. It was as if he didn't want them to be there, thought Lily. So, after he had signed their books, they said goodbye and left.

'What did you think of Farley – how he looked?' asked Harry casually as they walked back to Christ Church.

'He was much too thin.'

'I wonder when he'll fetch up here again?'

Let's hope never, Lily thought. I belong to Harry now. I'm in love with Harry. I'm going to marry Harry, and all Max would do for me is mess things up, destroy my peace of mind.

'I don't want to talk about Max Farley,' she said firmly. She held the book he'd signed against her beating heart, resolving she would read it soon.

Max couldn't believe it was the same Red Queen.

He'd left behind a gawky whippet of a sometimes slightly spotty adolescent girl. He'd come back to a woman: a rounded, curvy woman with fuller, redder lips and with a woman's clear, translucent skin. A woman dressed in even crazier clothes than those she'd worn when she'd first come to Oxford, but which somehow looked amazing on the person who had made them, even though they would have looked like fancy dress for lunatics on anybody else. A woman Harry touched and stroked and patted constantly. It was as if he needed to assure himself that Lily was a solid presence, hadn't vaporised.

'Africa the next time, is it?' chirped a reader who'd rushed into Blackwell's as the shop was closing. He signed her book – and wrist, she had insisted, even though her husband stood there scowling – in red ink. 'What are you going to do in Africa?'

'Go for a little stroll along the Nile, along the Congo – I rather like big rivers – and try to climb Mount Stanley,' Max replied.

'I didn't know you were a mountaineer?'

'I'm not – I shall be learning mountaineering as I go along. Or in this case, up.'

'Where will you get your gear?' enquired the husband, as his wife continued simpering, as the staff began to clear the table of Max's few remaining unsold books, as the shop itself prepared to close.

'I won't have any gear as such,' said Max. 'I'll be wearing T-shirts, jeans and trainers.'

'Surely lots of companies in the UK would sponsor you? They'd provide you with the proper gear?'

'Yes, but my publishers want me to suffer. Do everything the hard way. Do my best to lose some fingers, toes or even more important parts of me.'

'Why's that?'

'So they can sell more books. The man who spends his working life in some oppressive office, and hates his boring job, likes to know that travellers get frostbite, dysentery, yellow fever and various other horrible diseases, get locked up, go hungry ...'

'When you come back from Africa – that's if you do come back – where will you be going next?'

'I'll be off to India, or anyway that's the plan.'

Chapter Ten

'We got our Firsts then,' Harry said delightedly.

'Yes, well done us,' said Lily.

Harry had slaved his socks off and he deserved his excellent result. Lily, however, couldn't quite work out how she had managed to get a First, but somehow it had happened.

'We must find a place to live in Oxford,' added Harry.

'Or maybe move to London?'

'But we both love Oxford, don't we? Maybe we could buy a house here? Or at least a flat? My parents will be happy to help us out, provided we get jobs. We'll both need to find jobs. Or I shall, anyway.'

'Oh, don't you worry, I'll definitely find a job,' said Lily.

'What are you going to do?'

'Well, you know how much I love to sew? I'll turn a hobby into a career. I'll be a second Biba.'

'What's a Biba?'

'Oh, come on, Harry – even you have heard of Biba! I'm going to design and sell my own collections. I've already made the first ten things. They'll be my samples, and—'

'I mean you'll need a proper job, my darling.' Harry ruffled Lily's hair indulgently. 'One that pays a salary.'

'This will be a proper job – you'll see.'

But Harry wasn't convinced that making dresses would or could turn out to be a proper job, and so he got his hair cut, bought himself a suit in Savile Row – his parents paid – and went for Civil Service interviews.

He or his tailoring made a very good impression and, a few months later, Harry was in post and in the fast stream for promotion. He joined a cabinet minister's staff as his most junior aide. Soon, it was all *Sir Nicholas Barlow says* – and there was apparently no subject in the world on which Sir Nicholas Barlow was not a great authority.

Then it was *Nicholas Barlow thinks*.

Then *Nicholas told me*.

Then *Nick mentioned this in confidence*.

Then *Nick has a place in Somerset and says the shooting's splendid and I must go down some time*.

Lily grew extremely tired of hearing about Nick, who – Harry said – was going to be prime minister in less than ten years' time, and Harry meant to be his private secretary – the great Sir Nicholas Barlow's PPS, the power behind the throne.

'A certain earnest, puppyish way round older men that could be quite misleading.' Minnie had put her clever finger on it years ago. Harry definitely wasn't queer, physically at least. But he was a hero-worshipper: Max throughout his childhood, and now it seemed that Nick had taken Max's place.

Minnie was similarly underwhelmed by Lily's choice of job.

'A seamstress? What a tragic waste,' she said. 'You got an excellent First, for heaven's sake, so you could do all sorts of things – provided you don't marry that boring little man, of course, and then become a baby-making factory yourself.'

What's it to you, thought Lily. Why do you still want us to meet up? Surely you know other people you can push around? These days, there must be at least a hundred brand new undergraduates hanging on your every word? Well, I'm not your student any more. You're not my tutor. So ...

'It's because I haven't quite given up on you,' said

Minnie, reading Lily's mind. 'What about applying for a junior fellowship?'

'I don't want a junior fellowship.'

'Lily, as I've told you, when we met on your first day in Oxford, I thought you could be special. Since then, you've done a lot of silly things. You've made some dreadful choices. But you could still be special.'

'I'm definitely going to be special. I'll make my name in fashion. I intend to be another Biba.'

'Do you now?' Minnie smiled sarcastically, like a Cheshire cat. 'I'll observe your progress with amusement – and with interest, obviously.'

I'll show you, Lily thought, and paid a local printer to run off a thousand leaflets, business cards and flyers. She traipsed around North Oxford pushing these though letterboxes.

She waited for some orders to arrive. No orders came. Maybe she had priced the clothes too high, she wondered, even for North Oxford? She didn't see how she could sell them any more cheaply, and still make a profit – even a small profit.

Or was it the clothes themselves? 'They're gorgeous, but they're also most unusual, and so – how shall I put it – I think they would be difficult for anyone not young and tall and thin to wear,' mused the ladies' fashion buyer at Oxford's biggest and best department store. 'I'm very sorry. They're beautifully made, but I don't think they'd work for us.'

'Oxford's full of female students, they're all young, and some of them are thin and tall,' said Lily.

'But they still live in jeans. They probably don't have a lot of money to spend on gorgeous clothes, and if we sold your lovely dresses at our usual mark-up, they would be priced out of most students' reach.' The buyer shook her head in sympathy. 'They're not all earls' or bankers' daughters, are they?'

The fashion buyer might be right, thought Lily, at least as far as Oxford was concerned. She lugged her case of samples down the Banbury Road, back home to the tiny flat on the top storey of a Gothic horror that looked as if it ought to be the attic setting for *The Yellow Wallpaper*, complete with scoured and crumbling plasterwork.

Their particular attic was up four long flights of stairs and looked across a wilderness of gardens, all brown and muddy in the chill of winter. The rooms were dark and draughty. 'It will be fine in summer,' said Harry optimistically. 'When the sun comes round it will be full of natural light.' Well, thought Lily, it was foul in winter, cold and damp, with windowpanes that rattled and doors that didn't fit.

She knew her parents didn't approve of this arrangement, of as-yet-unmarried people moving in together, living in sin, as Lily's mother would have put it. But that was just too bad.

Mum, I'm definitely getting married, Lily didn't say, because she knew the M word would have been a cue for Mum to start to plan a big church wedding, and it wasn't going to happen. It looked as if her brilliant career in fashion might not happen, either – or not in Oxford, anyway.

'Why don't you apply to join the Civil Service?' Harry asked, when Lily came back home dispirited day after day.

'I can't imagine anything more gruesome.'

'You're still determined to be – what is it – a Biba? Okay, give it a few more months, my darling, then we'll see. You might find your sewing will need to stay a hobby, after all.'

Quietly determined to prove Harry and Minnie Rushman wrong, now Lily made her mind up that if bloody Oxford didn't or couldn't appreciate her talent, she would take her talent somewhere else. She would go to London. She packed her case of samples and started trawling through the dirty, crowded streets, being shown a hundred doors, but finally ending up in Camden in a tiny, quirky shop where the proprietor was – oh, thank you, God – enthusiastic.

'I'll take seven of this one,' she told Lily, smoothing down the velvet bodice of a long-sleeved day dress. 'Two tens, three twelves and two fourteens, all slightly different so they'll be one-offs, sale or return, of course. But I know my customers and I'm sure these will sell.' Lily could have kissed the woman's feet.

The dresses sold, the woman in the shop was thrilled – almost as thrilled as Lily was herself – and ordered twenty more. Lily worked into the small hours, diligently machining, and soon began to realise that success might have its downside in exhaustion and sore fingers.

I'll have to take on staff, she thought. But then I'll make no profit. I could source cheaper fabrics. But the people who buy my clothes want decent stuff, not rubbish. These are heirloom dresses ...

'You ought to go to India, you know,' the woman in the shop observed to Lily when, almost catatonic with fatigue, she finally delivered the new consignment, yawning and apologetic for the slight delay caused by John Lewis running out of one particular shade of heavy silk. 'All the prices for high quality fabrics are much lower there. Get on a cheap flight to India, buy in bulk – fabrics, trimmings, threads – then get it all shipped over here. I have a friend in Delhi who would be very pleased to have you visit, put you up and show you round. I can give you contact details, names, addresses. You should book your flight.'

'So there's this place in Delhi – it's called Chandni Chowk,' said Lily. 'I could source the most amazing fabrics there, apparently, and buy them at low prices, too.'

'It's a long way to go to buy some cloth,' said Harry, as she'd guessed he might.

'This won't be just any cloth. This will be the kind of stuff I need to make the sort of clothes I want to sell; that I know I can sell! Oh, Harry – I have such big plans! I'm starting small, I know, but when I get home again, I'm going to advertise for a machinist, train her up. Then I'll get another machinist, then a third, a fourth. I'll run the business from this flat at first, but soon I'll have a shop – or even shops. It's all going to work out, I'm certain. Please believe in me?'

'Oh, I do believe in you,' said Harry. 'But what are you going to do for money, for investment?'

'I won't need investment, not at this stage. I have a bit of money Granny left me. It's been held in trust for me, but now I'm twenty-one I'm going to be able to get it out and use it.'

'How long will you be away?'

'About a week, I think, or possibly a fortnight.'

'I don't think I can get the time off to come with you.'

'You don't need to come. Harry, I'm a big girl now.' Lily kissed his cheek. 'You mustn't worry. I'll come back to you, my darling, and I'll bring you lots of lovely presents. I'll find you something special.'

Part 2

January 1970
–January 1984

Chapter Eleven

Lily had confidently expected sunshine, but on that winter day she walked out of the airport into a smut-stained, stinking Delhi fog.

'You want taxi, madam?'

'Mine good taxi, very cheap!'

A cacophony of voices beat her jet-lagged eardrums, while a hundred hands pulled at her sleeves.

'Madam, my taxi best in all of Delhi. You come now!'

'Madam, where you want to go? I take you anywhere in city, it's no problem!'

'Lily? Lily Denham?'

'Sita Banerjee?' Disoriented, gritty-eyed, Lily almost fell over the tiny Asian woman who was smiling up into her face.

'Welcome to India, Lily!' said Sita Banerjee. 'I hope you had a pleasant flight? Where's your case? I have a taxi waiting.'

Sita's mother was as small as Sita, and Lily felt as if she took up all the space and oxygen in their minute, already cramped apartment. 'You must call me auntie,' said Mrs Banerjee authoritatively as she took Lily's case and passed it to a servant, or a man who Lily guessed must be a servant, anyway. 'So, now – you must make yourself at home. You must take a shower, then you must eat.'

You must, you must, you must, thought Lily …

'You must not go out dressed up like that,' said Mrs Banerjee the following morning, as her cook and sweeper stared at Lily in her jeans and T-shirt and shrugged and shook their heads in disapproval. 'You will definitely be courting trouble if you do.'

'What should I be wearing, then?'

'You must dress more modestly. You must not draw attention to your body, especially to your bottom or your legs.'

'You mean I should wear a sari?'

'No, most Western women find saris very difficult, so Sita has gone out to buy some salwar trousers and a couple of tunics for you, which we hope you'll love. They're very comfortable and stylish, too.'

She didn't like being told what she should wear. But when Sita turned up with the trousers and the tunics, which were actually very attractive, Lily thanked the Banerjees and asked how much she owed them.

'No, no, they are gifts!' cried Sita, looking horrified.

'Gifts,' repeated Mrs Banerjee. 'Go to your bedroom now and try them on.'

'Yes, you look very nice,' said Sita, twenty minutes later, eyeing Lily up and down and nodding her approval. 'So ... shall we go out? I'll show you round the fabric shops in Chandni Chowk and Nehru Place. You're going to believe you are in fairyland! But give yourself time to acclimatise and, however much you like what you are shown, don't be tempted to buy anything at all today.'

'How shall we get to the shops?' asked Lily as they left the apartment building. 'Do we walk? Or do we catch a bus?'

'It's not safe for women to walk alone down certain streets in this part of the city,' said Sita, with a shudder. 'As for buses: women – particularly foreign women – unaccompanied by men should never use a bus. They'd risk being sexually assaulted, robbed or worse. We shall take a taxi.'

They stood on the pavement waiting for a rickshaw taxi.

As they waited, male pedestrians and men on motor cycles grinned and shouted comments across the street to Lily.

'Why are they grinning?' she asked Sita. 'What are they going on about?'

'I don't like to tell you,' said Sita, reddening. 'Lily, just ignore them and, for goodness' sake, please don't smile back! They are very ignorant, foolish fellows who have nothing else to do.'

'Go on, Sita, tell me what they're saying?'

'When we are in a taxi, then I'll tell you.'

'So?' said Lily as the taxi merged into the traffic.

'Hijra,' muttered Sita.

'What?'

'Hijra – it means eunuch. They think you look like a man, but like a woman too. You are so tall and slender and you stare at them, you see. You look around you all the time. But, as a woman, you should keep your gaze fixed on the ground.'

'I see.' Lily couldn't decide if she was horrified or mortified or what. 'I've come to look at India, not at pavements,' she objected.

'All the same, try not to look men in the eyes,' said Sita. 'It confuses them. Ah, here we are now – this is Chandni Chowk, where you will find the most amazing fabrics in the whole of India!'

The fabric shops and stalls in Chandni Chowk were certainly amazing. Sita took Lily down a street jam-packed with shops and stalls that sold all manner of fabrics, trimmings, threads and other haberdashery. Lily began to visualise the clothes she could create from all these beautiful materials. She watched entranced as merchants unspooled bolts of cloth across their counters and their cutting tables. She stared in wonder at the flashing colours.

'Yes, madam, all is washable,' a merchant promised Lily.

But Sita didn't believe him. 'You wash that hand-blocked fabric, you will ruin it,' she said. Then she harangued and argued with the merchant until he shook his head and finally admitted washing this one would be foolish, but with this other fabric, madam, there would be no problem.

'Now I shall show you bead and buttons,' Sita said, dragging Lily out of one particular shop and promising they would come back tomorrow. She finally let Lily spend a few rupees on buttons, beads and bells, but insisted all the serious spending must wait until her guest had seen more shops, had got a handle on the prices and felt confident enough to bargain. 'Otherwise, these fellows will rob you blind,' said Sita, 'and we can't have that.'

Over the next few days in Delhi, Lily visited the various fabric markets, honed her bargaining skills and ordered many bolts of cloth for shipment back to the UK. She couldn't believe this stuff was all so cheap. The quality was excellent, so how and why – don't argue, said her other self. Just buy.

Sita introduced her to her friends, who were all extremely tiny and extremely beautiful, with curving hourglass figures and flashing coal black eyes. All traditionally dressed, they turned out to be lawyers, doctors and accountants, and they all spoke English perfectly. They giggled at the hijra business, and Lily realised ruefully that nobody would ever mistake one of these gorgeous Asian beauties for a man.

'Today, I must get something for my boyfriend,' she told Sita, the next time they went out.

'What does your boyfriend like?'

'I don't know, to be quite honest,' Lily admitted. 'He's not really into stuff. I mean, he doesn't seem to need possessions. He's always buying gifts for me, but never seems to want things for himself.'

'Gadgets – men like gadgets?' offered Sita. 'Or weapons – knives and daggers?'

'A dagger's not a present!' Lily glanced towards a silversmith, who was working at a pavement stall. 'One of those silver boxes might be good. He could keep his cufflinks in it.'

'What about some ties?'

'Oh, yes – silk ties,' said Lily, smiling. 'Yes, I'm sure he'd like those very much. Or I could buy the fabric and make them for him, couldn't I?'

'Yes, you could,' said Sita. 'A present made with love is always special. Lily, I think your boyfriend is a very lucky man.'

Sita and her friends took Lily to a Hindu wedding, where she saw such magnificence she couldn't help but stare. 'But everything is borrowed,' whispered Sita, as Lily stood there in her borrowed finery and goggled in astonishment. 'The wedding clothes, the wedding horse, the wedding thrones, the wedding jewellery – well, some of the jewellery – it must be returned.'

Special occasion clothes, thought Lily. I could make them, couldn't I? When I get married, I don't mean to wear a ghastly white meringue myself, and why should anybody else, unless it's what they actually want?

Oh, she had such plans!

She was enjoying her time in Delhi, certainly, but she couldn't wait to get back home to put these plans straight into operation. This was it – she knew it. This was going to be her future. As a hotshot businesswoman, she would revolutionise the wedding industry …

Sita was a lawyer who worked three days a week.

Mrs Banerjee had lots to do, chivvying her servants and spending hours and hours on the phone, chatting to her friends. Lily knew her way round Delhi now – or part of Delhi, anyway – and thought she would be fine going out alone.

She hadn't yet been on a bus. She decided that today she would go on a bus. She'd dress exactly how she wanted, too. She'd had enough of wearing floppy Asian garments, so she put on jeans and a new T-shirt she'd made for this adventure, white with sprays of pink and mauve embroidered flowers scattered across the front. While she'd been out with Sita, she'd seen other women – and some of them were Asian – wearing jeans. Why shouldn't she?

Mrs Banerjee was busy arguing with her laundry man when Lily pussyfooted past, calling she was going out and yes indeed, she would be home for supper, certainly, and yes, she'd get a taxi. No, of course she wouldn't walk.

Outside on the pavement, she went into a shop and asked where she could find a bus to go to Chandni Chowk. She meant to buy some special trimming for a wedding dress, perhaps her own.

She caught the bus – quite literally, because in India buses didn't stop. Passengers just climbed on board and disembarked at traffic lights or when the bus slowed down, avoiding cows; the skinny, mournful, dozy cows that wandered everywhere, scavenging from piles of rotting rubbish, eating shredded plastic bags and other litter, trying to get run over.

Lily made her way along the aisle of the bus and found a seat next to an old man in a dhoti and a dirty turban. He shuffled up a bit and moved a basket so she could have more room.

She thanked him and he grinned, patted her knee, and

then he started chatting. He sounded kind and friendly and very soon some other men joined in with him, all laughing, chatting and patting Lily gently on her shoulders, arms and knees …

Sita had just been being over-cautious, obviously. The bus was very crowded and, as the only European on board, she got some stares. But she smiled and nodded and some of the men smiled back.

Although the patting was a bit annoying, it didn't seem particularly sexual, just friendly. She was being patted like she herself might pat a child or dog. Nobody touched her chest, her neck, her thighs …

She decided she and Sita must have walked down some of these long streets before. Yes – there was the silversmith, busy working at his stall. She must be near her destination now. She looked across the aisle to a woman who was sitting with a toddler on her lap. 'Chandni Chowk?' she asked and pointed to a narrow side street.

The woman merely glanced at her then slid her gaze away.

'Yes, madam – Chandni Chowk is that way,' said a man in polyester slacks and a white shirt. He pointed to the street that Lily thought she recognised. 'You get off at the lights here, walk a hundred yards along that alley, and you'll find Chandni Chowk.'

'Thank you,' Lily said. At the lights, of which no one took notice anyway, she swung herself from off the moving bus, as she'd seen Indians – well, male Indians – do. It was just as well that she was wearing jeans, she thought. Such a manoeuvre would have been impossible in a sari, and quite difficult in a tunic and the baggy salwar trousers she'd been wearing recently.

The alley was dark and stank. She hurried, trying not

to touch the walls or tread in anything disgusting, while people coming the other way pushed past, trod on her toes, and in the darkness various hands groped at her legs and chest.

A couple of thin pariah dogs were following her now, and whining hopefully. 'Stay away from street dogs,' Sita had advised on her first day. 'They all have rabies.'

Getting anxious, Lily started hurrying, then running, weaving in and out of throngs of people, willing the alley to spit her into a familiar street. But instead more people crowded round, and then her bag was snatched. Somebody had evidently cut the strap, and other hands grabbed at the bag itself, so now she'd lost her money and her cheque book.

She must have been pushed against a wall, and that was how she'd hit her head – on something sticking out, a bracket or a sconce? Or had someone whacked her with a cosh? As she fell into the muck and mire, she panicked, wondering if this was it: if she would lose her life.

'Sir, sir, come, sir – British madam hurt!' Max's landlord shook his shoulder. 'Sir, we think she dead!'

Yes, thought Max, she might indeed be dead. Yet another stupid foreign woman had gone wandering on her own down side streets in a country where a woman walking by herself was almost always going to be a prostitute – fair game.

The British madam – that's if she was British, not American or German or any other nationality – was lying face down in the dirty alley where Max was renting two small, foetid rooms on the top floor of a crumbling tenement, and writing up his notes on trekking in the Himalayas.

113

She was being tended by two men who were no doubt also frisking her for change and jewellery. He felt her pulse. It was beating strongly, so she wasn't dead, or even almost dead. But she did seem to be unconscious.

'You'd better bring her to my room,' he said, in dreadful Hindi. 'I'll see what I can do.'

The two men lugged the woman up the stairs and laid her down on Max's charpoy bed, and then they and the landlord hung around.

They grinned and winked at Max, who grasped their meaning, but didn't want to argue. He gave them all some low denomination notes, the sort he'd give a porter. 'I'll keep the lady here until she's feeling better, until she can tell me who she is and where she's staying,' he said, or hoped he'd said.

The men grinned more, winked more, made a whole range of various rude gestures, then they left.

The British madam's body twitched. He hoped she wasn't seriously hurt and wouldn't need a doctor or a hospital because he'd have to go and tell the police there'd been an incident, and this would hold him up.

He pushed the shutters back. The woman was lying on her face and he could see some blood where she'd been hit with something hard and heavy on the head. He fetched some water and began to sponge away the blood, realising now she had a lump the size of half his fist – where she'd been mugged, presumably? He hoped the bastards hadn't cracked her skull.

She moaned a little and then stirred. She twisted round to look at him and then he got the shock of his whole life. 'Max?' she began, and frowned at him. 'What are you doing here?'

'Why were you in the alley?' Max shook his head. 'It's

all right, don't answer. I know I must be hallucinating and imagining this.'

'Then we're both hallucinating. But, to make quite sure, let's do a test.' Lily tapped him gently on one knee. 'You felt that?'

'I did.'

'So this is real. What happened to me?'

'You were mugged, I guess,' said Max, who knew he was still staring in astonishment at this bedraggled woman who looked so much like Lily. 'What are you doing in Delhi?'

'I'm buying buttons, trimmings, fabrics.' Lily began to struggle to sit up and so Max put one arm across her shoulders, giving her support.

Yes, this was Lily.

'Where's Harry?' he demanded.

'Oh, he's in the UK,' said Lily, shrugging. 'I'm staying with some friends. I came out on my own today. I meant to catch a bus to Chandni Chowk. I lost my way.' She smiled at him. 'Or perhaps I didn't lose my way at all?'

'You're very lucky to be alive.' Max wrung out the sponge and offered it to Lily so she could wipe her face. 'Where do these friends live? I'll go and find a taxi, take you home.'

'But now we've met, I want to stay with you!'

'You have concussion, Lily.'

'I have my heart's desire.' Lily leaned towards him. She kissed him on the mouth. 'This was meant to be. It's karma, kismet, fate. My God, this T-shirt's filthy.' She stripped it off and then she wound her arms around his neck and pulled him close. 'Max, make love to me?'

'What? Lily, I think you ought to see a doctor, get that bump checked out, and maybe have an X-ray—'

'You don't want me.' Lily kissed him once again. She

started to undo the buttons on his shirt. 'How can you not want me, Max, when I want you more than life itself?'

Afterwards, he gazed at Lily, looking deep into her eyes. She smiled like a lazy cat, and he could hardly credit that barely half an hour ago she had been lying practically unconscious in a dirty alley.

So was this fate, as Lily had insisted, was this karma, was he being given a second chance, was he being offered an opportunity to change, to settle down with the one woman – with the only woman – he would always love?

He turned away, stared at the wall. What would it mean, to change and settle down, become a caged and fettered prisoner with a mortgage and a starter home, spending holidays with in-laws, never free to roam or ramble, never—

'Max, my darling?' Lily touched his hand. 'What are you doing? You look miles away.'

'I … I was just thinking.'

'About what?'

'Oh, nothing, really. How do you feel now?'

'I'm in a state of bliss,' said Lily. 'What shall we tell Harry?'

'We won't tell him anything!'

'Of course we will. We must! We'll need to tell him the engagement's off, that now I'm going to be with you.'

'You don't mean that.' Max stroked her hair back from her face. 'Yes, what we did just now was wonderful, amazing, life-affirming, all those things. But you're engaged to Harry. You belong to Harry, and the life you'll have with Harry is the life you want.'

'How do you know what I want?'

I heard what you said to Minnie Rushman in that café in

St Giles, Max thought sadly, knowing there was no way he could ever tell her that.

'I'm a wanderer, a traveller,' he said at last. 'I'll never put down roots. I'll never want to stay in just one place for months, for years, for life. You want a husband, children and a home. You know you do. But I'm a loner, not a marrying man, a family man.'

'You could be.'

'No, I couldn't.'

'You're rejecting me.'

'I want to make you understand it wouldn't work between us and we'd be mad to try to make it work because we'd only end up making one another miserable.' Max reached for his clothes. 'I'd better get you back to where you're staying.'

'I don't want to go. Max, do you love me?'

'Yes, I do.'

'So isn't love enough?'

Mummy, I miss you.

Please come home.

I love you.

'I don't think love can ever be enough.'

'What do you mean?' demanded Lily, trailing one long finger down his chest. 'When we have love, don't we have everything?'

'Love needs feeding, nourishing; and, unless it's nourished, it will die.' Max caught her finger, pushed her hand aside. 'I can't feed or nourish you. I can't give you anything. You and me – you know we have no future. So come on, put your clothes on, and I'll take you back to where you're staying, if you can remember the address?'

'It's all over, is it, just as it was getting started?'

'Lily, nothing started.'

'What we did an hour ago – are you saying it was a mistake?'

'It was a big mistake.'

Lily realised it was no use. She could talk, persuade, cajole forever but Max wouldn't change his mind. So she put her dirty clothes on, let him find a rickshaw taxi, let him take her back to Sita's place.

He explained extremely briefly to a disbelieving Mrs Banerjee that Lily had been mugged. Since he had happened to be in the vicinity, he had brought her home. He didn't add they were already acquainted. Sita evidently wasn't there. Or she didn't come rushing to the door, in any case, asking Lily where on earth she'd been or what she'd done to get into this state.

Sita's mother didn't ask Max to come in, presumably because there were no other men in the apartment and it would not be decent. So, after saying goodbye, he disappeared. Mrs Banerjee did some tutting then pushed Lily into a hot shower to wash the filth away.

Chapter Twelve

Lily still couldn't decide if she had dreamed it or if it had been real. After all, how likely was it she'd meet Max in India? When she'd fallen over in that alley, or been pushed, she knew she had lost consciousness for at least some minutes – minutes in which there had been time to dream. Yes, meeting Max and making love to Max: it must have been a dream.

The mugging, though – that had been real. The bump was there, she'd lost her handbag and her clothes were filthy. They'd been handed over to the dhobi, who returned them two hours later, boiled and starched, the embroidery on her T-shirt ruined, her jeans now able to stand up on their own.

'Who brought me back here?' she asked Mrs Banerjee.

'Oh, some hippie fellow,' said Sita's mother carelessly. 'One of those long-haired, bearded layabouts who ride in coloured buses, have no morals and are always playing guitars. You had a fortunate escape from him.'

'Did he give his name?'

'No, and I didn't ask for it. I do not wish to know such awful people and you shouldn't know them, either. They are a disgrace to civilized society. You are a very foolish girl, you know. You're lucky to be alive.'

Harry met Lily at Heathrow. 'Darling, it's so good to see you!' he exclaimed. He took her in his arms. He hugged her tightly. He swung her round and round.

'It's good to see you, too,' she said. 'But could you put me down?'

'Why, is something wrong?'

'No, nothing's wrong, but I'm so tired.' She forced a smile for him then winced. 'Ouch – please don't stroke my hair.'

'Why not?'

'I had a little accident, fell over, and the bump's still sore.'

'Poor love,' said Harry sympathetically. 'Okay, let's get you home to Oxford. You can tell me all about it: where you went and what you did and who you met. I'm longing to hear everything.'

After an early supper, they went to bed, made love, and it was nice. Harry was considerate and kind, pulling her on top of him and being careful not to touch her head. They woke up to a chilly winter morning, comfortably spooned.

'Missed me, did you, sweetheart?' murmured Harry as he nuzzled at her neck.

'Yes, a bit,' said Lily.

'Just a bit?' Harry pulled her round to face him, kissed her sweetly on the mouth. 'I was rather hoping you would say you've missed me lots.'

'Okay then, lots.' Lily knew she wasn't being fair to Harry. 'Sorry, darling. I'm still tired and jet-lagged and when I'm tired, I'm scratchy.'

'You didn't sleep last night?'

'No, all I did was doze. I took some sleeping tablets in the end, but still I couldn't settle.' She looked at him, at his kind, handsome face. 'I missed you lots and love you lots,' she added, meaning it. How could she not love this gentle, generous man? How could she not want to be his wife? How could she have gone to bed with Max? What had she been playing at? I shall not give Max another thought, she told herself.

'I brought you this.' At breakfast, she gave Harry

the little silver box. 'I was thinking you could keep your cufflinks in it. Or your paperclips. Or something, anyway?'

'It's very pretty – thank you, love.' Harry looked so gratified that Lily felt ashamed.

'I know we should have done this sooner,' Harry said as they were having dinner that evening. 'But, to tell the honest truth, my mother couldn't find it.' He produced a purple velvet box and put it on the table. 'Go on, look inside,' he added, smiling.

Lily opened it and stared.

'What do you think?' he asked.

'It – it's gorgeous, Harry! A family heirloom, is it?'

'Yes, it was my grandmother's.' Harry picked up the diamond and emerald engagement ring and slipped it on her finger. 'A perfect fit,' he said with satisfaction. 'Just like you and me.'

But I've been told that that emeralds are supposed to be unlucky, Lily thought. My mother always said so, anyway. 'I won't wear it every day,' she told him. 'It's too precious. I wouldn't want to lose one of the stones.' It's totally impractical and it will snag material as well, she added to herself, but didn't say.

As they lay in their double bed that evening, legs entangled as they read their current books-at-bedtime, warm and cosy and secure as freezing rain poured down, lashing the windows, Lily told herself again that this was what she wanted. She would be Harry's wife. One day, they'd have a gorgeous house: a Georgian rectory or similar, in a pretty village. Harry would do well in his career. They'd have half a dozen clever, beautiful, good-natured children just like him, and they would all be happy.

What about her own career, then? Oh, she would have

that as well, of course. She'd juggle, wouldn't she, like modern women do?

The fabrics, trimmings, buttons and the rest of all the stuff that she had bought in India arrived intact, and Lily got to work. She had lots of orders from the shop in Camden to fulfill, and sewing kept her sane.

Or at least it kept her mind off Max, who would insist on visiting her in her dreams. But in her dreams he told her they'd get married on a beach in Trinidad. They'd cross deserts, ride on camels, live like Lawrence of Arabia. They would build themselves a boat and sail all round the world ...

'Go away,' she told him angrily. 'You said you didn't want me and now I definitely don't want you.'

'What?' asked Harry, woken by her muttering to herself. 'Who don't you want?'

'Oh, nobody,' said Lily. 'I was dreaming.'

She started looking at shops in Oxford and in less expensive parts of London. She made plans. She realised she couldn't run this business entirely on her own. She needed to employ someone to do some of the cutting and the basic sewing. She had to buy a second sewing machine. She found her granny's money was running rather low and so she asked about a bank loan, completed reams of paperwork, and made some paper patterns for a range of new designs.

But by late February, she was being sick each morning. She was getting fatter. She had swollen ankles, too.

She didn't want to see her own GP because this doctor was Harry's doctor too, and – patient confidentiality or non-confidentiality – she did not quite trust him not to share her news with Harry, if in fact there was some news. There shouldn't be because she had her loop.

She went to see a duty doctor at a drop-in clinic in the suburbs. After confirming Lily was expecting, the doctor asked if she was planning to keep the baby, if she was in a relationship, if she had a roof over her head.

'I'm engaged,' she said. 'I'll be getting married in the spring.'

'You're not annoyed with me, I hope?' she asked him, after she told Harry he was going to be a father.

'I'm surprised,' said Harry. 'I thought you had a period last month? You have a thing, as well – a loop, an IUD?'

'Yes, but the doctor told me pregnant women often get a bit of breakthrough bleeding they mistake for periods. It's all to do with hormones settling down. As for my loop – they sometimes fail.'

'What about the baby, Lily, will it be all right? What if it gets tangled in the loop?'

'The baby will be fine. The loop is very small. Apparently the baby comes out holding the contraption in its fist. Harry—'

'What?'

'You don't seem very pleased. Do you want me to get rid of it?'

'No, of course I don't!' cried Harry. 'I'm surprised, that's all. God, how could you even think of killing our defenceless little baby?'

'It's not a baby yet. It's just a blob.'

'It's a baby.' Harry looked at Lily. 'We're going to get married anyway. We'll be parents sooner than expected, but that will be fine.'

The wedding was arranged for April. Lily hoped she wouldn't be too fat to fit into the dress she had designed.

Wasp-waisted and long-sleeved and made of heavy

scarlet silk she'd bought in India, adorned with gold embroidery, not boring white on white, she wanted to be noticed and remembered, but noticed and remembered because she looked astonishing, not because she looked as if she must be up the duff.

Maybe she should buy herself a corset? Or would it squash the baby? She'd change the pattern, she decided. She would – regretfully – forget the narrow waist. She'd redesign the dress on Empire lines and add some floating panels. These would hopefully conceal her shape and look romantic, too.

'But I need him here,' insisted Harry, when Lily said perhaps they ought to go ahead without waiting for Max. 'He's my best friend. Who else would I have for my best man?'

He wrote to various consulates and made a hundred phone calls and finally he managed to track Max down in Kerala, where he was in an ashram helping some weird cult or other build a shrine. He left a message with someone in the ashram who promised on his honour to deliver it. 'Max will come, I'm certain,' he told Lily.

She was not so sure because Max would be travelling to the UK on some banana boat or cargo ship, so how could he possibly arrive in time? But he did arrive and, like her parents who had muttered about getting married in a local church and having a half a dozen bridesmaids, but who finally accepted this would never happen, he behaved impeccably.

Oh, why had he not misbehaved? thought Lily. Why had he not helped her out? Why had he not grabbed her hand and dragged her back along the aisle, out of the door, and why had they not jumped into the taxi he had waiting round the corner to speed them to – well, where?

It was because he had more sense than she did, obviously. As he'd pointed out in India, as a couple Max and Lily had no future. What they'd done had been a big mistake.

Minnie was invited but she didn't come. Maybe that was just as well, decided Lily, for if Minnie Rushman had seen them all together, she'd have no doubt worked out what was going on and said they were all fools.

Chapter Thirteen

Max let the white sand trickle through his fingers.

The wedding had been at least two months ago, but it was still a nightmare that played incessantly inside his head.

When Lily had turned away from Harry, saying she needed air, he'd hoped, he'd prayed – but why should he have hoped or prayed, when he had told the girl he loved they had no future, when he'd said that what they'd done had a been a big mistake?

As she had whispered her wedding vows to Harry, he'd realised he was the one who'd made the big mistake.

What did she mean by wearing that red dress? It was as if she wanted to announce to everybody that she was a scarlet woman: that her lover and her husband were standing there together, side by side. No, that was ridiculous. He knew very well she just liked red.

As they'd walked back down the aisle as man and wife, Harry had looked so happy that his face had almost shone. But Lily had looked as if she might be physically sick. All through the ceremony, her complexion stayed a ghastly shade of greyish-green, and at the reception afterwards she had seemed distracted and had eaten hardly anything.

Max stared out at the ocean, hearing all the shouts and yells of laughter as young, fit Australians whooped and played. Yes, there were other women – a million other young, attractive, interesting women. There were a hundred thousand women here in Oz alone – countless blonde and tanned and gorgeous girls who would go anywhere, do anything, in bed or out of it. They'd all read Germaine

Greer in the original Australian. They'd all renounced monogamy, commitment, family values. They had no time for patriarchal attitudes. When they wanted sex, they wanted only guilt-free sex and it had to be on their own terms.

Lily had been right to marry Gale, he thought, while he was in a sweltering-hot, tin-roofed bar that evening, outlining all his latest travel plans to half a dozen boys and girls who told him he would definitely not survive a hike into the outback.

'Or not if you go solo, anyway,' said one.

'Scorpions or spiders, wolves or dingoes: they'll see to it you leave your bones in some bleached desert or some dried-up riverbed,' added an older drinker, a sun-scorched, grizzled veteran. 'Go walkabout alone, mate, and you won't be coming back.'

'Okay, okay,' Max muttered to himself, while more Australians told him all about Australia's red heart and the many dangers to be found there. 'But I'll be going by myself. It's in my contract.'

It would not have worked with Lily.

It could never work with Lily.

So what do I care if I come back or don't come back?

Although her girth increased alarmingly, and she often felt so ill she thought she must be dying, Lily carried on making clothes and also making contacts, getting orders here and there from various small London shops, determined her new business would eventually be a big success.

But then the shop in Camden closed because its lease ran out. She had some cancellations from the other shops. One had cash flow problems and one began to source its stock from big suppliers who could undercut a smaller business.

Then she saw a range of dresses very similar to the kind she made, but at half the price she had to sell them if she was to make a profit, in a high street chain store. You should sue, she told herself. But she didn't have the means or energy to take the store to court.

She used some of the fabrics that she had bought in India to make some gorgeous bedspreads which upmarket shops in Oxford wouldn't stock at more than cost, even though they were unique and beautifully made. 'We can import this stuff direct from India for a third of what you want to charge us,' they told Lily. 'Yes, they're lovely, but we need to price realistically.'

She didn't argue, didn't point out that her creations were one-offs, because she was too tired.

Then her doctor said her blood pressure was far too high and she would be at risk of complications if she didn't give up work and rest.

'It's just as well,' said Harry. 'Now you will be able to enjoy your pregnancy. Our baby will be healthy, happy, strong and well-adjusted.'

How did Harry know? Oh, he had read a book about it by a famous gynaecologist and a famous obstetrician, with a foreword by a famous child psychologist. 'Do you want to read it, too?' he asked.

'Only if at least one author is a woman who has had some children of her own,' said Lily as she heaved herself up off the sofa and lurched off to the bathroom to be violently sick again. 'Men know nothing about pregnancy. This morning sickness business, for example – why does it go on all day? It's supposed to stop after the first few weeks, so why am I still throwing up?'

'I'll look it up,' said Harry, glancing at his growing pile of how-to-have-a-baby books. 'I admit I'm ignorant,' he added. 'But I'm very keen to learn, you know. I want to be involved as much as possible.'

'I wish you could have this baby for me, then,' said Lily.

'It's a privilege, surely, giving birth?'

'Only if you're into masochism,' Lily told him, deciding she was never going to go through this again.

As she turned into a human hippopotamus, Harry got more and more excited and more knowledgeable. The catalogue from Mothercare became his book-at-bedtime and he ordered new stuff every day: a Moses basket, bedding for it, packs of cotton towelling nappies, tiny socks and bibs.

'What about a steriliser for the bottles?' he enquired as he was making yet another list. 'Or are you going to breastfeed? Breast must be best, of course, because it's natural. But it must be your choice.'

'I haven't really thought about it yet.'

'I'm sure they'll mention it at natural childbirth classes.' Harry looked up from his list. 'You're still going to the classes, aren't you?'

'Sometimes,' Lily fibbed because she hated them and hadn't been for weeks. Why had she signed up? Oh, Harry had read something in the *Oxford Mail* about the wretched classes and nagged her into going along.

But lying on a rubber mat in some malodorous school gymnasium, and learning various relaxation methods from some middle-aged North Oxford woman who apparently had no children of her own, but who droned relentlessly about the miracle of birth, about how if it was managed properly childbirth could be practically painless, so most healthy women should not need analgesics, had no appeal at all. Lily was not a martyr and had long ago decided if it hurt, she wanted every possible analgesic straight away.

'You should go every week, you know,' said Harry.

'Yes, I know,' said Lily, yawning as she wondered what might be on the telly. She fancied half an hour of melodrama, preferably starring actors dressed in farthingales or togas; something far removed from real life. Or her real life, at least.

'But natural childbirth in a GP unit or at home: it's not the only way,' continued Harry. 'Some women tend to need the reassurance of the latest in technology, and they're the ones who'll want to be in hospital. So we must consider all our options. What about a water birth – that sounds rather fascinating, doesn't it? But you're the mum-to-be and so, of course, your wishes must be paramount. This month's *Parents* magazine says no one should be trying to influence you on your choice of birthing methods or your other wishes one way or the other, so—'

Lily tuned out and wished that none of this was happening at all.

By the third trimester, she was bleeding constantly, she had awful stomach cramps, and she got dreadful vertigo whenever she climbed stairs. She did her best to hide all this from Harry, who she knew would worry and start scrabbling through his books so he could worry even more.

But he found the bloodstained towels, he watched her double up in pain, and one evening he laid down the law. She had to go to A & E.

'Okay, some pregnant women lose a little blood from time to time, but I'm worried you might be miscarrying,' he said as he strapped her in her seat and drove her to the hospital, where she was admitted straight away and told she would be staying.

'What, until I have the baby?' she demanded.

'Yes, until you have the baby,' said the obstetrician. 'Your blood pressure is off the scale. Your life's at risk.'

'What about the baby's life?' asked Harry.

'Yes, that too.' The doctor looked at Lily. 'We need to try to get you to full term. But I must admit right now that this is looking doubtful. An emergency Caesarean might be on the cards for you.'

'Let's hope it won't come to that,' said Harry. 'We would like our baby to have as natural a birth as possible.'

'I'll be a second Biba.' Lily remembered saying that a mere six months ago. The words came back to mock her pitilessly.

Harry said they ought to move out of their top floor flat because it wouldn't be the ideal place to bring up children.

'Where would you like to live?' he asked.

'I don't mind – you choose. It's not as if I'm going to be able to come with you and argue, stuck in here.'

Harry chose a worker's terraced cottage on the borders of North Oxford, in a street where lots of other parents of babies and young children lived.

These parents were professionals, not workers. A dozen of the houses in the street belonged to various colleges and were rented out to college servants, but nowadays no other workers could afford North Oxford. They lived in Blackbird Leys.

While she was in hospital, Lily had a lot of visitors: relations, parents and other expectant mothers from her natural childbirth class. She was also visited by Molly Fox, the former Molly Yardley, who was now settled permanently in Oxford with her engineering junior fellow of a husband, who Harry said she must have frightened into getting married.

Molly was pregnant, too. The child was going to be a genius. Molly had arranged it. While it was *in utero* she read it *Middlemarch* and *David Copperfield* and

Mrs Dalloway so it would learn to love great literature. She spoke to it in French so it would be bilingual. She played it Mozart symphonies, Elizabethan madrigals and Gershwin so its tastes in music would be catholic but intelligent. She ate a lot of fish because she'd read somewhere that this would help increase its brainpower. 'Obviously I'm going to feed my baby for two years at least,' she said, when the eternal breast-or-bottle stuff came up in conversation like a perennial weed. 'Some women feed for four or five years, actually, so I might do it, too.'

Lily decided privately that feeding anything that walked and talked would be disgusting. But she also thought it likely Molly would be able to feed a dozen babies for a full decade or more, because her breasts had grown enormous. So huge, in fact, that people – even nurses – stared in wonder.

'I doubt if you'll be able to nurse your child,' said Molly as she studied Lily critically and clearly found her wanting. 'You're absolutely tiny. You won't make sufficient milk to feed a hamster, let alone a baby.'

We'll soon find out, thought Lily – and she did.

It all began at midnight on a Thursday with her waters breaking. 'As you've been telling me for months, birth is a natural process,' she reminded Harry, who came rushing to the hospital and asked repeatedly how she was feeling, if she was all right, if he should go and try to find that nurse who'd said to sit down here by Lily's bed and wait. 'You'll worry yourself into an early grave. Then I'll be a widow and this poor child will be without a father.'

The nurse came back and she was carrying Lily's file. 'We're going to take Mum to the labour ward now,' said the nurse. 'We need to do some girl stuff. You can see her later, Dad.'

'Do I go home or wait?' asked Harry.

'Go home,' said the nurse decisively. 'It's likely to be hours yet. We'll phone you when things start to get exciting.'

'Perhaps I'll wait,' said Harry. 'I'll go to the canteen and get a coffee, read my book.'

The girl stuff proved to be the ultimate in humiliation, as a different nurse arrived with bowls and tubes and razors, ready to subject her victim to the mysteries of shave and enema.

'Let's make you all pretty there for Doctor,' said the new nurse, flourishing her razor then whipping off all traces of anything that might risk making anyone un-pretty.

The enema that followed wasn't pretty in the slightest. 'Just hold on as long as you can manage, Mum, and then we'll get you to the loo,' chirruped a different nurse.

'Where's my husband?' Lily asked as the next part of the dreadful business was getting under way, making Lily think of camping holidays in France when she had eaten something disagreeable and subsequently paid a heavy price.

'You can't see him yet, my love.'

'I don't want to see him. I want one of you to tell him something.'

'What?'

'When I get out of here, I'm going to divorce him.'

'You don't mean that, Mum.'

'Oh yes I do.'

Lily had never known such pain was possible. Surely having to go through all this torture infringed her human rights?

'I need a shot of morphine,' she told Harry, who was

133

sitting at her bedside mopping Lily's forehead with a flannel and presumably supposing this was useful. 'The stuff they give to soldiers who've had their legs or other bits blown off – I want some now.'

'No you don't,' soothed Harry. 'We opted for as natural a birth as possible. All this is a natural process. So, if you breathe deeply, and do all the other exercises you learned at natural childbirth class, you're going to be fine.'

'A lot you know about it.'

'Of course – I've read the books.'

Oh yes, the books ...

'So, darling,' added Harry, 'when you feel the next contraction coming, take a gulp of gas and air and try not to tense up. You need to ride the pain, not fight it.'

'Your hubby's right.' A midwife, who had just popped in to see how Mum was getting on, smiled reassuringly. She had a dekko, as she put it, at her patient. 'Yes, I'd say it's almost time to push.'

'Only almost?' Lily sobbed. 'I just want to get this damn thing out!' As a new contraction hit with all the force of buildings falling down and burying everybody in the rubble, Lily grabbed the midwife's hand. 'God, I've had enough of this!' she wailed. 'I want an epidural! I want that Caesarean you promised me! Go and find that doctor who knows about emergency Caesareans and said I'd probably need one!'

But she didn't get an epidural or Caesarean. She just got the absolutely useless gas and air. Since, according to the midwife, she was very tight, some butcher came and slashed her with a scalpel and, five or six hours later, when she was exhausted and past caring that Harry was sitting at her bedside still, and still offering words of wisdom from some book that had been written by some man, she finally gave birth.

'What is it, then?' she asked him groggily.

'A perfect little girl,' said someone. 'Well done, Mum – she's beautiful!'

Lily shut her eyes.

'You need to wake up, darling. You need to nurse her, or you'll never bond,' said Harry, laying something damp and squirming on her chest. 'See, we have a gorgeous baby daughter!'

'Go away and take your daughter with you,' whispered Lily, whose throat was sore from screaming. 'I want to go to sleep.'

But they wouldn't let her sleep because now it was stitches time, and here was a tired junior doctor who looked all of twelve, and who cheerfully told Harry she'd be his first human patient, though of course he'd practised on bananas loads of times.

'Just this last procedure, love, and you'll be done,' said Harry, who was holding his new daughter in his arms and cooing like a pigeon.

'I thought I told you to go away?'

'Why don't you and Baby come with me, Dad?' said a nurse. She ushered him away. 'I'll take Baby to the nursery. You come back this evening, when you and Mum have had a little rest.'

Molly had her baby that same week, and of course for Molly the giving birth stuff was so beautiful, so spiritual that she had felt – no, she had positively known – a birthing woman was a kind of goddess.

'I knew what it was like to be at one with nature,' she told Lily dreamily. 'As Fiona came into the world, I felt connected to our mother earth in the most primaeval and elemental way.'

She had ridden the pain. She had pushed when she was told to push and not before. She had not been cut, she had not torn, and so she hadn't needed any stitches. She'd probably taken the placenta home then boiled and eaten it, thought Lily, shuddering. According to a book of Harry's, some madwomen did.

But, as for breast or bottle – as it happened, it was Sarah Lily Gale who was nursed on mother's milk for several months, while Fiona Fox had to be put on Cow and Gate. Two weeks after giving birth, Molly got mastitis and her milk supply dried up completely.

'You put the evil eye on me,' said Molly.

Lily thought she was joking.

So she laughed.

Chapter Fourteen

After all her stitches had dissolved, and after sitting down became less painful and less like perching on a barbed wire fence, Lily supposed the hideousness of childbirth had been worth it.

She had a baby, anyway, and the baby was adorable. Or while she was asleep she was adorable. The trouble was she didn't often sleep. She was too afraid of missing something. On those many evenings when she refused to settle, when she had been bathed and fed, was warm and dry, but still she cried and cried, Lily didn't know what to do with Sarah or herself except join in and cry in harmony.

So Harry did the rocking. Harry did the soothing. Harry lulled and crooned for hours and hours while Lily slept or tried to sleep, but this was very difficult with Sarah's hideous racket going on and making Lily's milk flow like a torrent in primaeval, elemental sympathy.

'You don't need to tie yourself or Baby to a strict routine,' said one of Harry's books. 'Whenever Baby cries, your milk will flow. Yes, Baby crying is Nature's clever way of telling you it's feeding time!'

'This infant is insatiable,' sobbed Lily in the small hours of one awful morning, as Sarah sucked and sucked and sucked and Lily knew that she was teetering on the very edge of sanity.

One little push …

She couldn't sleep, and so she was beyond exhausted, her hair a mass of elf-locks, her eyes inflamed and bloodshot, her breasts engorged and sore. 'She's a piglet, not a human being,' she told Sarah's doting and besotted father.

'She's just beautiful,' said Harry, taking Sarah as her mother finally unlatched the child. He rocked his little daughter in his arms and, suddenly quite calm and rational, the baby gazed at him with dark-lashed eyes of deepest navy blue. 'She's Daddy's gorgeous girl. Daddy loves his girl to bits. She loves her daddy, too.'

'She doesn't love her mummy,' reflected Lily sadly. 'I'm a disappointment as a mother. I expect she ordered Julie Christie, Dusty Springfield or Marilyn Monroe.'

'I'm sorry, sweetheart?'

'I was saying—'

But it was obvious to Lily that Harry wasn't listening to a single word she said.

As Sarah grew and flourished, passing every single baby milestone well ahead of expectation, smiling, sitting up and rolling over, grabbing anything and everything, it soon became apparent to Lily that Harry had been born to be a father.

She, on the other hand, was not a natural mother, and she knew it. Oh, if only it were otherwise! Yes, she loved her baby, and yes she would have given her life for Sarah. But the endless mewling, the relentless round of feed-and-change and feed-and-change and feed-and-change, the feeling that she always had to be on high alert and did not dare relax for half a heartbeat, made her want to scream and beat her head against a wall.

I'd never hurt my child, she thought. I'd sooner die the most protracted, painful death devised than cause my daughter one second of distress. But those awful stories about mothers who threw themselves and their new babies into raging torrents or into the paths of speeding trains now made a dreadful kind of sense.

'Why don't you have a day out on your own?' suggested Harry as he winded Sarah expertly after her evening feed. 'I mean, without the little one? Leave some bottles in the fridge for me on Saturday and I'll look after Sarah. You could go shopping or have lunch with Molly? I expect her husband would look after Fiona for a day.'

'Going anywhere with Molly Fox would drive me crazy and our daughter's making a good job of that already,' Lily told him.

'But Molly is your friend,' said Harry.

'Molly Fox is not my friend! She's just someone I know, worse luck.' Lily started crying. She couldn't seem to help it. She'd never been a sobber or a wailer, but these days tears came easily. 'I don't have any friends.'

'Of course you do,' said Harry. 'All those girls at LMH – you must have liked a few of them? What about those women at your natural childbirth classes, don't you want to keep in touch?'

'Maybe I could ring one of them up.'

'You do that,' said Harry. 'What's the matter, darling?' he asked Sarah, who was fidgeting on his lap and making grunting noises, the sort that often heralded a pooh.

Sarah twisted round, stared up at Harry, and then grinned gummily. 'Da-da-da!' she cried. Yes, her first word was Dad, and Lily suddenly knew that she was the outsider here. She was alone.

Chapter Fifteen

Max wondered if he'd always be a loner. It wasn't as if he didn't have any friends. He had a million friends. He easily made friends – and dropped them just as easily.

Harry Gale ... yes, once he had loved Harry like a brother. But then Lily came along, and now Harry and Lily were a couple, and so Max was excluded. Or so it seemed to Max. When he was offered a new contract to write a book about the Middle East, he accepted straight away. It meant he'd be away for a whole year, or maybe more.

'Try to get yourself blown up. Or, even better, kidnapped; chained to a dungeon wall by some mad faction that thinks it's doing the will of God. Or sold into slavery, perhaps – that might be interesting,' his publisher continued as he gave Max lunch in a new-up-and-coming, almost-but-not-quite-designer restaurant. 'Get beaten up. Get stabbed. Get a disease or two and almost die. Make friends with those BBC types, try to get into a war zone, take some snaps of starving children, eh?'

'I'll do my best,' said Max.

'Good show,' said his publisher. 'Naked ladies seem to sell a lot of books,' he added thoughtfully. 'But, apart from belly dancers, you won't get too many photographs of naked or near-naked ladies in the Middle East. So you'll need to go for blood and gore. Maybe we could send you to the Congo next? There must be naked ladies in the Congo?'

'You think that's all I need to sell more books – some photographs of naked ladies?'

'They won't do any harm to sales. I'll tell you that for

nothing, sonny boy. Most men like photographs of naked ladies. They find them therapeutic.'

Lily was distressed by the derailment of her plan to be a second Biba. She hoped this setback might be merely temporary, because in spite of everything she still loved to sew. She found it therapeutic. While she tacked and hemmed and smocked, she found she could be almost calm. While she was calm, the baby was less querulous as well.

So she sewed mother-and-baby outfits made of matching fabrics: soft cottons, fine-ribbed cords and velveteens. Harry took photographs of his two girls and put them in an album. No one would have guessed that Sarah's gorgeous smiles were solely the result of Daddy's clowning and cajoling, and were always just for Daddy.

I will not be jealous, Lily told herself, adding she was glad, she was delighted that Harry and his daughter were so close, that – unlike Molly Fox's husband – Harry hadn't grumbled because their firstborn hadn't been a son.

A year went by and things got slightly better. Sarah was still Daddy's little girl and didn't seem to care too much for Mummy, but Lily found she could accept it – more or less.

Maybe it was natural for girls to love their fathers more than mothers? They practised being women on their fathers, didn't they, learned to flirt and wheedle and how to get round men? Sarah was already a tremendous little flirt.

Max seemed to have vanished from their lives. They hadn't heard from him for eighteen months or more, which Lily told herself was good, was great. Now that she had lots to do at home, she could go for weeks – okay, be honest, for a couple of days – without giving him a single thought.

'Let's meet up soon,' said Max. He was briefly back in the

UK and phoning Harry at his office. 'You're in London most days, aren't you, Gale, masterminding running the country? Let's have lunch – my treat.'

'No, you come to Oxford,' Harry told him. 'Come for a weekend, why don't you? Stay with us – there's room. You could see Lily and meet Sarah.'

'Sarah?'

'She's our daughter.'

'Oh – congratulations, Dad!'

See Lily – maybe not, thought Max. But he couldn't avoid her all his life, and now she was Harry's wife and mother of his child …

'We can take her to the Parks,' said Harry, making it sound like a big adventure. 'We go there most Saturdays while Lily goes to Waitrose. She loves to run around. Or rather bumble round. She can't quite manage running yet. Max, would you consider being Sarah's godfather?'

'I don't believe in God.'

'You don't need to believe in God. It would be unofficial. But I should like you to have a special place in Sarah's life. Maybe you could be a sort of uncle, if you don't want to be a godfather?'

'Okay,' Max replied.

'You don't sound very keen.'

'You took me by surprise, that's all.' Max rummaged in his biscuit tin of platitudes for the right thing to say. 'Yes, of course I'll be your daughter's godfather. I'd like that very much. Uncle sounds like somebody who smells of musty tweeds and stale tobacco, but godfather sounds rather grand. What shall I need to do to be a proper godfather? Buy your little girl a silver spoon?'

'Of course, and pay her fees to Roedean.'

'I'll expect *my* god-daughter to get a scholarship.'

Going to the Parks on Saturdays, commuting into London throughout the working week and pushing papers round a desk, thought Max – live dangerously, Harry ...

Maybe this was fate taking a hand, he told himself, as he caught the train to Oxford on the Friday afternoon, arriving at the love nest well before he thought the master would be home, and hoping to catch Lily by herself.

He supposed the baby would be there. But didn't babies spend most of their time asleep? So perhaps he'd have a chance to talk to Lily, ask if she was happy, if she'd made the right decisions, if, if, if ...

Stop all this, he told himself. You heard her tell her tutor she was going to marry Gale, and that was what she did. But what if you pushed her into marrying him by saying all that I'm-a-loner and you-know-we-have-no-future stuff in India? She's a wife and mother now, of course, but even so – perhaps it's not too late to tell the truth? She ought to know the truth.

Footsteps – she was coming down the hallway now. Max drew breath, his declarations, explanations and apologies all hovering on his lips.

The front door opened and Harry stood there beaming at him with a dark-eyed baby in his arms. 'Welcome to the pigsty,' he began. He backed off down the hallway, which was very narrow and full of baby stuff. 'Please excuse the mess.'

'Why are you back so early?'

'I always try to get away by lunchtime on a Friday.'

The baby was a miniature Red Queen, perfect in every way.

She had little pearls of teeth, enormous black-fringed eyes – they'd been navy blue at first, said Harry, but gradually they'd changed to Lily's grey – a searching and interrogative stare that made her look as if she meant to cast a spell on you, or subject you to a devastating cross-examination, and a totally enchanting smile.

'This is Max,' said Harry.

'Max,' repeated Sarah, squirming in her father's arms. 'Daddy, get down now.'

'She's very busy. She always has a lot of things to do,' said Harry as his daughter toddled off and started trying to electrocute herself by jabbing with a stubby index finger at a socket in the hall. 'Sarah, leave the plugs alone. They're dangerous, okay? She's interested in everything, you see. She has a very high IQ, and she—'

'Hello, Max!'

Lily came out of the kitchen, scooped up Sarah, kissed Max on the cheek. But even that slight, momentary contact made him tingle with desire, and he knew he shouldn't have come to Oxford.

He should not be in this little house that smelled of drying washing, of something he suspected must be Sarah's dirty nappies, of bland and basic cooking, and was full of baby clutter. You couldn't move for clutter.

He should have stayed in London, met Harry in a restaurant or a pub, spent an hour or two with Harry on their own and talked about their schooldays, about Harry's boring job or his own travels – nothing more.

'Supper's almost ready,' added Lily cheerfully. 'It's only pasta whatsit, I'm afraid, but it will fill us up. Harry, please could you strap Sarah in her booster chair?'

Supper was a gruesome business. Sarah threw her pasta everywhere, banged on the table with her spoon and dropped sauce on the tablecloth, which luckily was plastic, and emitted sudden high-pitched squeals for no good reason. She was never told by either parent to sit up straight, be quiet, eat up, or otherwise behave.

The wine was fairly decent, though – a good Italian red. Lily and Harry seemed to drink a lot of it, he noticed.

Grunting like a pig, Sarah shovelled food into her mouth with both her chubby hands and then she lobbed some pasta at her father, scored a direct hit all down his shirt, and clapped her hands, delighted.

'Tinker,' Harry said and grinned, as if the infant had done something clever. He poured himself another glass of wine then drank it down in one. Max didn't blame him; if the child had thrown spaghetti and tomato mush at him, he'd have grabbed the bottle, used a straw.

Max ate his spaghetti whatsit. After pudding, Sarah quietened down a bit, so it was possible for the adults to talk.

'Now, Max, tell us all about your travels?' Lily was looking rather flushed, and he had a sudden vision of her naked in that room in Delhi, when she – no, don't go there.

'How many women have you loved then left?' She twinkled at him from underneath her long black eyelashes. 'I'll bet you've been breaking hearts in all five continents?'

'I've been much too busy to break hearts,' said Max, who could see his hosts were very mellow now, but who wasn't drunk or anywhere near approaching drunk himself. He didn't dare get drunk.

'You sowed all your wild oats while you were still a student, did you?' Harry chuckled like somebody's uncle. 'Lily, you'll remember what a randy bastard old Max here used to be?'

'You got through all of Somerville and half St Anne's, I do believe?' Lily giggled drunkenly. She glanced at Sarah, who was slumped in her high chair, eyes closed and drooling. 'This poor baby's practically asleep. I'd better take her up and get her settled. You boys can do the dishes and reminisce about old times. Harry, I've put Max in Sarah's room so she'll be in with us tonight.'

On Saturday morning, Lily went to Waitrose. Max and Harry took the baby to the Parks. Harry carried Sarah in a pink and purple canvas sling affair. Max thought it made him look ridiculous.

But the baby clearly loved to snuggle up to Daddy, to dribble down his sweater, chew his cuffs. When they got to the Parks, she bumbled round the shaven lawns, giggling when Daddy rugby-tackled her and growled like a bear. The outing was cut short today because, as Harry put it, Sarah suddenly filled her pants.

'You'll want to settle down one day, you know,' said Harry as they made their smelly way back to the clutter-burrow.

'You mean I'll want a wife, a home, a baby?'

'Yes,' said Harry. 'I can recommend all three.'

'I have lots of things to do before I settle down.' Max shot a glance at Sarah, who was beaming as if she had done something very clever, not merely crapped herself. 'Places to go, you know?'

'Where will you be off to next?'

'My publisher suggested I should try the Congo or Somalia or Sudan.'

'All those places welcome tourists, do they?'

'Yes, with Kalashnikovs and rocket-launchers, usually; they're big on hospitality. I might have some bits missing when I get home again. Or I'll come back in a body bag. Or not come home at all.'

'Why do you do it?'

'Go travelling, you mean?'

'I can understand the travelling. But why do you go to dangerous places where you're likely to be killed?'

'You could get killed yourself crossing St Giles.'

'I suppose so.' Harry shrugged. 'Lily should be back, so let's go home and have some lunch. She said she's making cassoulet for supper and I know that takes a while – most of the afternoon, in fact.'

'What does she usually do all day, your wife?'

'Well, she looks after Sarah, obviously. She's a mother, after all, and let me tell you it's a full time job.'

'So it's all worked out?' said Max.

'What do you mean, worked out?' asked Lily, pouring oil into a frying pan.

'You know what I mean.'

Harry was upstairs changing Sarah, so Max sat down at the kitchen table, watching Lily slice up garlic sausage, duck, pancetta. 'This is the life you want?'

'Yes, of course,' said Lily, opening a can of beans. She poured the beans into a saucepan. 'Do stop trying to make trouble, Max.'

'I'm not trying to make trouble.'

'Good.' Lily turned to meet his gaze. 'You rejected me – don't you remember? But it was for the best. I love my husband and I love our child. I love our life in Oxford. I'm a very lucky woman.'

'Who's a lucky woman?' Harry came into the kitchen carrying his daughter in his arms. 'Gosh, that was a behemoth of a pooh,' he told them, grinning. 'You must weigh ten pounds less now, little tinker. Lily, maybe she should keep off the bananas for a while. Oh, and I'm really sorry, but while I was changing madam here, she grabbed one of your books and I'm afraid it's rather chewed.'

'It doesn't matter,' Lily said.

But Max heard the sharpness in her tone and knew it did.

He couldn't bear it any more. 'I've just remembered I promised to have dinner with my father this evening,' he lied. 'So although it's been great to see you lovebirds, soon I'll need to go and catch a train.'

'What a shame you can't stay longer,' Lily said, not looking at him, sounding – if she sounded anything – relieved.

'Yes, it's a shame, but there'll be other times,' said Harry.

Chapter Sixteen

When she and Sarah started going to the local mother-and-toddler group, Lily saw a woman she had noticed at natural childbirth classes who'd been expecting twins. How did anybody cope with giving birth to two when giving birth to one was more than agony enough?

'I had a Caesarean,' the woman said. 'I demanded one and, let me tell you, when I demand, I get. Where did you buy that gorgeous dress for Sarah?'

'I made it.'

'Did you really? It's absolutely beautiful! I don't suppose you'd like to make a couple of them for Jessica? I'd pay you for your time and skill, of course.'

'You wouldn't need to pay me anything,' said Lily, blushing at the woman's praise. 'Just buy the material and bring it round and then I'll make it up. I love to sew.'

Gina turned out to be someone who appreciated quality. She liked a garment to hang properly, to have a generous hem, neat cuffs, bound buttonholes and double seams. When she came to collect the clothes for Jessica, she said Lily should go into dressmaking as a professional.

'You'd make a mint,' she added.

'I don't think so.' Lily shook her head. 'I tried it and it didn't work out.'

'What happened?'

'I made some dresses for a shop in Camden. They sold well, and so I went to India to source a range of fabrics, trimmings, buttons, all that stuff.' Lily sighed. 'Oh, I had such big plans! But then the shop went out of business. I had a complicated pregnancy. I spent three months in hospital, and after Sarah came along, of course there was the sleep thing.'

'Yes,' said Gina. 'I know about the sleep thing.'

'What did you do before you had the twins?'

'I was an accountant. Jeff's a lawyer. I met him when a client was accused of corporate fraud, and – well, the rest is history! But my family's in tailoring. I like to sew myself, although I'm not as good as you. I know all about lapels and linings. I can roll a seam. I know you should always soap an interfacing—'

'Why would anybody soap an interfacing?'

'When professional tailors use interfacings in lapels or cuffs, they rub them lightly with a bar of soap. Then, when they machine the garment, all three layers of fabric stay together and don't ruckle up.'

'That's a handy tip,' said Lily. 'Thank you.'

'You're most welcome. While I was growing up, my grandparents and parents worked long hours. After school, I always did my homework at the factory, sitting at a workbench, surrounded by great piles of half-made garments and watching the machinists. Tricks of the trade – well, they run into thousands, and I probably know them all. Or most of them, at least. See you at the madhouse for cash-and-carry coffee and stale Garibaldis on Tuesday afternoon?'

'Yes, we'll be there.'

As they drank their nasty instant coffee and watched their offspring reinforce old-fashioned gender stereotypes that, in spite of middle class conditioning, seemed bred in the bone – as the boys attacked or killed each other with plastic guns and swords, and as the girls undressed their Barbie dolls then crayoned make-up on their plastic faces – Gina shared more tricks and tips with Lily.

'Look at Molly Fox's child,' she added, breaking off from telling Lily she should always pin a garment crossways, at right angles to the seam, and then it wouldn't matter if she accidentally machined across a pin or two. 'What's she doing to that Barbie? Lots of latent anger and aggression there, I think.'

'It's hardly latent,' whispered Lily as they watched Fiona Fox dismember Birthday Barbie then throw the head and limbs across the room.

'She's going to be in therapy before she's five years old, you mark my words,' said Gina. 'Anyway, as I was saying: I can work a perfect buttonhole in thirty seconds flat. The stuff they sell in chain stores nowadays – my grandfather despairs of it. But when I showed him something you had made for Jessica, he said: this girl is good.'

'I'm very flattered.'

'I know how to run a business. So ...'

Lily felt a tingle of excitement.

'... why don't we set up a company selling children's clothes in pretty, non-iron fabrics? Kits for customers to sew at home, or ready-made?' suggested Gina.

'We could use my original styles and patterns to make the clothes distinctive?'

'Yes.'

Lily's excitement mounted. This could be her second chance, and this time she would get it right. 'Do you think your grandfather could get us fabrics wholesale?'

'He'll do anything for me.'

'Let's go for it,' said Lily. 'What shall we call ourselves?'

'Something snappy and alliterative, I think?' Gina glanced down at the daisy pattern on her blouse. 'Daisy – Daisy what?'

'Daisy Designs?'

'That's it.'

So they got started with a loan from Barclays Bank, setting up their sewing machines on Gina's kitchen table, keeping bolts of fabric and big cardboard cartons of buttons, zips and other haberdashery in Lily's sitting room.

'No,' she replied, when Harry said why take out loans when his own parents would probably fund their first few months? 'I must do this myself.'

'But Mum and Dad would love to help,' said Harry, looking wounded. 'We'd only have to ask and they'd stump up five thousand or whatever it is you need. I'd like to help you, too.'

'Okay, wash up occasionally, get home in time to put Sarah to bed at least three times a week and – best of all – believe in me.'

Gina told Lily how much they could spend, which didn't seem very much at all to Lily. But she accepted Gina understood the money stuff.

'We grow slowly first of all,' said Gina, who had done the business plan for Barclays, then marched into the Oxford branch in high heels and a business suit and scared the local manager into giving them a loan at a good rate of interest. 'We try out small ranges of no more than half a dozen styles. We don't try to run before we've even learned to walk. We're going to need to price this stuff quite high. Otherwise, we'll be working for a pittance or nothing at all.'

'Okay,' said Lily. 'Who are our customers, then?'

'Professional women mostly, like I told the bank – lawyers, doctors, senior civil servants – they'll want stuff ready-made. Dons' wives too, but they're a different market. They'll want cut-out kits and then they can tell their friends they made the clothes themselves. So now we'll need to start a mailing list. Who do we know? Who do our husbands, aunts and uncles, parents, brothers, sisters, cousins know? Who's your dentist, who's your doctor, who is your solicitor, do they have husbands, wives, do they have children?'

They wrote down several hundred names, designed a basic catalogue, sent copies to their friends, relations and acquaintances, then prayed.

They got some orders. Professional women seemed to like the clothes. Lily hoped their children liked them too, weren't being forced to wear them just because their mothers said so.

Dons and dons' wives, doctors, lawyers, doctors' wives and lawyers' wives – as Gina had predicted, these were their first customers. The other obvious Oxford target market – the earth mother brigade – resisted until Lily said: maybe we ought to try a range in hessian, hemp and linen?

Yes, it creased, and these days almost everyone liked man-made fabrics, cotton and polyester blends you didn't need to iron.

'But perhaps the earth mothers like creases?' she suggested, adding you could spot an earth mother at fifty paces because they were always creased themselves. Creases were more natural and, after all, these women seemed to go for unshaved legs and unplucked eyebrows and no make-up, and these were natural, too ...

'Let's do it, then,' said Gina.

'But can we afford it?'

'No, but let's live dangerously for once. We'll soon find out if the workhouse orphan look is going to catch on.'

Lily was proved right – the hemp and linen were a big success. Soon, Oxford toddlers dressed like workhouse orphans were everywhere along the Woodstock Road and Banbury Road.

'What about boiled wool and Harris tweed for winter?' Lily asked as they watched their profits grow and grow. 'Tweedy Sherlock-Holmes-style hats for five-year-olds and a range of pre-shrunk coats for kindergarteners?'

'Now you're talking.'

Gina's North Oxford kitchen was enormous. She had a Swedish nanny to look after the children, too. Nanny kept the children busy, so no sticky fingers marked the fabrics.

But even Gina's kitchen soon became too small. So they found a place in Cowley Road, a workshop with three cutting tables and two heavy-duty sewing machines. They recruited half a dozen part-time workers, women who were quick and nimble and who wanted jobs where they could have the radio on, work flexi-time and gossip while they cut and stitched and pressed.

'We're a pair of geniuses, to have thought of doing this,' said Gina happily, as she sighed with satisfaction over the accounts for their first year. 'Now we need to raise our game. We need a glossy catalogue next season, professional photography, full colour.'

'We don't need a professional photographer. Harry takes endless photographs of Sarah and he's good. So he can help with that.'

Harry was delighted to be involved at last and photographed both Jessica and Sarah and Jessica's twin brother Tom looking cute in the new autumn ranges. He studied the new catalogue, approved it, and then he said that he and Lily ought to have more children – two or three, perhaps? Or maybe four? Sarah shouldn't be their only one. 'Only children being lonely children and all that,' he added, glancing at their daughter who was sitting in a corner of the kitchen, playing happily by herself and burbling to her family of rabbits, bears and ducks. 'After all, I'm one of two, and you are one of four.'

'I'm not sure about more babies,' Lily told him. She had not forgotten all the ghastliness of pregnancy and childbirth. She didn't suppose that many normal women could actually enjoy the process, unless swelling up until they were the size of whales was their thing. 'You didn't actually mean three or four?'

'Perhaps not three or four, then, but I think a couple would be good. Since I got promoted, we can certainly afford to have another one.'

'What about my business?'

'You'd need to take some time off, obviously. Then, afterwards, we would have various options – playgroups, nannies, childminders. We could work something out. Mrs Fraser from next door, she already babysits for us. She might like to do some childminding in the daytime? Or—'

'You've made your point,' said Lily. 'But what's the mighty rush? Harry, we're both young. So surely we could wait a while before we get a second scream machine?'

'Sarah's of an age when she needs playmates.'

'Yes, but playmates don't have to be siblings. I have three brothers and when we were small I hated them. I'm not keen on them now.'

'But you'll think about another baby?' he persisted. 'As I said, we can afford it.'

'Maybe, if we do without the yacht.'

'Darling, please be serious?'

'Okay, I'll think about it,' promised Lily. 'But I don't want another baby for at least a year or two.'

'When Sarah goes to Rising Fives, perhaps?'

'Perhaps – but there's no hurry.'

Chapter Seventeen

Max had been very busy. He'd travelled all around the Middle East and, though he hadn't managed to be kidnapped, jailed or chained to any dungeon walls, he'd still got into various kinds of trouble.

Yemen was difficult because he had run out of currency. This was his own fault because he hadn't done the necessary research. He hadn't realised that Yemenis didn't haggle and that if he tried it he was likely to be stabbed.

All Yemeni men wore daggers, knives or carried other weapons. They clearly found it odd that Max went everywhere unarmed. 'Hey, Americano, British, you want dagger? You want AK47?' was the constant cry when he was in a souk or market. 'You want qat?'

No, he didn't want a dagger or an old Kalashnikov. But he did want qat. He needed qat because in Yemen nothing ever happened without qat. When you visited a Yemeni, for whatever reason, in a public office, in a government building or at home, to get a visa or to hire a guide or to visit somebody who was going to put you up tonight, you took along a bush of qat.

Then you sat and chewed its leaves until viridian spit ran down your chin and all your teeth turned green. Then, if you were Max, you got so wired you couldn't sleep. Then you had to drink some bootleg brandy to relax you. Then you got a hangover. Then you slept off the hangover and then you started all over again. Thanks to qat, most of his time in Yemen passed in a befuddled haze.

Iran had been a challenge because although his Arabic was passable, his Farsi was a joke, and there had been a big misunderstanding between him and another man who wore a golden earring, which he found out later was apparently a symbol of availability. Why hadn't he known that?

He spent some time in hospital in Israel recovering from being beaten up in Gaza when he was mistaken for an army spy. When he got out of hospital he found a room to rent in an apartment in Jerusalem. He wrote his book about the Middle East and then, although he couldn't have said why, he found he was reluctant to move on.

'What shall we do today?' asked Zara, who was a librarian at the university and with whom he shared the small apartment in Jerusalem and nowadays a bed.

This had not been the plan. Zara Stein had advertised a room to let, to a journalist or academic, preferably. Max had needed somewhere to recuperate and write. Zara seemed to need someone to love and, in his weakened physical and mental state, Max found he appreciated loving.

'You told me you would like to see Masada,' added Zara. 'So if you're feeling up to it?'

'You could drive us, could you?' Max flexed or tried to flex his fingers, some of which had been smashed up when he'd been beaten and were not yet able to grip or hold a steering wheel for more than half an hour at the most.

'Yes, I'll drive us. Max, we've been together now for thirteen months and nineteen days.'

'We have?' Max shook his head in disbelief. 'As long as that?'

'As long as that – I've counted.' Zara smiled. 'We get on very well, don't you agree?'

'Yes, yes … we do.'

'Where my parents live is on the way. We could break

our journey there, stay overnight. I've told them all about you and they said they'd like to meet you.'

'Yes, okay.'

'What do you mean, okay?'

'I'd like to meet them, too.'

Max couldn't quite believe he'd just said that. Meeting parents sounded serious! But he was fond of Zara. More than fond and, if he couldn't have Lily – which he knew he couldn't, even though he also knew that Lily was a witch who'd cast a spell upon his heart and soul that never would be broken – maybe it was time he settled down into a permanent relationship with a woman he might learn to love?

A woman who understood he was a traveller and would always be a traveller? A woman who had read his books, admired them? A woman who was independent, clever, who had a life she loved here in Jerusalem, who didn't want to be a wife, a mother – she had told him so herself?

Sarah started Rising Fives and loved it.

Rising Fives was run by Mrs Harley who Lily soon decided was a witch because the children all adored the woman and nobody was ever naughty, rude or difficult at Mrs Harley's Rising Fives.

'Daddy, Mummy, Mrs Harley says we have to grow a bulb,' said Sarah. 'We have to get a hyastink, and then we plant it in a pot, and then we put it in the dark, and when it starts to grow we take it out, and then we water it, and one day it will be a flower. Daddy, can we go and buy a hyastink?'

'Yes, on Saturday,' said Harry.

'Mummy, you come too,' invited Sarah.

'You go with Daddy, just the two of you,' said Lily. 'Saturday's your special time together.' Much as Lily tried to force herself, she couldn't get excited about hyastinks.

Mrs Harley said that next week they would build a castle. So could everybody bring in cardboard boxes and the tubes from loo rolls, kitchen towels? Arts and crafts, thought Lily. I can do arts and crafts.

'What are you going to do for soldiers, sweetheart?' she enquired, determined this time she would show an interest, get it right. 'Make them out of Plasticine? I could help you make some soldiers. I'm quite good at modelling.'

'We're not having soldiers, Mummy.'

'What, a castle with no soldiers? So you'll have no weapons, cannons, siege engines? No vats of boiling oil?'

'Vats of boiling oil?' repeated Sarah, looking puzzled.

'Or perhaps it's going to be a non-defensive castle?' added Lily. 'One designed for pacifists?'

'Shut up, Lily,' muttered Harry.

'Mummy, you don't need to help,' said Sarah. 'Daddy will find some tubes and boxes, won't you, Dad?'

So Lily went into the sitting room and fished the copy of Max's latest book from underneath the sofa where she had hidden it. The book had come while Harry was at work. She hadn't told him, although she didn't know exactly why, because of course the package had been addressed to both of them.

As she read Max's words, she felt connected to the writer. She fell out of that stolen punt into that cold, dark water. She scrambled up that wall to jump down into Magdalen. She was in that little room in Delhi where she'd kissed him, and they – no, she must not think about it.

She was Harry's wife and Sarah's mother, not a traveller's

concubine. She poured herself a glass of Chardonnay and started reading guiltily.

The following afternoon, while Sarah was at Rising Fives, Lily got a phone call at the workshop. Sarah had tumbled off a climbing frame. She wasn't hurt, said Mrs Harley. She'd fallen on the play-mat, then rolled over, then got up again. But she was a little tearful now. So she'd probably like her mum to come and take her home.

Lily felt the panic rising in her throat like vomit and rushed over straight away, slewing awkwardly into a parking slot that was too tight, then racing for the hall.

'We're sure she's going to be fine,' said Mrs Harley cheerfully. 'We know she didn't bump her head. But she's a little shaken and she's clearly feeling rather sorry for herself.'

Lily took one look at Sarah's tear-streaked face, realised she must be in pain and drove her to the hospital, where she called Harry from a pay phone in the waiting room. Harry left his boss Sir Nicholas to his own devices and got on the next train back to Oxford.

'How long have you been waiting?' he demanded when he came running breathless into A & E.

'Two hours at least,' said Lily, looking round the crowded waiting room at various drunks who'd fallen over in the street, at workmen who had cut themselves on chainsaws, at people who had burned themselves in accidents at home. 'I asked a nurse again about ten minutes before you came. She said another hour at least. Sarah needs to go to X-ray and it seems there's quite a queue. Then, if she's broken anything, she might need a general anaesthetic.'

'It's a disgrace,' fumed Harry. 'I'll speak to Nick about

it. I'll make sure he takes it up to ministerial level, asks questions in the House. Come to Daddy, poppet?'

Sarah squirmed off Lily's lap and went to sit on Harry's.

As another hour went by, she whimpered once or twice, but mostly she was silent. 'Where does it hurt?' asked Lily.

'All over, Mummy – my whole arm is sore. It feels like someone stamped on it.'

'My poor baby.' Lily would have given anything to take the pain away, to choke it down herself. 'Let's hope it won't be long before you're seen.'

'I'm hungry, Dad,' said Sarah.

'You can't have anything to eat until you've seen the doctor, love,' said Lily.

'I don't want to see the doctor. I want to go back to Rising Fives.'

'You're never going back to Rising Fives,' said Harry, who sat stroking Sarah's soft, black curls as yet another hour ticked by.

'Sarah Gale?' A tired-looking doctor, radiographer – somebody in white, in any case – materialised in front of them. He had a set of notes. 'Sarah's for an X-ray, is that right?'

Two or three hours later, they'd been given the all-clear. Sarah was very bruised and shaken up, but it appeared no bones were broken. So she would soon be fine again.

'We'll need to find a different playgroup, crèche, whatever you want to call it,' Harry said as they were driving home. 'One where they watch the children all the time. One where they take proper care of them. By the way, you promised that when Sarah started Rising Fives, you would think about a second baby.'

When Sarah was at last in bed, dosed up with Calpol and sleeping fitfully, Harry and Lily went to bed themselves, where Harry fell on Lily with such a fierce urgency and grim determination that she was at first surprised and then impassioned, clawing him and biting him herself, something she had never done before.

Afterwards, she found her nails were dark with gore. She must have gouged long channels all down Harry's back. Later, looking in the bathroom mirror, she saw her neck and chest were red, inflamed and angry-looking, scraped and bruised by Harry's desperate kissing. Poor Harry – she had felt him come with a great shuddering gush and he had been in tears as he had finally relaxed.

After her experience with the loop, these days she was on the pill. But she knew this wasn't foolproof either, and she thought, if she'd conceived tonight, this would be a child of fire and blood.

Chapter Eighteen

Max was standing underneath a waterfall deep in the South American jungle, washing off the blood.

He had been so stupid. He had broken his own rules. Well, that was nothing new, of course. He broke them all the time. But what he'd just done here in Colombia – a dangerous, lawless country he knew very well indeed, around which he had travelled several times before – had been spectacularly idiotic, even for Max Farley, adventurer and traveller and fool. It was as if he had a death wish, and perhaps he did. What use was his life to anybody, after all?

It had not worked out with Zara Stein. She had been so adamant that it would be all right – her parents wouldn't mind that he was British. But they did. They minded very much. They had not forgotten the mess the British made in Palestine before the state of Israel was created.

He wasn't Jewish. Also, it transpired that Zara had a childhood sweetheart in the army who ticked all the boxes and both sets of parents expected her to marry him.

'It's okay,' he said, when Zara tearfully admitted that she and Ben were practically engaged. 'It probably wouldn't have lasted, anyway.'

'But I wanted it to last,' she'd sobbed.

'Well, all good things – you know?'

'You're angry with me.'

'Zara, I'm not angry.' Max thought, what right have I to anger, when my own heart belongs to someone else and always will? 'I wish you well and happy. It's been very good between us, but it's over now. So no hard feelings, right?'

'I won't forget you, Max.'

'Perhaps you should.'

After Max had said goodbye to Zara he went to South America again and collected some material for another book. As he was about to try to find a vessel on which he could work his passage home, he had an invitation – a summons, actually – to meet a cocaine baron who had read some of his books and heard Max was in South America. How had he heard? Max didn't know. But he guessed that if you were a cocaine baron in Colombia, you probably heard everything there was to hear.

The meeting had gone well. The baron proved to be a genial host who wanted to explain to Max that he was just a farmer, that coca was a crop like any other, supporting several thousand families in this part of Colombia alone, and bringing welcome income so their children went to school. It was a useful anaesthetic, it was the perfect natural remedy for altitude and travel sickness, and if people buying it decided to abuse it, how could they blame him?

Max had made a lot of notes, confident he'd get a series for the Sunday papers out of it.

But when a South American man invites you to his home, you should be on your best behaviour. You shouldn't speak to his wife without permission. You shouldn't chat up his daughters.

You definitely shouldn't go walking, talking and eventually having sex with a cocaine baron's daughter in his jungle fastness deep inside the rainforest while you are the cocaine baron's guest, and expect to get away with it. Although, of course, Max did expect to get away with it.

But his guardian angel had obviously been on holiday, because he and the daughter had been caught. Max had been badly beaten up and sliced with a machete. The daughter got locked up and Max did, too. But he had escaped, and now the baron's men were after him.

He sorted out his wounds as best he could – the one from the machete was bleeding rather badly – and then he set off again, hoping he was going in approximately the right direction.

This time, his guardian angel did her stuff. The boat was there. The jerry can of fuel was there as well. He had been prepared to row, but miraculously the engine deigned to start.

As he chugged along a tributary of the Rio Negro in the hired boat that he had had the foresight to tie up and hide for just such an emergency, he thought of Lily and was comforted. He imagined her in Oxford, baking bread and making pies and polishing the furniture and doing whatever else a housewife did. She probably had another child by now: a little boy, a second Harry Gale.

He really ought to write to them, he thought, or even try to make an international call. He decided if he ever got out of this jungle, if the cocaine baron's rabble didn't catch him, crucify him, cut his balls off, he would phone his friends.

Cut his balls off …

Maybe he should give up sex? Life had been much easier when there was no sex involved: when he had been at school.

'When can I go to school?'

Sarah couldn't wait to go to school.

But which school should they choose? There was a tussle about that. Harry was all for sending Sarah to an independent school where the children wore a special and distinctive uniform, the various components needing to be bought not from John Lewis or from Marks and Spencer, but at huge expense from Elliston and Cavell, Oxford's main department store.

'Why can't she go to the local primary?' asked Lily.

'I don't want our daughter to mix with yobs and bullies.'

'Harry, you get those at any school.'

'But we can just about afford to send her to a decent school and give her a good start in life, which she might not get if she went to the local primary.'

'I went to a state school. My father's a headmaster in a state school. The local primary's a lovely school, with good facilities and motivated teachers. I want her to go there.'

'I've already put her down for St Cecilia's and paid the first year's fees.'

'You've done what?'

'You heard me.'

'So I have no say in this?'

'I thought you would be fine about it.' Harry had the grace to look a little bit ashamed. 'Let's start her off at St Cecilia's, shall we, see how it all works out?'

'You should have talked to me about it first.'

'I'm sorry, darling. But I only want the best for Sarah. You know that. Mum and Dad have said they'll help with fees and buy the uniform and all the other kit.'

'Oh, so Mum and Dad have known for ages, have they? When did you propose to break the news to me?'

'I've said I'm sorry. As you say, I should have talked to you about it first. But it's not long now before she goes to school, and St Cecilia's has a waiting list, so I just thought ...'

Harry did seem reasonably repentant. He had that look most children get when they've done something wrong and wish they hadn't because they knew they'd hurt somebody else. 'I promise you if she's unhappy at this place we can discuss it and we'll think again,' he added, looking at Lily with brown puppy eyes. 'Please could we be friends again?'

'I'll see.'

'I'll take you to the Ritz for a weekend, for a whole week.'

'Do you know how much that would cost?'

'We'll get a second mortgage.' Harry walked the fingers of one hand up Lily's arm. 'Mum and Dad could come and stay with Sarah while we go and have some grown-up fun. By the way, have you thought any more about another baby?'

'I'll let you know.'

'I rather think the time is right, don't you?'

'Oh, darling, please stop nagging? We don't need to be in any hurry to have another child!'

But Harry nagged and nagged and nagged about a second baby. So because she loved him and could see how much it seemed to mean to him to have a second child – perhaps he'd like a son, she thought, a boy to kick a football, make aeroplanes from balsa wood, go fishing – she made a decision.

'You'll be pleased to know I've thrown my pills away,' she said.

But time went on and nothing happened. 'It could be down to stress,' suggested Harry. 'I was reading something in the *Guardian*'s women's pages about how being stressed can stop a healthy woman getting pregnant. All she needs to do is get sufficient sleep, eat properly and relax. Perhaps you ought to give up work? Or could you take a little break, at least?'

'No, I couldn't,' Lily said. 'Daisy Designs is doing really well. We want to find some factory space next spring, employ more people and start selling our best new lines abroad. Darling, I'm not stressed, I promise you. I'm busy and enjoying life. Sarah's doing well at school and you've just been promoted. We don't have any money worries and we're fit and healthy. We're lucky, can't you see? We have so much already. So perhaps it's greedy to want more?'

'You don't want another baby, do you? I wouldn't mind betting you're still on the pill.'

'Of course I'm not!' cried Lily. 'I don't lie to you!'

'I know you don't, my love. I shouldn't have said that, but—'

'It's all right,' said Lily, who'd actually considered staying on the pill in spite of what she'd said to Harry and who now blushed guiltily. 'But, sweetheart, we have Sarah. She's a real daddy's girl. She thinks the sun shines out … you know she does. Why isn't she enough?'

'What happens when we're old? When looking after us is solely down to Sarah? How is she going to manage?'

'She'll probably have lots of cousins, friends; they'll help her out. Or we'll go to the workhouse. Harry, we're not even thirty yet! We won't be old for ages. So, please – stop all this worrying and fretting?'

But Harry kept on worrying and fretting. He suggested Lily ought to go and see a doctor. 'It might be your tubes,' he said. 'They could have got bunged up.'

'Or maybe it's your tadpoles.' Lily laughed at Harry's frown. 'Maybe they're too fat and sluggish nowadays – like you. I ought to put you on a diet. Maybe you're the one who needs to see a doctor, eh?'

She poked him in the stomach, which, thanks to fifty press-ups every morning before he left to catch the train to Paddington, was washboard-hard and flat. Otherwise, of course, she wouldn't have done it. But Harry didn't laugh.

* * *

'Señor, this hurt, it is no laughing matter.' The cargo vessel's doctor in Caracas, where Max finally ended up, added he'd been lucky.

If that machete slash had been a fraction of a centimetre closer to his heart, he would have bled to death. What had he been doing, and where had he been, to be so badly wounded?

'I got into a fight.'

'Some fight, señor.' The doctor grimaced. 'What happened to the other guy?'

'You'll pass me fit?' demanded Max impatiently.

'Yes, but it's against my better judgement,' said the Venezuelan doctor. 'Señor Farley, if you've had enough of pre-Columbian ruins, of rainforests and frogs in all the colours of the rainbow, if you're anxious to get home again, why don't you do as other Europeans do? Why don't you take the plane?'

'I need to go by ship, it's in my contract,' Max replied. 'I don't have the air fare, anyway.'

'Your embassy would help you.'

'But I would prefer to work my passage.'

'This is also in your contract?'

'Yes.'

'I never heard of such a thing.' The doctor shook his head. 'You want my verdict? You are one crazy Englishman.'

They got the verdict. Lily was a fully-functioning, super-fertile female. So Harry had to be the one with problems. 'There are so many causes of male infertility,' the doctor told them carefully, so carefully that Lily almost pitied the poor man. When he'd been a student, he'd clearly failed the module on giving people awful or unwelcome news.

'What are these causes, then?' growled Harry.

'You might feel well, but if your work is stressful, if you're skipping meals or if your diet isn't balanced, you could be malnourished and lacking in those vitamins and minerals that help maintain fertility. I can prescribe some supplements. Or maybe you contracted an infection some time after your little girl was born.'

'What do you mean, contracted an infection?' Lily saw that Harry's face was mask-like, drained of all its normal colour. 'I'm prepared to swear on Sarah's life that I have never, ever been with—'

'Mr Gale, nobody is suggesting that you have been unfaithful to your wife,' the doctor told him hurriedly. 'What I mean is, something like a bout of influenza or bronchitis can compromise fertility in men.'

'You had that really awful dose last January,' Lily reminded him. 'You were off work for weeks.'

Harry stared at her in stony silence.

'We'll start a programme of investigation,' the doctor told them cheerfully, clearly happier now he had delivered the bad news and could begin to talk about this couple's family prospects for the future, which apparently were fairly bright. 'Nine times out of ten, we manage to identify a cause of infertility, and very often we find a solution. We have an encouraging track record of success.'

'Harry, shall I drive?' asked Lily as they walked out of the clinic into the bright sunshine of what was for other people just an ordinary, boring day. 'You've had quite a shock, and you—'

'I can still drive, you know.'

'I was only offering.'

Harry was silent driving home and Lily was silent, too. She couldn't think of anything to say that wouldn't make things worse. She could hardly say it didn't matter because it clearly did, at least to Harry.

She was secretly and rather guiltily relieved. She didn't want another baby. Yes, she would have welcomed one more child into the family. But she didn't want to incubate it or give birth to it.

She didn't want Harry to be miserable. So now she started to think about adoption. Maybe this could be the right solution for them both, whatever Harry's long-term prospects? She decided when the time was right she'd mention it. But not yet while he was feeling wounded, while he was so unlike his usual happy, genial self. He hardly spoke for several days, not even to his daughter, except to say:

'I'm going out.'

'I don't want any supper.'

'I don't want to talk.'

'Leave me alone.'

'Daddy isn't feeling well,' said Lily, when Sarah asked him what was wrong and merely got a shrug.

'Does he have the measles?' Sarah asked her mother. 'Fiona Fox had measles. She didn't want to eat or talk and she had spots inside her mouth and all over her chest. Dad, have you got measles?'

Harry shook his head.

'Perhaps you need some vitamins?' suggested Sarah. 'Mrs Wallace told us we all need lots of vitamins. Otherwise, we die. We did a project in our science group. Why don't you take some vitamins? You could try some of mine. The orange ones are nice. They taste like Smarties.'

Sarah fetched the bottle from the cupboard. She tipped out half a dozen tablets, offered them to Harry. 'You have some of my vitamins and then you'll be all right.'

Although he'd wondered if the South American doctor had a point and if he was quite fit enough to work his passage home, Max found the voyage back to Europe was all right.

The crewmen on the huge container vessel were an interesting lot: Polish, Maltese, Russian and Sri Lankan. So Max had lots of opportunities to pick up smatterings of different languages.

He wrote several postcards to Sarah and her parents, postcards chosen on his various travels and which lived in various backpacks: photographs of Nineveh, Jerusalem and Bethlehem, of Rio de Janeiro, Buenos Aires and Caracas. These days, he was something of a maverick authority on the Middle East and South America, his two favourite places in the world.

'You write home to wife?' one of the other seamen asked, as he watched Max addressing postcards.

'No, to friends – amigos,' Max replied.

'Why write amigos? You a man – you drink beer with amigos, you not write to them.' The seaman looked at Max suspiciously. It was as if he thought this weird Englishman must really be insane and might be dangerous as well.

Max thought the seaman could be right about insanity. What normal person did what he did? He tucked the postcards back inside a pocket of his rucksack. He didn't know if he'd post them. So why did he write to his amigos?

He supposed he liked to think of them at home in Oxford: Harry, Lily and their miniature Red Queen. He didn't want their lives. But there was something very reassuring about the thought of people being calm and ordinary, and managing to be happy nonetheless. Maybe there were special pills for calm and happiness? Or even pills for making extraordinary, mad or downright weird people ordinary, and maybe he should take them?

The special pills were useless.

As for all the other stuff – the multi-vitamins and herbal supplements, the diets featuring broccoli and asparagus and a whole range of other, weirder things – Harry said he might as well have gone to see a witch doctor for all the good they'd done.

'What about adoption?' suggested Lily. 'Harry, if you'd like more children, that's okay by me. Why don't we make enquiries about fostering, adoption?'

'No.'

'Why not?'

'I know there are children out there who need parents,' Harry admitted. 'But I also know I couldn't raise somebody else's child.'

'You were anxious Sarah shouldn't be an only one, and I'm sure I could love a child who wasn't biologically my own.'

'I don't think I could do it. But, on the other hand, you don't really want to have another baby, do you?'

'I'm not as keen as you. Pregnancy and childbirth are no fun for anyone who's not a total masochist.'

'But they're natural and normal, aren't they?'

'So are cholera and typhoid.'

Yes, a part of Lily was relieved. Perhaps she'd never have to incubate another pumpkin now? She wouldn't have to grunt and sweat to push the pumpkin out. She wouldn't have to change the pumpkin, feed the pumpkin, burp the pumpkin, let the pumpkin chew her nipples off and vomit down her top.

She didn't really want another child, another challenge.

She had one of those already in the form of Sarah, who was busy shaping up to be a great dictator. At present, she was mostly a benign one. But there was and always had been something about Sarah that made you do her bidding. Once she had decided on a course of action, both her parents knew that it was pointless to resist.

'Dad, you have to let me have a bike,' she said. 'One with three speed gears. Otherwise I'll get a complex and you'll need to spend a fortune sending me to child psychographists.'

'Do you know anyone who sees a child psychologist?'

'Yes, Alan Flynn in Mrs Ryder's class. Alan doesn't come to school on Tuesday afternoons because his mother takes him to a child psychographist who wears a spotty tie.'

'Why is that?' asked Lily.

'Perhaps he hasn't got a stripy one?'

'Why does Alan see a child psychologist?'

'Oh, he pulls his hair out then he eats it, because he has a complex. He says he has a complex because his father went away and won't come home again. It costs a lot of money to see a child psychographist, so Alan's mother says. You don't want me to pull my hair out, do you?'

Sarah got her bike with three speed gears.

But sometimes Harry laid the law down. 'No riding on the roads before you pass your Cycling Proficiency,' he said. 'It's parks and cycle tracks for you until you do.'

'Mum?' said Sarah hopefully.

'Pass your test and then we'll see,' said Lily.

'Why are you both so horrible? You don't want me to have any fun! Fiona rides her bike to school.'

'Fiona probably has more sense than you,' said Lily.

'But I don't want sense. I want some fun. I wish I was grown up.'

Chapter Nineteen

'Mum, it's somebody called Max! He says he wants to talk to you,' called Sarah, who had answered the extension in her parents' bedroom.

Lily picked up the receiver on the downstairs phone. Max, she thought, and now her heart began to thump against her ribcage. She slumped against the banister feeling winded. But then she told herself to get a grip.

'Max, what a surprise,' she managed. 'Gosh, we haven't heard from you for years! W-where are you?'

'Oh, I'm back in Blighty,' Max replied. 'I got home a few days ago. I thought, why don't I give the Gales a ring, find out how normal people pass their time?'

'Where have you been?'

'You didn't get my postcards?'

'Did you send us any?'

'I'm almost sure I posted one or two. Your postman must have lost them. Or he binned them. Did you see that story about a Yorkshire postman who had two bedrooms full of undelivered letters, parcels and what-have-you in his flat?'

'These postcards you might or might not have sent?'

'They'd have come from Argentina, Chile, Colombia, the Congo, Russia and the Middle East.'

'So you're now a world authority on everything?'

'Well, almost everything. I've climbed a few more mountains. I've met some very curious people. While I was in South America, I got friendly with a group of monks who were running Christian missions saving souls in the favelas of Brazil, but who were also running drugs to the

United States and laundering money for the president of Haiti. I wrote a series for the *Sunday Times*.'

'I didn't see it.'

'Then I spent a few months in the Congo looking at gorillas and volcanoes. I saw where the fastest lava flow in human history engulfed a district half the size of France in twenty minutes. I've walked some of the Silk Road, dodging bullets, bribing undercover Russian policemen, fighting off advances from boy prostitutes in high-heeled sandals, eyeliner and lipstick. Oh, and I've been followed by a thousand rabid dogs.'

'It all sounds like a normal Saturday in Soho Square.'

'Of course, and it was often rather tedious and routine. But there were a few dramatic moments. A German scientist introduced me to a family of gorillas. One big male came up to me and grabbed me, dragged me to his nest of grass, which was full of shit and worse, and then he sat on me.'

'He must have been attracted by your aftershave.'

'Yeah, I'll know for next time – leave the Aramis at home. God, those guys are heavy! I lost my camera, rucksack and all my notes in Lebanon when I was robbed at gunpoint in Beirut. I shall have to write most of the book I'm doing next from memory. But at least I have some photographs. I'd sent some rolls of film back home two days before I got myself attacked. Lily, do you think we could meet up?'

'I'll have to check the diary. We're quite busy. I run my own business nowadays – well, I have a partner, actually – and we're taking on more workers all the time. Sarah's started school, and Harry's doing twelve hour days in London, or he's in Nick's constituency, and we—'

'I was rather hoping that I could meet you, singular – not you and the family.'

'Oh.'

Lily's heart was hammering fit to jump out of her body, and a terrifying mix of feelings – excitement, anger and arousal being the most prominent – churned inside her head. 'Max, I need to go,' she said. 'I'm sorry, but I have a hundred thousand things to do.'

'Please – you have to see me.'

'Why?'

'We need to talk.'

'It's like I said – I'm busy.'

'Maybe you could write to me care of my publisher? The address will be inside my books. We could meet in London some time, have a drink, perhaps? I'll hope to hear from you.'

Lily disconnected and stared down at the phone. She wasn't going to London, definitely. She didn't want anything to do with Max.

Max, Max, Max – why did it make her colour rise merely to say his name? Merely to whisper it inside her head? He turned me down, she told herself. I would never have been enough for Max. I love Harry. I am Harry's wife.

But sometimes being Harry's wife was hard. Since his diagnosis, he was often difficult and moody.

Then, however, he'd do something generous and thoughtful, like book tickets for a show in London he knew they'd all enjoy. Or organise a weekend in a European city, fly them all to Paris, Rome or Florence, and they'd have a lovely time, forget about their problems and be an ordinary happy family again.

'Mum, I've got the letter about pottery,' said Sarah.

'What?'

'You know – the class on Saturdays? Fiona Fox is going. What's the matter? You look really strange. Your face is white, but round your neck you've gone all red.'

'I feel a little dizzy.'

'Sit down on the stairs, then. I'll get a glass of water for you. Mum, why were you talking about aftershave?'

'I wasn't, was I?'

'Yes, you were – he must have been attracted by your aftershave, that's what you said. So who is Max?'

'He's one of Daddy's friends. We used to know him when we were all students here in Oxford. He's your godfather as well, but unofficially.'

'Why haven't I met him, then?'

'He spends a lot of time abroad. You did meet him once, but you were just a little baby.'

'Why did you say you had a hundred thousand things to do?'

'Sarah, don't you have a school project?'

'We need to talk,' he'd said. The following day, she found a postcard of the Mona Lisa, wrote a couple of lines to Max and then, before she had a chance to change her mind, she posted it.

Lily had combined their meeting with a visit to a wholesaler. At half past five she would meet Harry and go back home with him. Sarah would be taken home from school and given supper by Fiona Fox's mother Molly.

'I have a child and husband, don't forget,' she said to Max when she arrived in Leicester Square, the most public, unromantic place to meet, with its hurrying crowds of tourists and its litter and its dirty pigeons.

'I won't forget,' said Max, and kissed her lightly on the cheek. As Lily felt the pressure of his mouth against her skin, she knew this meeting was a big mistake. Wife and mother – none of that made any difference, for the heat of him, the scent of him, the warmth of him, were irresistible.

They had to be resisted. I should leave now, she told herself. I should go to Paddington at once and get a train to Oxford. I'll ring Harry at his office, say I have a headache and I've gone home earlier than planned.

But first things first.

'What did you want to talk about?' she asked.

'Oh, nothing in particular,' said Max.

'You mean you've dragged me all the way to London to say nothing in particular?'

'Lily, I would like to talk to you. What's wrong with that? Shall we find somewhere nice to have a drink?'

'I must go,' said Lily, torn between relief and disappointment. He hadn't changed his mind. They'd been friends, then – very briefly – lovers. Now they were friends again. 'I need to get my train.'

'Yes, of course, but if you've time – one little drink, perhaps?'

'I suppose so, now I'm here.'

Lily let him take her to a pub in Holborn where they had their little drink and Max asked after Harry and Sarah, told her bits and pieces about his recent travels. Then he asked: do you have time for dinner?

'No,' she said. 'I must get home. I'll go and find a taxi.'

'Oh – okay.' Max followed her into the street and then he flagged one down.

'I meant just for me,' she told him as the cab drew up but he didn't show any sign of leaving. 'Goodbye, Max.'

Max didn't say goodbye. 'I don't think pretty women should travel by themselves in taxis,' he said softly. 'Anything might happen in a taxi.'

Then they were in the taxi and were sitting side by side. Lily edged away from him and stared out of the window.

'Red Queen, don't worry,' he whispered as he kissed her

cheek again. 'I won't do anything as obvious as grope you in a taxi.'

'Shut up, Max,' said Lily, scrubbing at her face. 'I know you're arrogant enough to think I'm mad about you. Well, here's news – I'm not.'

'I know you're not, and that's why I left Oxford.'

'You mean you didn't like it when I took up with Harry. But you were busy shagging your way through all the women's colleges and it wasn't as if you wanted me.'

'When you got engaged to Gale, you broke my heart,' said Max. 'I wanted to forget about the pair of you. But it was just impossible.'

'I'm meeting Harry here,' said Lily as the taxi stopped outside the station. 'So if you don't want to see him?'

'Actually, I think I do.'

'Look who I met in Praed Street!' Lily cried.

'Farley, you old devil!' Harry was clearly thrilled to see his friend. 'Come back with us,' he added, when they'd done the back-slapping and man-hugging routine. 'Come and stay for a few days, a week or two, catch up with us, see Sarah. She's not a tiny baby any more. She's quite the little lady. You won't recognise her now.'

He took Max by the arm. 'You don't need to go home and get your stuff. We'll find him a toothbrush and pyjamas, won't we, Lily? A change of clothes? It will be like old times!'

Max and Harry talked and laughed the whole way back to Oxford. Lily sat and gazed out of the window, wondering how on earth she'd handle this when they got home, what she would do, what she would say.

They collected Sarah from Molly's house.

'Say hello, Max,' said Harry as his daughter scrutinised the stranger.

'Hello, Max,' said Sarah, holding out her hand for Max to take, a princess condescending to a junior ambassador from somewhere unimportant, a place that had no gold or silver mines.

Sarah's demeanour managed to be both charming and disdainful, Max decided. Yes, she was her mother's child all right.

'I'll get the supper going,' Lily said.

'Do you need any help?' asked Max.

'No, you stay in the sitting room, relax and talk to Harry. I'll get you both a beer, shall I? Sarah, will you come and lay the table in the kitchen, please? I'm afraid it's only boring sausages and chips,' she added. 'So it won't take long.'

'You're looking rather flushed, love,' Harry said. 'I hope you're not sickening for something?'

'No, I'm fine,' said Lily. 'It was cold outside but now it's rather hot in here. Perhaps we ought to turn the heating down.'

'Perhaps,' said Max and met her gaze. 'You're sure you don't want any help with dinner?'

'I'm quite sure,' said Lily, and Max saw she was blushing even more. 'You stay there,' she added sharply, as if she were talking to a disobedient dog.

'How was school today?' asked Harry after all the adults had had supper and sorted out the kitchen.

'We had a test in history,' said Sarah, who was sitting on her father's lap, his hands wrapped round her waist, and playing with his fingers. 'Fiona Fox got ninety-two.'

'But you got?' prompted Harry.

'Ninety-eight!' crowed Sarah.

'Well done!' cried Harry.

'Yes, clever girl,' said Lily, feeling only very slightly smug because her daughter could beat Fiona Fox.

'Mum, will you play draughts with me before I go to bed?' asked Sarah, sliding off her father's lap and reaching for the draught board.

'Yes, of course,' said Lily. 'But you usually play with Dad. What's different tonight?'

'Daddy always beats me.'

'No, I don't!' objected Harry.

'Or you let me beat you. But Mummy does her best to beat me. So when I beat Mum, I really win.'

'Max and I are going to the pub, in any case,' said Harry, getting up and stretching. 'Come on, Farley – shift yourself. We're wasting drinking time.'

'She's still your only one, then,' Max observed as he and Harry had a pint together in The Lamb and Flag. 'I thought you'd have a football team of ankle-biters around the place by now: one Gale for every number on the Beaufort scale. Sarah's obviously Strong Gale. Why don't you have a Moderate Breeze and Hurricane as well?'

'Oh, we discussed it and decided we didn't want more children,' Harry told him. 'Lily didn't much like being pregnant. Sarah was quite a demanding baby and Lily found it hard to cope. Where will you be going next to get yourself arrested, jailed or killed?'

'Somewhere hot and dusty, I expect, where democracy's a dirty word and I can meet all sorts of shady characters. Then I'll write about them for the *Sunday Times*.'

'Do you think you'll ever settle down?'

'Get a proper job, you mean? A mortgage on a house out in some suburb? No chance of that,' said Max. 'But I almost envy you: the family man who's living in his perfect house, which must be worth a packet nowadays, with his perfect wife and perfect daughter.'

'Yes, I'm very lucky,' Harry said.

Chapter Twenty

Max ran along the towpath of the Oxfordshire canal, trying to exhaust himself, but failing. He was far too fit to be exhausted by running anywhere in Oxfordshire where there were no clouds of biting insects, no sudden violent, terrifying storms, no near-intolerable humidity, no angry people chasing him with axes, guns, machetes or firing poisoned arrows at him.

How did people live such tame, safe lives and not go mad with boredom? You could die of boredom, he was sure. He pounded on and on and on, passing other morning joggers easily, even though he wasn't wearing running kit himself, just his usual uniform of T-shirt, jeans and trainers.

Obviously, Lily wasn't interested in him. When he'd kissed her in that taxi, when he'd willed her to respond to him, when he'd wanted her to kiss him back with all the passion he'd unwittingly unleashed that afternoon in Delhi, she'd flinched and pulled away.

Nowadays, she was a perfect wife and perfect mother. So he would have to be a perfect godfather to Sarah.

Max was a perfect godfather, thought Lily. It wasn't so much that he was good with children as he didn't even seem to notice that Sarah was a child. He talked to her as if she were grown up.

They went off on a private expedition to Oxford's two most interesting museums – the Ashmolean and the Natural History – and Sarah came back full of wonder with a notebook just as full of notes.

'These are hieroglyphics,' she explained, showing her

parents pictograms she'd copied that spelled out *queen* and *beautiful* and *red*. 'Max bought me this book from the museum shop in the Ashmoligan that tells you all about them.'

'Ashmolean,' corrected Harry.

'Yes, that's what I said. So I can write in hieroglyphics now, you see, like in a secret code.'

'I hope you'll sometimes write to me?' said Max. 'After I go away again, I mean?'

'I will. I promise,' Sarah told him. 'I could write to you in hieroglyphics, couldn't I?'

'Yes, and I'll write back.'

'When are you going away?'

'The day after tomorrow,' Max replied.

'What?' demanded Lily harshly, making everybody stare. 'I ... I mean why so soon?'

'Yes, why?' asked Harry. 'What's the rush?'

'I suppose I have a date with destiny,' said Max.

Sarah clearly missed him went he left.

'When will he be coming here again?' she asked.

'I don't know,' said Harry. 'Maybe in a year or two? He spends most of his time abroad, you see.'

'But when he's been abroad, he comes back home and writes a book about it. He told me. It's his job.'

'Yes, he's a travel writer.'

'Why can't I read his books?'

'He doesn't write for children. But you can read them, if you like.' Harry pointed to the top shelf of the bookcase at a row of hardbacks. 'See ... they're all up there.'

'When I'm grown up, I'm going to travel, too. I'm going to find things out. I'll go to Egypt and sail in a felucca up the Nile like Max, and then I'll write about it. Mummy, I think Max is nice. Why don't you like him?'

'I do like him, Sarah! Why—'

'While he was here, you hardly ever spoke to him.'

'Of course I spoke to him.' Lily didn't dare to look at Harry. 'But Max is Daddy's friend, you know, and Dad and Max are men. So they talk about the stuff that interests men, like politics and sport and drinking beer.'

'Dad, did the Egyptians drink a lot of beer?'

'I expect so; building pyramids is thirsty work.'

'Did they play football?'

'Yes, with their enemies' heads,' said Harry. 'I believe they ate a lot of onions, too.'

'Max didn't tell me that.'

'He might not have heard about the onions. Maybe you could tell him when you write to him?'

'Pyramids are tombs, Dad – did you know?'

'I might have heard it somewhere.'

'I wouldn't want to be shut up inside a pyramid. I don't want to be cremated, either. I want to be buried in the earth, under a tree, so I'll be food for worms. When people are buried, worms can eat their bodies and that's how worms survive, by eating bodies. We learned about it in our science class. How do I make sure that I get buried, not cremated?'

'You put it in your will.'

'How do I make a will?'

'You get a piece of paper. You write down what you want to happen to the things you leave behind, your toys and books and clothes and jewellery – who should inherit them – and also what you want to happen at your funeral. Then you sign and date the will. You'll need to get two of your friends to sign below your signature. They will be your witnesses. You need to have two witnesses.'

'Fiona Fox and Alan Flynn will do. Dad, will you and Mum be buried and be food for worms?'

'It will be our pleasure, poppet.'

'What about Max, will he be buried, too?'

'Maybe, if they ever find his body,' Harry said.

'Oh, Harry ... don't!' cried Lily.

Max wrote to Sarah now and then – a postcard from Somalia, a letter from Sudan. He usually wrote some of the text, and always signed his name – or Lily thought it had to be his name – in hieroglyphics.

Sarah kept the correspondence in a wooden box bought from a jumble sale at school, a box that she had decorated with some hieroglyphics of her own.

Lily assumed they must say things like *Sarah Lily Gale* and *Strictly Private* and *Mum & Dad Keep Out*.

'How is Max?' she asked one morning while she and her daughter ate their breakfast, while Sarah giggled over something Max had written in a letter from Morocco. 'What's so funny?'

'While he was swimming, a jellyfish attacked him and stung him on the foot,' said Sarah. 'All his toes swelled up. He had to hop around for days. Look, he's drawn a picture of him hopping. Some jellyfish are poisonous – did you know?'

'What else has he been doing, apart from getting stung by jellyfish?'

'Oh, climbing mountains and riding on a camel in the desert and eating goat and talking to some – Beddings?'

'Bedouins.'

'Yes. He says to give his love to the Red Queen. He must mean the one in the museum, mustn't he? He's looking forward to seeing us again when he gets home. But he doesn't know when it will be. Mum, he says he's going to be in Libya for a while and if I want to write to him I'll need to send a letter to the post office in Cairo. Then, when he's back in Egypt, he can ask for it.'

The post office in Cairo …

Lily told herself to stop it, not to be so damned ridiculous. This was not a coded message or an invitation. She must not write to Max.

Although she was always thinking and preoccupied, and therefore tended to bump into things, Sarah was not particularly clumsy. But sometimes she fell off her bike and sometimes took a tumble playing games – like children do.

One evening after netball practice, Lily found her daughter sitting in the kitchen, looking very miserable and cradling her arm, the one she'd fallen on when she was little.

'Does it hurt a lot?' she said, when Sarah asked if she could have some Calpol.

'Sometimes, yes,' said Sarah, whose usual attitude to bumps and scrapes and coughs and colds was stoical. She never made a fuss about grazed knees and hardly ever asked for medicine of any kind.

So Lily was alarmed.

'What kind of hurt?' she asked. 'A sharp pain, a dull ache?'

'Sometimes it's a sort of stabbing pain, especially after netball. Later on it aches. But when I'm in bed it sort of tingles and I don't know what to do with it.'

'You mean it often hurts? Why didn't you tell me?'

'I didn't think there was anything you could do.'

'Let me feel it, sweetheart? I promise I'll be gentle.' Lily carefully ran her fingers down her daughter's arm. She thought it seemed a little knobbly here, a touch misshapen there.

She told herself that she was probably imagining things

and Sarah just had growing pains, whatever they might be. 'But I'll take her to the doctor anyway,' she said when she and Harry were in bed that evening.

'Yes,' he said. 'We'd better sort it out.'

Sarah's GP felt she looked a little bit anaemic. So he took some blood to check up on her general state of health. Then he felt along her arm and said he thought she ought to have some X-rays.

The X-rays seemed to indicate a little abnormality. So then she saw an orthopaedic surgeon. 'There must have been a break here, after all,' the surgeon said, and pointed to an X-ray. 'You can see where the bone has knitted, here and here and here.'

Yes, he added, minor breaks were often very difficult to spot, especially in children, and Sarah's would have been a tiny one. But now the bones here in her lower arm were growing slightly misaligned.

'She should have a minor operation,' said the surgeon. 'It isn't an emergency, so she'll go on a waiting list, but I feel she'd be better off for having this procedure.'

'Do I get a plaster?' Sarah asked him.

'Yes, from your fingers to your elbow. We do pretty pink ones nowadays.'

'Any time off school?'

'Only a few days. But you shouldn't play games for a few weeks. Do you ride a bike?'

'Yes, but only in the parks or places where there isn't any traffic. Mum and Dad won't let me ride on roads.'

'Mum and Dad are very sensible. Okay, carry on riding in the parks. But always look to see where you are going and, after you've had the operation, don't fall off your bike for a few months. How do you like school?'

'It's all right.'

'She does very well at school,' said Harry.

'What do you do for pleasure?'

'I play netball, I make models, and at weekends I do pottery.'

'Perhaps give up the netball for a while and, when you go to pottery classes, just make pots and models on the workbench – don't use a potter's wheel.'

The surgeon turned to Lily. 'By the way, when Sarah has this operation, we shall need to have some blood on standby.'

'Why's that?' she asked, alarmed. 'You told us it would be a minor operation. Why—'

'There's always blood available for any patient undergoing surgery. It's just standard practice. As I expect you know already, Sarah's blood group is extremely rare. So, rather than rely on banks, I wonder if whichever of you shares her group would give a pint of blood this week, and then another pint in four months' time, and so on and on until we have a good supply?'

'Obviously,' Harry said.

'Yes, of course,' said Lily.

'Do you know your blood groups?'

'I must have known mine once, when I was pregnant,' Lily told him. 'But I can't remember now. Harry?'

'I don't know mine.'

'Let's get you tested, then. We'll find a nurse to take a sample from you both. Please don't look so worried, Mrs Gale. As I said, this having blood on standby – it's normal practice nowadays, even for the simplest operations. We like to be prepared.'

Chapter Twenty-One

Harry and Lily had just finished breakfast on the Saturday the letter came. Lily had started loading up the dishwasher, so when they heard the rattle of the letterbox Harry went to fetch the post.

'Anything exciting?' Lily asked.

'A letter for our daughter from her godfather, postmarked Cairo six or seven weeks ago,' said Harry as he sifted through the mail. 'A water bill, a postcard from your parents, and this one's from the Radcliffe. They'll have got the test results. You or me, then – heads or tails? Do you want to open it?'

'No, my hands are wet.'

So Harry opened it and read it. Then he stared at it for a long time.

'What's the matter?' Lily asked. 'What's wrong?'

Harry looked up again and met her gaze. 'Anything you need to tell me?' he began. 'Anything I ought to know and should have known for years?'

Lily saw his face was greyish-white, like unbleached linen. She felt a sickening, churning mix of terror, hopelessness – but also huge relief that Sarah was at weekend pottery class. So she wouldn't hear the conversation Lily and Harry were about to have.

'I ... I don't know what you mean,' she said.

'I mean you've made a fool of me.'

'Harry, what exactly does the letter say? Your daughter needs an operation, and—'

'But it would seem she's not my daughter.' Harry handed her the sheet of paper. 'You lied to me,' he said.

'I have never lied to you!'

'All right, perhaps you didn't need to lie because of course I never asked if Sarah is my child. But if I had asked you, Lily, what would you have told me?'

'I'd have said she's yours, of course!'

'As you see, the letter says they'll need to use blood from the bank,' continued Harry. 'That's because they can't use yours or mine. Obviously, I'm not a doctor. I don't know precisely how it works. But if Sarah doesn't share your blood group, she must share her father's, mustn't she?'

'I don't know!' cried Lily. 'Maybe some of us inherit blood groups from our grandparents or other ancestors?'

I have never lied to you.

Lily thought about that time when she'd been drunk. When she had been late for Minnie's party. When she'd told Max and Harry she was going to be sent down. But that had been a joke. A punishment for telling her that Minnie was a dragon or whatever, wasn't it, and if Max and Harry had been seriously worried, if they'd marched straight off to see the principal, to explain that it was all their fault, she'd have owned up long before they got to LMH. She wouldn't have let them make fools of themselves. But now it seemed she'd made fools of them both.

She glanced at Max's letter lying on the kitchen table.

Harry saw her looking, tracked her gaze. 'Did you ever sleep with him?' he asked. 'Did you have sex with Farley?'

'No,' said Lily.

'You swear on Sarah's life?'

'I won't swear anything on Sarah's life!'

There was one good thing, she thought – since the standby blood would now be coming from the bank, the operation would now go ahead a little earlier than planned.

They got a date and Harry marked it on the calendar in red. As this date grew closer, she almost managed to convince herself her husband was so silent because he was so worried about Sarah.

He spent a lot of time in London, leaving Oxford very early every morning and returning very late, because of course his work distracted him from what was going on at home. But she knew that he'd been busy putting two and two together, that he'd made a perfect and irrefutable four.

'She's Farley's daughter, isn't she?' he asked one evening, after Sarah was in bed and Lily was sitting at the kitchen table, sorting through some paperwork.

'Why do you think that?'

'I don't just think, I know. I can see it now. She has Farley's eyes, his nose, and when she smiles she looks exactly like him.'

'You're imagining things. She looks like you.'

'Did you go to bed with him or didn't you?' Harry leaned across the kitchen table and took Lily by the shoulders, dug his fingers deep into her flesh. 'Lily, look at me!' he growled, shaking her hard. 'Did you have sex with Max?'

She thought: I could deny it. Harry couldn't prove it now and, if Max doesn't tell him, there is no way he could ever prove it.

She'd been to the reference library in St Aldate's where she'd looked up blood groups. She'd researched who could inherit what, how it all worked, what were the rules. She'd discovered that although it was unlikely Sarah could be Harry's daughter, it was not impossible.

There are documented cases where these rules are broken. So if you don't share one of your parents' blood groups, don't jump to conclusions.

'Did you have sex with Max?' repeated Harry.

'Let me go. You're hurting me.'

Harry gave her one last shake but then he let her go.

'Well?' he demanded.

I could still deny it, Lily told herself. But what would be the point of lying any more?

'Yes, I did,' she said.

'Where and when was this?'

'The time I was in India.'

'So the two of you arranged it, did you? All that stuff you told me about buying fabrics – that was just a cover? You were really going to meet Farley?'

'No, it was an accident. We met by chance.' Lily grabbed him by the hand and made him meet her gaze. 'Harry, we did! You must believe me!'

'You're telling me that in a country that must have a population of about a billion, you met Max by chance and then had sex by accident?'

'I know it sounds ridiculous, but that was how it happened.'

'You were engaged to me.'

'I know.'

'Do you regret it?'

'You mean going to bed with Max?' asked Lily. 'Yes, of course I do.'

'Why didn't you tell me?'

'You'd have been so hurt.'

'You thought it was appropriate to deceive me?'

'Harry, this is history. We're a family now. We're Sarah's parents. Please – can't we get over it, move on? Why should we destroy our happiness?'

'You never loved me, did you?'

'Yes, of course I did! I do! I love you very much!'

'I don't believe you.' Harry turned away. 'I loved you

194

and Max, you know. He was my ideal brother. As for you –
you were my heart and soul.'

'Please don't hate us, Harry,' pleaded Lily. 'We didn't
mean to hurt you. Max and I – we love you.'

'It sounds like it,' said Harry.

'All the same, it's true. Anyway, we don't have time to
argue because we need to find him.'

'Why?'

'Well, obviously we might need Max's blood.'

'So you finally admit it, do you? You've known all along
that Sarah isn't mine? You know Farley is her father and he
knows it, too?'

'Max didn't – doesn't – know. Harry, I want Sarah to be
yours. I have always thought of her as yours, and so has
Max. She could still be yours, you know. I think it's very
likely. Or at any rate it's not impossible.'

'You had sex with Farley and you came home pregnant
with his child.' He glanced towards the silver box in which
he kept his keys. 'You brought me a consolation prize. Did
you think that spending a few rupees on a bit of ethnic
rubbish would make everything all right?' He picked the
box up, threw it and it smashed into a mirror, shattering it.

That evening, Harry went to sleep in the spare room.
'Dad gets very tired these days,' said Lily, when Sarah
noticed Harry wasn't sleeping with her mother any more. 'I
toss and turn a lot, so I disturb him.'

Chapter Twenty-Two

Lily hoped that Max would soon be found.

But in spite of Harry pulling various strings and calling in some favours from people in the Foreign Office, and in spite of embassies and consulates all round the Middle East and Africa being asked to look for him, Max could not be traced. Since he wrote that letter postmarked Cairo, he'd presumably moved on.

'Maybe he's in South America?' suggested Lily. 'Africa, the Middle East and South America – they're his favourite places. He writes about them most.'

'I'll go and see his publisher,' said Harry.

'What if he won't talk to you?'

'He will.'

It was difficult to be with Harry, but Lily was more concerned about her daughter. Since Sarah had been told she'd have her operation soon, she'd been unusually quiet.

'You mustn't worry, darling,' Lily said. 'The surgeon is a very clever man and while he operates you'll be asleep. You won't feel any pain.'

'I know that, Mum,' said Sarah. 'We did anaesthetics in biology last term. I know how operations work.'

'Then you'll know more than I do! Listen, when you've had the operation and you're feeling better, maybe we could have a little holiday? Do you fancy anywhere? Maybe we could go to Egypt? We could see the Pyramids, the Sphinx, ride on a camel, maybe?'

'Do you think Dad would come with us to Egypt?'

'Yes, of course.'

'But he might be busy at the office. He seems to spend a lot of time there nowadays. He's hardly ever here at home with us.'

'Yes, he does work hard. Sarah, would you like hot chocolate? I was just about to make some.'

'Maybe later, Mum. I have a lot of homework.' Sarah grabbed her schoolbag and lugged it up the stairs and shut her bedroom door.

'What happened?' Lily asked when Harry said he'd spoken to Max's publisher.

'At first he said he couldn't give me any information. It might endanger Farley. But I have my methods.'

'Do you mean you threatened him?'

'The Revenue's been watching him for years and trying to catch him out. When I said I was a civil servant and added that I know some tax inspectors, he was quick to tell me that he'd commissioned Farley to get himself into Tibet; to walk around then write about the place. I can't believe the British reading public needs to know about Tibet. But, anyway – if Farley's in Tibet, he's very likely to get himself arrested. They'll lock him up and lose the key.'

'Why would they want to lock him up?'

'Tibet is under Chinese occupation. I dare say Farley won't have bothered with a visa and he's also likely to be carrying US dollars. So anyone who picks him up is going to assume he's working for the CIA.' Harry smiled a mirthless smile. 'Chinese interrogators don't have a reputation for being kind to spies.'

Lily didn't want to think about Max being caught and tortured by the Communist Chinese. She'd read about the occupation of Tibet in various Sunday supplements, and now she shuddered. 'Sarah has her check up at the hospital on Friday,' she told Harry. 'Do you want to come?'

'Of course.'

'All right, but I just thought with work and everything—'

'You never think.'

'It's for half past ten, and so you should be able to get away by lunchtime.'

'I don't need you to organise my life.'

'I was only trying to—'

'Well, don't.'

When they saw the surgeon, they said nothing about Max, about the possibility he might be Sarah's father and therefore the right person to give blood.

Sarah had her operation and the surgeon told them he was confident her arm would now grow straight and give her no more trouble.

'It went very well,' he said. 'So you should have her home in three days' time. As for her aftercare – all you'll need to do is stop her racing round the place and falling over. Yes, it's easier said than done, I know.'

'May we see Sarah?' Lily asked.

'Of course,' the surgeon said. 'But she's still going to be a little groggy. So you mustn't expect to have a conversation yet.'

'As you see, she's fast asleep,' the sister said when they were shown into a little side room on a children's ward. 'You can say hello, of course. You can hold her hand and smooth her hair and she might realise you're here. But she had a lot of anaesthetic, so it could be a while before she wakes and talks to you. One of you could go home and get some sleep. Oh – excuse me, someone's paging me.'

The sister left them standing by the bed.

'You go,' said Lily.

'No, you go,' said Harry. 'Do you have your keys? I'll see you in the morning. By the way,' he added as he turned away from Lily, 'last week, I went back to that fertility clinic and I saw the doctor who said I could be under stress, malnourished or recovering from an infection. I had some other tests. As it turns out, I'm not malnourished and I haven't had an infection. I have a condition.'

'What condition?'

'I can't remember what it's called, but basically it means I'm shooting blanks. I always have been and I always will be. Sarah's not my child.'

'Harry, surely there's a chance, a possibility—'

'There's no chance at all.'

'It's not appropriate to talk about this now. So, if you're staying, I'll go home.'

As Lily pulled her coat on, Harry grabbed her by the forearm. 'You might think you've won,' he muttered. 'But whatever games you've played, however many men you've had, remember Sarah is my child in law and you will never take her from me.'

Lily went home to an empty house half-wishing she could go to sleep and not wake up again, but instead, she passed a sleepless night.

She didn't know what to do. She was sorry Harry had been hurt by people he had loved. She pitied him and longed to make amends. Although she loved her daughter, she wished she'd never been to bed with Max.

The following morning, she took Harry's razor and a change of clothes into the hospital. He took them, kissed the sleeping child and then he went to catch the train to London.

Lily sat down at the bedside, held her daughter's hand and stroked her fingers and willed her to wake up.

At lunchtime Sarah did.

'Hello, darling,' whispered Lily. 'It's so good to have you back with us! How do you feel now?'

Sarah looked at Lily but didn't speak – instead, she turned her head away and wouldn't say a word.

The following day, although she was awake, was eating stuff like porridge, jelly, custard and ice cream, was breathing normally, and so her doctors said she could go home, she wouldn't speak to Lily or to Harry.

'Give her time,' the sister said. 'She's had a general anaesthetic and perhaps her throat is rather sore still – from the tubes, you know? Sometimes it can take a while for children to come round, I mean completely, be their normal selves again.'

Chapter Twenty-Three

When they all got home again, the silence was unbearable.

Lily talked to fill it, but Harry wouldn't talk to Lily.

Sarah wouldn't talk to anyone.

She didn't appear to be in any pain. Although she was in plaster from her fingers to her elbow, the cast was very light and didn't seem to trouble her at all. She managed to get washed and dressed unaided. As for eating – Lily thought her throat could not be sore, because she managed crisps and bacon sandwiches followed by a Crunchie.

'Do you want go to school today?' asked Lily, on the fifth day home from hospital. 'You will need to talk, you know, at school.'

Sarah shrugged.

'I'll pack your lunchbox for tomorrow, shall I? You can sort your books and pens out – yes?'

Sarah shrugged again.

The following morning, she got up, got washed, got dressed, ate breakfast. She let her mother drive her to her school. 'Darling, do you want me to come in with you?' Lily asked. 'Speak to Mrs Woodley, maybe?'

Sarah shook her head, got out and disappeared.

Lily thought: she'll probably be fine at school. She'll chat to all her friends and let them sign her plaster and everything is going to be all right.

But it was not all right.

'Hello, love – good day?' asked Lily, when she went to meet her daughter after school.

Sarah merely shrugged and then walked off.

'Why won't you speak to me?' Lily hurried after Sarah. 'Do we need to get some throat sweets?'

Sarah shook her head.

'Mrs Gale, may I have a word?' Sarah's teacher Mrs Woodley called to Lily from across the playground then came hurrying up. 'Sarah isn't quite herself today,' the teacher said. 'She's been very quiet – in fact, she hasn't spoken to anyone at all – and this is most unusual for Sarah. She's normally a little chatterbox.'

'I think her throat must still be sore,' said Lily. 'After all, she had an anaesthetic. Lots of tubes, you know? I'm sure she's going to be okay tomorrow, aren't you, love?'

Sarah didn't answer and was silent all the way back home. When she and Lily walked into the house and Lily went to put the kettle on, Sarah carried on upstairs and shut her bedroom door.

At first, the staff at school were understanding and made allowances. But later, as the days then weeks went by, Lily got such looks, there was such muttering and whispering whenever she was in the playground waiting for her daughter, that she began to understand how it must feel to be a social outcast, a pariah.

Then Molly Fox, the mother of Fiona Fox and chairman of the PTA, decided it was time to have a little word with Lily.

'I don't think Sarah ought to be in school until she's better,' Molly said. 'I've been talking to the staff and parents, and everybody says she's being deliberately disruptive.'

'Molly, she's been poorly!'

'As well as this not speaking stuff, she's acting strangely, too. Do you know she's made her will? She got Fiona and another friend to witness it. I think that's very morbid, children making wills. Why would she think of such a thing?'

'Why wouldn't she? Amy makes her will in *Little Women*, which is one of Sarah's favourite books.'

'I still think it's odd,' said Molly, narrowing her eyes. 'She's always been a little strange, your Sarah, hasn't she? She must take after you.'

'What's that supposed to mean?'

'When we were at college, you told me you could put the evil eye on people. When I had Fiona and my milk dried up, it was because you put the evil eye on me for saying you'd have trouble feeding babies because you were so small. You're a witch and Sarah has inherited your powers.'

'I don't have any powers!'

'I think you do, and so does Sarah.'

'Why would you think that?'

'She fixes netball matches, doesn't she? She stares at people so they fail to score. While she and Fiona were playing in that tournament last year, Fiona's team was winning. But suddenly Sarah started staring. She was willing Fiona's team to lose – and lose it did.'

'Molly, you're absurd.'

'I don't think so.' Molly tossed her flaxen hair. 'Your mother was a gypsy, after all, and everybody knows how gypsies—'

'Mum was born in Birmingham!' cried Lily. 'She grew up in a terraced house in Smethwick.'

'You say that now because you want to be respectable. But I haven't forgotten what you said when we were students.'

'Molly, I was joking.' Lily sighed. 'You're letting your imagination run away with you. Perhaps you ought to find yourself a shrink?'

Three days later, Lily cursed herself for putting thoughts into the head of Molly Fox.

'Mrs Gale, I'm well aware that Sarah's been in hospital,' the headmistress observed, as she and Lily sat facing one another across Mrs Godfrey's polished desk on which lay Sarah's personal file. 'We – the staff here – we all understand that going into hospital can be very difficult for a child. We've tried to make allowances. But it's been weeks and weeks. We think your daughter needs professional help.'

'What sort of help?'

'Perhaps she ought to see a child psychologist?'

'Sarah doesn't need a child psychologist.'

'We feel it might be useful.'

'As I understand it, psychologists help people who self-harm, are traumatised or even mad. My daughter isn't mad.'

'What does Sarah's GP think?' asked Mrs Godfrey. 'I assume you're seeing her GP?'

'Yes, of course we're seeing her GP. He's known Sarah since she was a baby and he's satisfied there's nothing physically wrong. He told us it's a passing phase and not to worry. Sarah isn't traumatised and she'll come out of it.'

'I'm not a doctor, obviously, but my personal feeling is your daughter has a problem. When one child has a problem, the other children notice. Some of them are bound to be affected. This month, there have been several instances of students copying Sarah's most unfortunate behaviour. A parent has expressed concern—'

'You mean complained.'

'I mean expressed concern.'

'Molly Fox has been to see you, hasn't she? What exactly did she say to you?'

'The parent stressed most forcibly that her intention was to help your child. She also asked if I would keep her comments confidential and I agreed to do so.'

'I know it was Molly Fox. She thinks Sarah puts the evil eye on people and I do it too. Mrs Godfrey, Molly Fox is crazy. How could you even start to think she should be taken seriously? Anyway, what sort of help did she suggest? Does she want Sarah taken into care?'

'There was no such suggestion, but—'

'She thinks I'm a witch. She told me so. Perhaps she'd like to burn me at the stake? Why don't we do it in the playground? The PTA could toast marshmallows, bake potatoes, couldn't they?'

'Mrs Gale, I'm not prepared to tell you who said what. But I have to say I feel the parent had a point. Since Sarah has been back at school, the other children in her class have been somewhat unsettled. We don't know why Sarah doesn't speak. But I suspect she wants to draw attention to herself, to make herself seem special. As I just explained to you, other pupils have begun to copy her behaviour, have refused to answer questions. They've started staring at the staff and at each other just like Sarah does. I hadn't actually noticed this myself until the parent mentioned it to me. But now I can see it all the time. Sarah stares at people in a most disturbing way. She upsets them. She is a disruptive influence.'

'I'll take her home,' said Lily. 'I'll take her now and I'll explain that she must start to speak again.'

'Mrs Gale, I must repeat that I feel Sarah needs to see a child psychologist. So I hope you and your husband will consider it. Otherwise it might be necessary to exclude your daughter from the school.'

'Temporarily, you mean?'

'I hope so, but if matters don't improve, if her behaviour stays completely unacceptable—'

'You can't expel my daughter just for being ill!'

'I get letters every day from parents who would like to send their children to this school. I could fill every student's place twice over, three times over.'

Blackmailer, thought Lily.

'Give me a few days at least,' she said.

Lily drove them home. She left Sarah drawing something at the kitchen table and went round to call on Mrs Fraser, their neighbour who'd known Sarah all her life and been her babysitter countless times.

Mrs Fraser said she thought that Sarah's doctor talked a lot of sense and Sarah would grow out of this – this phase, this funny spell, whatever you liked to call it. So Lily shouldn't worry.

'I know you need to work, my dear,' added Mrs Fraser. 'But I'm here at home most days. So, while Sarah's having a little break from school, I'll pop round from time to time and she can pop round to me. You and Harry, you can rest assured your little one will be all right.'

'You really think it's just a phase?' said Lily hopefully.

'Yes, I do.' Mrs Fraser patted Lily's hand. 'Your Sarah's at that awkward age. She's not a child any more, but she's not grown up, and she hasn't long come out of hospital. I brought up six, they all had phases, and they all grew out of them.'

But Sarah's phase went on and on and on.

'I don't know what to do with you,' said Lily as the three of them sat in the kitchen one evening, pushing cooling pasta round their plates and hardly eating anything.

Sarah shrugged.

'Harry, you ask Sarah why she isn't speaking.'

Harry shrugged as well.

'Harry, Sarah, please will you stop doing this to me?'

cried Lily. 'Sarah, darling, you must talk to people! When they speak to you, you need to answer!'

Sarah ate a piece of pasta, chewing it reflectively.

'Sweetheart, what is wrong with you – will you try to tell me? Maybe I can help you? I know you like to go to school. But, if you upset the other children and your teachers, you will be excluded, and is that what you want?'

Sarah sat in silence.

'Please say something?' Lily begged. 'I know – I'll get some notebooks for you, shall I? I'll get a dozen notebooks. You can write down what you want to say. Maybe you could keep a diary, too? A sort of journal, if you like?'

There was yet more shrugging.

'I must go to work today,' said Lily the next morning. 'Only for an hour or two, and Mrs Fraser's promised to call round to see that you're all right. But, if you want to come with me, of course that will be fine. You could sit in the office, couldn't you?'

Sarah shrugged then walked out of the kitchen and went up to her room.

On her way back home from work, Lily bought a range of pretty notebooks, and Sarah wrote her name on all of them. She drew some pictograms in one, but wouldn't explain their meaning to her mother.

'She's not going to talk to you,' said Harry.

'I'm her mother!'

'You feel this means she owes you something?'

'What do you think she might have overheard in hospital?'

'Why don't you ask?'

'As if she'll tell me!' Lily felt herself well up. 'Please, Harry, can't we stop all this? Why do you want to tear our family apart?'

*　*　*

Max came back from the Far East and started writing up his notes on all his wanderings in Tibet, a dismal place in which an ancient civilisation was being torn apart.

He wondered about going to Oxford, seeing Lily.

Or should he leave well alone? As he'd sorted through the piles of mail that he'd found lying on the doormat of his rented flat, he decided if he found a postcard or a letter postmarked Oxford, he'd phone Lily.

There was nothing.

He should have been in Egypt, researching Coptic culture and traditions. But he wasn't fit enough. While he'd been in Italy last month, making his way home to the UK, he'd met a Greek professor who was interested in ancient trade routes between Italy and Egypt, and also between Italy and China. Did the Ancient Romans get as far as China? It was likely, the professor said – the Jews did, after all, and so why not the Romans, the Persians, Abyssinians?

Max had always thought he could eat anything – rats, cats and bats, slugs, snails and scorpions, he'd probably ingested all of those at various times – and live to put it in a book. But when he went to dinner with the professor, he'd got shellfish poisoning. He'd never been so ill in all his life. He thought he'd die.

When he didn't die, he found himself reflecting on his own mortality and wondered if he ought to make his will. But who should be his major beneficiary? Or only beneficiary? He supposed his god-daughter, the junior Red Queen?

Now he was in London, he'd go to see a lawyer, he decided, and he'd make it all official. But first he needed a few days to rest and get his strength back. At the moment, he could barely find the energy to walk and talk.

Chapter Twenty-Four

The days dragged on and Lily almost came to feel that it would always be like this, that she and Harry would still live together but hardly ever talk, and Sarah wouldn't speak again at all.

She filled a dozen notebooks, though, with various pictograms and hieroglyphs. Why hieroglyphs, thought Lily fearfully. Maybe she'd forgotten how to write?

Maybe the GP was wrong? Maybe this non-speaking wasn't just a passing phase? Maybe Sarah had forgotten how to speak, and wasn't merely being awkward, stubborn, difficult? What if she wanted desperately to talk, but couldn't find her voice? What if she couldn't hear? What if they'd given her too much anaesthetic? What if she had been damaged? What if all the doctors were in cahoots and covering up for one another and – what if, what if ...

Or should Sarah see a child psychologist?

I'll take her back to the GP, decided Lily. I'll demand referrals. I'll get specialists involved. We have to sort this out once and for all.

'Next week, we're going to see the doctor,' Lily told her daughter. 'You've been ill for far too long. We need to make you better.'

Sarah looked alarmed then grabbed a notebook and scribbled furiously. *I'm not ill and I don't need a doctor!!!*

'We'll see,' said Lily, thinking: well, that's something. At least you still know how to write, and I know you can hear.

But she had awful nightmares in which Sarah needed something desperately, urgently, but couldn't ask for it, that she was drowning and couldn't scream for help.

Then there was a new development.

'Hello, Mrs Gale.' It was Sunday morning and Fiona Fox was standing on the doorstep. 'I came to see how Sarah is today.'

'She seems okay,' said Lily carefully.

'Oh, do you mean she can talk again?'

'No, she's still not speaking to us.' Lily couldn't see Molly Fox's yellow Mini Cooper in the road. So she assumed Fiona must have walked from Summertown. 'Does your mother know you're here?'

'She and Dad have gone to church. I said I had a stomach ache, so Mum said stay in bed.' Fiona shrugged. 'I know you and Mum don't like each other very much. But Sarah is my friend. We made our wills, you know. I witnessed Sarah's and she witnessed mine. We signed them in our blood.'

'Oh, right,' said Lily. She repressed a shudder. 'I see you have your book bag.'

'I thought Sarah might be interested in what she's missed at school.'

'Why don't you go upstairs? I'll bring you both some milk and biscuits, shall I?'

'Thank you, Mrs Gale,' Fiona said politely.

Lily heard Fiona knock on Sarah's bedroom door, heard Sarah open it, then heard Fiona say *hello* and *how are you?* There was no response from Sarah, but Fiona didn't come downstairs again. She stayed an hour, but promised she'd be back on Tuesday while her mother took her usual Bible study class.

'You must say you're coming here,' said Lily. 'Otherwise, she'll worry.'

'She won't worry, Mrs Gale. I'll be home before she's even left the church. So she won't know I've been here, anyway.'

'I still think you should say you're seeing Sarah.'

'There are lots of things Mum doesn't need to know, and this is one of them.' Fiona looked at Lily. 'Mrs Gale, I want to help my friend. I'm not a spy for Mum.'

'I never thought you were,' said Lily, reddening. But you *are* a mind reader, she thought.

Fiona came two or three times a week and stayed an hour or more. Lily wasn't happy about Molly being deceived, but she couldn't bring herself to ring the woman, and she thought if Sarah liked to see her friend, which evidently she must do ...

'See, it works,' she heard Fiona say one afternoon, then there was an alarming smell of burning.

'What are you two doing?' Lily shouted.

'Science homework, Mrs Gale!' Fiona shouted back. 'We're using glass and solar energy – that's from the sun – to burn a hole in paper.'

'You be careful!'

'Oh, we're *always* careful, Mrs Gale!' Fiona carolled cheerily, reminding Lily of her mother Molly, which was sad because she rather liked Fiona Fox.

Chapter Twenty-Five

'You wish this child to be sole heir?'

The lawyer looked at Max, his eyebrows raised. 'Mr Farley, you're a wealthy man. Your father left you everything. He and your mother were divorced, of course, and you have no other blood relations, no dependents. But surely there are various people – friends, maybe – whom you would wish to benefit? Perhaps you should consider setting up some charitable trusts?'

'I've considered everything, and this is what I wish to do,' said Max.

'Very well.' The lawyer nodded and picked up his pen. 'Where shall you be going next, if I may ask?'

'Egypt, then the Lebanon.'

'A very dangerous place, by all accounts. So I feel your decision to put everything in order is a wise one. Let's call my secretary, shall we? She can be your second witness, that's unless you'd like to ask somebody else?'

'Let's get it done today.'

'You're sure?'

'I've never been so sure of anything.'

So the lawyer buzzed his secretary. 'By the way,' he added, turning back to Max, 'I've very much enjoyed your books on South America and the Middle East. You do have some adventures! You've just been to Tibet, I think? How is it coping, ruled by the Chinese – is everything quite ghastly?'

'It's worse than ghastly,' Max replied. 'I still have nightmares.'

Lily still had nightmares about Sarah, in which she had no

mouth and therefore couldn't have spoken if she'd tried. But nowadays she hoped Fiona might be helping Sarah in some way, so she put seeing any doctors, counsellors or psychologists on hold.

'What do you and Fiona talk about?' she asked one day, after Fiona had gone home. She had not been keeping track of all Fiona's visits, but was aware she must have now been coming for several weeks, or maybe it was months.

Sarah looked at Lily, shrugged.

'You mean you never say a word, not even to Fiona? She talks all the time to you. I hear her chattering and you giggle, too. Does she tell you jokes?'

Sarah raised one eyebrow. Then – miracle of miracles – she smiled a tiny, hesitant half-smile.

Lily almost fainted with the shock of it, but also with delight. 'I'm going to make some chocolate – would you like some?'

Sarah nodded.

'I have marshmallows, pink and white ones.'

Sarah smiled properly and Lily felt a surge of optimism. Maybe their GP was right? Maybe all this verbal non-communication was indeed a passing phase? Perhaps they'd turned a corner?

The sun came out just then and slanting rays lit up the kitchen, like in a Renaissance painting. So perhaps this was a sign, a blessing? Maybe Harry would come home tonight and say he felt they ought to draw a line under the past and be a happy family again?

At first, it looked like this might happen. Sarah was in bed. Lily was loading up the dishwasher when Harry came into the kitchen and sat down at the table.

'I've decided what we'll do,' he said.

This wasn't exactly how he was supposed to start the

conversation during which he'd say the past was past and now they must go forward. But it made a change from saying nothing.

'Do I get to share in your decision-making?' Lily asked him calmly and – she hoped – non-confrontationally.

'No, you don't,' said Harry. 'I want you to move out.'

Lily stared at him, astonished. 'You mean you want me and Sarah—'

'Only you.'

'Where would I go?'

'Well, that would be entirely up to you.'

'Please, Harry, don't do this to us?' asked Lily. 'Why don't we try to make this marriage work? We were very happy once and we could still be happy, couldn't we? You and me and Sarah?'

'This marriage is broken,' Harry said, 'and that's why I want you to go.'

'Who would look after Sarah?'

'She could have a nanny.'

'I'm not leaving,' Lily told him. 'This house is my home, my daughter's home, and if anyone's moving out, it's you.'

Max was afraid he'd broken something.

Along with other Western journalists and writers, he had had to jump down from the second storey of a burning building after it was shelled by God knew whom – Beirut was being attacked by every terrorist, extremist and his brother nowadays, it was a free-for-all – and, although he'd jumped on to the roof of an adjacent building, he'd fallen awkwardly.

'You all right, mate?' asked a big Australian cameraman who'd landed close to Max.

'I'm not sure yet,' Max said, wincing. 'How are you?'

'Just a few scrapes and minor burns – the usual,' the Australian replied. 'I've lost all my kit, of course.'

'God, that's rough.'

'I'll say it's bloody rough.' The Australian scrambled to his feet, brushed himself down. 'I'll have to send some telexes. Get authorisation to replace the stuff. I dunno how – it's not like I can go to Curry's, is it, pick out what I want and pay with flaming Mastercard? But now I need to find a beer or two. You coming, then?'

'I'm not sure if I can stand.'

'You've still got two legs, mate, haven't you? So that means you can stand.' None too gently, the Australian pulled Max to his feet, which made him gasp in pain and realise yes, the ankle must be broken. 'Let's get you to a bar.'

'I don't want to be a killjoy, but I think I need a doctor first.'

'I think you need a bar.'

The Australian lugged Max down a broken staircase, then along a street in which no buildings were unscathed, and finally into a gloomy cellar where there was a bar of sorts, full of foreign journalists and a few Lebanese.

Although the place was also full of smoke, it was just light enough for Max to check his arms and hands. He saw the burns were nothing. Or almost nothing, anyway. He'd had worse and they had healed, so these burns would heal, too.

But his ankle throbbed and burned like crazy. He flexed the joint and felt the bones grate almost audibly. It was the same ankle he had broken when he was fourteen. The one he had pretended didn't hurt, and so it had been weeks before he'd finally been shunted off to A & E, and it had never been quite right again. He didn't think he'd make it to the Syrian or Israeli border with a broken ankle, even if he strapped it up.

Maybe he could break his rules and hitch a ride with someone from the BBC or ITV, someone who was heading for Damascus or Jerusalem to send a news report or file a story? Or could he buy a horse? Or donkey?

As he was considering what to do, another huge explosion rocked the district and a new shower of masonry came down, making everybody choke.

Then everything went quiet – much too quiet. There was no light. Something warm was dripping on him and he knew it was most likely to be someone's blood. He tried to speak, call out, but couldn't because his mouth and throat were full of dust.

Perhaps the bar was now his tomb?

Over the corpse of their dead marriage, Lily and Harry reached an awkward truce. They – or Harry, anyway – tacitly agreed on a regime of strict non-interaction, of non-communication.

Whenever Lily walked into a room, Harry walked straight out of it. While she was in the kitchen, he was in the sitting room. Lily cooked for Sarah and herself at teatime. Harry cooked much later or didn't cook at all. Sarah spent most of her time up in her bedroom, sometimes with Fiona, but usually alone, filling notebook after notebook with – well, Lily didn't know, because everything was written in code or hieroglyphs or in both.

As Lily was working in the sitting room one summer evening, she thought she could smell burning. At first, she took no notice. Many of their neighbours loved a barbecue. The stink of scorching flesh often polluted the scented summer night. The Frasers were enthusiastic barbecuers, often getting their extended family round for burgers, chicken wings and sausages and other charred and mangled bits of beast.

But they were away on holiday, and so tonight it wasn't them ...

'Harry, are you in the kitchen, are you burning something?' Lily called. But then she realised he was most unlikely to respond. So she got up and walked into the hallway.

Smoke.

The crackle of a fire?

A fire!

'Harry!' Lily screamed in panic. 'Harry, I think the house is burning! Sarah's up there! Harry!' Lily raced upstairs. Wisps of smoke curled all around the door of Sarah's room.

You shouldn't open doors where there's a fire.

My child is in that room!

She wrenched open the door and charged inside.

The window was wide open. The fire had caught one curtain and it was blazing merrily. The through-draught fanned the flames so now they coiled towards the ceiling. She grabbed the as-yet-unscorched edges of the curtain, tore it down, threw Sarah's duvet over it, stamped out the wicked flames.

'Sarah!' she cried desperately.

Where was she?

Harry came panting up the stairs. He pulled open the doors to Sarah's wardrobe, cupboards, lifted up the lid of an old toy box she probably couldn't fit inside in any case, but still ...

'Sarah!' Harry shouted. 'Christ, where are you?'

She doesn't speak, thought Lily, who was pulling open doors and lifting lids as well. We've damaged that poor child so much she can't. Perhaps she never will again. But where the hell—

'Daddy!'

Lily stared around the room and wondered if she was imagining things. Although the fire was out, the draught was showering glowing shreds of burnt black fabric all over the carpet, filling Sarah's room with acrid fumes and making her and Harry choke.

Sarah screamed again, a bubbling wail. 'Daddy, Daddy, Daddy!' Outside – was Sarah calling to him from outside? But Sarah couldn't call him, could she? Harry rushed over to the window. 'She's out there,' he said. He climbed over the sill on to the sloping roof. Lily would have followed him, but—

'You stay there,' he rapped.

So Lily stayed, but leaned out and watched as Harry inched towards his daughter, who was clinging to the metal gutter above the dormer window of another bedroom, perilously suspended over a long drop of twenty feet on to a brick-paved yard below.

'Sarah, take my hand.' Harry held the sill of Sarah's window with his left and reached out to his daughter with his right. 'Grab my hand, my darling. You won't fall. I'll never let you fall.'

But Sarah held on to the gutter, obviously afraid to let it go.

'Sarah, let me help you?' Harry's voice was low, persuasive. 'Sweetheart, hold on tightly to the gutter with your right hand and let me take your left. Then I can help you climb back in your room.'

Still Sarah hesitated. But then, as Lily watched and Harry soothed, persuaded, Sarah stretched out her left hand. Harry grasped it, talked her into sliding her right hand along the guttering towards him, and finally he pulled his sobbing daughter into his embrace.

Lily helped them both climb back inside, and then, for several minutes, the three of them stood like a tableau, holding one another, shaking.

'Sarah, love, you spoke,' said Harry.

Sarah stared at him.

'You called out to me! Say Dad again?'

Sarah gulped.

'D-dad?' she faltered. 'Daddy?'

Then Lily saw the wetness on her husband's face, saw he was crying, too. 'Anybody hurt?' she asked them gently.

'I'm okay,' said Harry. 'Sarah, any burns or scrapes or grazes?'

Sarah shook her head.

'Lily, did you burn your hands?'

'No, thankfully.'

Of course she'd called for Harry, Lily thought, as she held him and Sarah close. Sarah's first word had been Daddy, after all. But that was fine, it was okay, because her daughter had found her voice again.

The fire engines arrived when there was nothing left to do apart from check the fire was out. So did Molly Fox, who had presumably heard bells – a neighbour must have called the fire brigade.

'You must come and stay at our house,' offered Molly, but to Lily's great surprise she said this very kindly and not bossily at all. 'You poor things, you've had a dreadful shock! Come round now, have showers and get yourselves into pyjamas. We always have some spare pairs in the jumble bag. The Mothers' Union ladies wash and mend and iron all the donations, so they'll be nice and clean. Please come and make yourselves at home.'

'Sarah, you can sleep in my bed,' said Fiona.

'Harry and Lily, you can have our bedroom,' added Molly. 'As it happens, I changed the sheets this morning.'

'Thank you, Fiona, Molly,' Lily said – and then, before she knew it, she'd burst into floods of noisy tears.

Molly hugged her like a mother, crooning softly, saying it was all right now, and things would seem much better in the morning. Lily let herself be hugged and thought, maybe she'd misjudged poor Molly all along?

Sarah told them later, in a mix of speech and writing, what had happened.

She and Fiona had been lighting candles, studying the effects of draughts on flames, how flames behaved in different circumstances, how much energy it took to blow a candle out. They'd written up their findings for Fiona's science homework and Fiona had gone home.

Sarah had carried on experimenting, finding out how close a piece of paper had to be to flames before it could catch fire, before it reached combustion temperature. Did it actually need to touch the flame? Or ...

She had worked it out. She had lit the paper before it came in contact with the flame. But then the paper had blazed up. She'd tried to throw it through the open window. But, as she had done so, one curtain had caught fire. She'd panicked and instead of making for the door, she'd climbed out of the window.

'Why did you do that?' asked Harry, puzzled.

'I don't know!' wailed Sarah.

'You must have had a reason, love?'

But do we need reasons, wondered Lily, for anything we do?

* * *

220

They stayed with Molly and her family for a couple of nights and then went home.

At Molly's, Harry and Lily were obliged to share a bed. Now Lily wondered if he'd like to share a bed again, if this might prove to be a turning-point in all the misery, if maybe they could start again.

It was not to be. Harry said until they got the decorators round, Sarah should sleep in the spare room. He'd sleep on the sofa.

He was sitting in the kitchen one evening eating dinner when Lily thought she'd give it one last try. As a family, they had come so close to tragedy that surely they could put the past behind them? Surely they could, should – they must – move on?

She sat down at the table opposite him and poured them both a glass of wine.

'You were wonderful that evening,' she began.

Harry merely shrugged.

'You rescued Sarah, and it was all thanks to you she found her voice again.'

Harry didn't speak.

Lily wondered if the voices in this house were rationed, if now Sarah had agreed to speak again, Harry was struck dumb.

'Harry,' she continued gently, begging him in silence to please stop being so stubborn, so unyielding. 'I know I've made mistakes. But, please – can't you forgive me? Why do you need to punish me? Sarah is your daughter, whoever was her father. We're a family. Why can't we forget the past and get on with our lives together? Be as happy as we used to be?'

'I don't love you any more.'

'You could be kind to me.'

'You want a husband who is kind to you but doesn't love you? You could see me every day knowing I don't love you and you could still want to be with me?'

'It's Max – you're jealous.' Lily took a gulp of wine. 'Harry, if I'd been to bed with someone else, and Sarah had been someone else's child, I'm sure you'd have forgiven me. You would still have loved me.'

'We can't test that theory, can we?'

'What do you want to do, then – separate or get divorced?'

'I suppose we see solicitors and talk about divorce.' Harry glanced at his own untouched glass. 'By the way, you drink too much, you know.'

After she began to speak again, Sarah was permitted to return to school and move up to the senior department with others in her age group, rather than repeat the year she'd partly missed, provided she agreed to see a child psychologist.

'All right,' Sarah told her school and parents, after long and private consultations with Fiona. 'But only if I must.'

Luckily, to Lily's great relief, the child psychologist turned out to be a nice young woman called Elizabeth. She didn't have a box of tissues on her desk. She didn't get her patients to lie down on a couch. All in all, she seemed extremely normal for a shrink.

She and Sarah seemed to hit it off. Elizabeth was interested in Egypt too. They appeared to spend most of their sessions talking about ancient writing systems: cuneiform and pictograms and hieroglyphs.

'What have you done with all your notebooks and those journals?' Lily asked when Sarah had been seeing the psychologist for several weeks. 'The ones you kept while you were ill?'

'You mean the ones I kept when I was mental, while I was behaving like a retard? You can say it, Mum.'

'There used to be a pile in your bedroom, but they're not there any more.'

'I didn't want them so I put them in the bin.'

'Why?'

'I told my shrink about them and said I didn't need them now and she said okay, get rid of them.'

'You like your shrink, then?'

'Yeah, she's cool. She talks to me as if I'm almost normal. It makes a pleasant change from people speaking to me in a sort of baby language, cooing at me.'

Lily wished her husband would see a shrink as well, or at least a counsellor. Somebody needed to talk – or even coo – some sense to him; someone from marriage guidance, possibly? But when she suggested marriage guidance, Harry said he had no need of marriage guidance. After all, he was no longer married, and didn't want to be, so what would be the point?

Okay, there was a piece of paper somewhere, but that was a formality, and when he got round to it he'd replace that piece of paper with a different one. But at least he didn't try to force her to move out.

Gradually, he moved out himself.

Chapter Twenty-Six

Several more months dragged by, with Harry spending far more time in London than was likely to be necessary, Lily thought, having Sarah there for weekends when they stayed in the apartment he had found close to the Foreign Office.

They had a lot of fun, or so it seemed. They went to theatres, concerts, exhibitions, had their meals in grown-up restaurants rather than McDonald's, stayed out well past Sarah's usual bedtime.

'What did you do with Dad?' she asked politely when she fetched her daughter from the station one Sunday afternoon.

Sarah was as usual laden down with loot – new clothes, new books, new records – as well as all the clutter it seemed she always had to cart around in various sacks and bags. 'It's just stuff,' she said, when Lily gave up asking what she'd done and asked what she'd been buying and then she turned to stare out of the window.

Lily nudged a plastic carrier bag emblazoned with a bleeding heart out of the way. She sighed, aware that if she wanted information, she would have to sift through all the debris on her daughter's bedroom floor to excavate the theatre programmes, exhibition catalogues, ticket stubs and leaflets and the like.

'Why don't we have our supper in the sitting room and watch a bit of Sunday evening rubbish on the telly?' she suggested as they stopped outside the house.

'Sorry, don't have time, got French and German homework and I have to finish it tonight. Mum, may I have some money?'

'It depends how much.'

'I need a twenty for new hockey boots.'

'I thought you had new hockey boots last month?'

'Somebody pinched them. Mum, don't be so awkward! I have to buy some new ones. Otherwise I'm going to get detention.'

'All right, but keep the new pair in your locker, don't leave them lying around.'

'Yeah, yeah, yeah,' said Sarah as she dragged her clutter up the stairs.

'What can I do?' asked Lily as she and Gina pored over designs for the next season. 'She's only twelve years old, not seventeen. When I was twelve, I was a baby. I was still in ankle socks and gingham. I didn't look like Miss Havisham's demented little sister.'

'They grow up faster nowadays,' said Gina. 'The average ten-year-old is going on fifteen. Tom's the same – communicates in grunts or not at all. He doesn't ask for money, just takes it from my purse. Jessica is moody and morose. She stays up in her room most of the time, listening to awful music with her friends and varnishing her nails. It's just their age. How is Sarah's schoolwork, do you know? Does she have too much of it and is she feeling stressed? Or is she being bullied? Does she have a crush on some weird boy?'

'I wouldn't know because she wouldn't tell me.'

'When she couldn't speak, that must have worried you,' said Gina. 'But now she can speak again – that's progress.'

'I suppose so.' Lily wondered about telling Gina everything – about meeting Max in Delhi, having sex with Max, conceiving Sarah. Gina knew about the separation, obviously. But she didn't know that Sarah wasn't Harry's child. Lily tossed a mental coin – heads she'd tell and tails she wouldn't tell. It came down tails. 'I expect you're right,' she said and turned back to the galleys of their latest catalogue. 'It must be just their age. I shouldn't worry, or not quite so much.'

'We'll laugh about it one day.'

'When we're wise old grandmothers and they've got adolescents of their own who drive them round the bend.'

'When they've got full time jobs and have to look after a family as well.'

'Oh, yes – they'll learn!'

Max thought: I'll never learn.

He'd got out of the bar in Lebanon. Three days after he and everybody else had been entombed, there'd been a temporary ceasefire. So rescue workers using pickaxes and shovels started sifting through the rubble. They'd called to ask if anyone was still alive, and passed down bottled water. Then, eventually, they'd dug him out.

The Australian cameraman had died, and so had almost everybody else. This, in spite of having a broken ankle, made Max feel that he must be immortal, singled out, a cat with ninety-nine, not just the usual nine lives. A doctor strapped his ankle up and, once it started to get better and he could put some weight on it, he'd set off on his travels once again.

But now the insect bite on his left arm, the one that he'd ignored for days, was septic, and he had run out of penicillin. He'd given the last of his supply to a village headman's daughter in the badlands of Uzbekistan, a place where it was very dangerous for him to be.

He had no visa and had crossed the border from Afghanistan without the necessary paperwork. So if anybody in authority should happen to pick him up, he was going to find himself in prison, being gnawed by rats.

He knew he had been stupid, that he mustn't stay too long, even though he looked like an Uzbekistani – more or less – with his heavy beard, in his ragged 1930s European jacket some departing sahib must have left behind when India was partitioned, in the baggy cotton trousers bought in a bazaar in Pakistan.

Tribal Pakistan, Afghanistan – both were perilous enough for European foreigners who were travelling alone, but being in Soviet Uzbekistan was downright suicidal.

Of course, he never could resist the downright suicidal. It made such great copy for the broadsheets, after all. It also sold a lot of books, and selling books was a necessity. Why write them otherwise?

Originally, he'd intended to be in Uzbekistan for just a week or so, for a mere chapter's worth of his next book. But now he was unwell and holed up in a village guest house, drinking tea that tasted of the blackened pan in which they'd boiled the water, and eating flatbread baked over a fire of dung.

The Muslim headman stopped by every hour to make a speech to him – a traveller of uncertain origin – about the hated Soviets: murderers and torturers and atheists and blasphemers all, every one of them destined for hell.

'But you're not a Muslim either, are you?' asked the headman as an afterthought, following one particularly vitriolic diatribe that Max had followed with some difficulty.

'No, I'm not a Muslim,' Max replied, in a mix of faltering Uzbek and appalling Russian. 'I'm a Unitarian.' This was the answer he always gave when asked about religion. He did not subscribe to any faith, but he'd always thought the Unitarians sounded like a decent set of chaps, as his old headmaster might have put it, and from what he knew of them they seemed to have their heads screwed on and no one hated them.

'Unitarian – what is Unitarian?' The Uzbek shook his head. 'I think you're a Persian. When I was a little child, a Persian merchant came here, selling Russian guns and samovars. You look and sound exactly like him.'

Max decided not to argue.

After the whole village – men and women, children, cats and dogs – had visited the guest house to goggle at the Persian and ask him why he'd come, what he was selling and why didn't he have a bigger pack, Max was allowed to rest, to try to get his strength up and hope nobody would inform the police there was a stranger in the village. He wasn't well enough to cope with prison.

He lay on a stained blanket on the floor of beaten earth, feeling sick and feverish, his broken ankle aching, his arm hot, red and swollen. It was at times like this he wanted Lily: to talk to Lily, share a meal with Lily like that lucky bastard Harry, the father of her child, who was bound to Sarah and to Lily by both love and blood.

'Unitarian – you are British, yes?' the headman's son demanded, when he visited Max the following morning, squatting on his haunches and watching while Max bathed his arm in a tin bowl of tepid, scummy water. 'Unitarian is a British faith?'

'It started in Romania and Poland. It's international nowadays, but there are many British Unitarians,' Max replied. 'I didn't catch your name?'

Zafir then introduced himself and told Max he had briefly studied civil engineering in Tashkent, where he'd learned some basic English, too. Then he had come home again to work on public highways, bringing with him, as Max later realised, dangerous opinions and unachievable ambitions, several pairs of tattered Levis and a second-hand black leather jacket.

'What is your profession?' he asked Max.

'I'm a traveller and historian.'

'Where do you come from, traveller-and-historian?'

'London,' Max replied.

'What's your name?'

'Max Farley.'

'You British, you are friends of the Americans?'

'We're in NATO, yes.'

'Mr Max,' Zafir said, speaking low. 'I have a wish to tell you. It is my dream to leave the Soviet Union and emigrate to Texas, USA.'

'Why Texas?' Max enquired as he rubbed Savlon on his arm, which he was relieved to see looked slightly better in the morning light: still red, but not so swollen.

'People rich in Texas, they have so many things – big steaks, big hats, big houses. Communism stupid, Mr Max, says we should not want to own things. Always people want to own things.'

'Yes, it seems most of them do,' said Max. 'Zafir, when I get home to the UK – well, that's if I do get home to the UK – I'll ask about a US visa for you, how to get one, shall I?'

'Too dangerous,' the boy replied and shrugged. 'I have my leather jacket and my jeans. The rest is just a dream.'

Like my dream of Lily, Max thought sadly.

He must try to get some postcards he could send to Sarah, he decided. But it would be quite risky, buying postcards, even if there were such things in south Uzbekistan. He rather doubted it. The Russians didn't advertise their factories or public buildings to the world, and anyone who showed a more than casual interest in them would be thought to be a spy – which Max supposed he must be, in a way.

All the same, he ought to write to Sarah. It was presumably what godfathers should do, and it was quite a while – at least three years or maybe it was more – since they had been in touch.

He wondered if she still wrote messages in hieroglyphs, if she'd kept the promise of her childhood beauty and grown up to be a pretty girl, if she was clever, if she had a brother or a sister now?

'How is Leila?' he enquired, hoping the broad-spectrum penicillin would help Zafir's sister. She had a septic sore all down the one side of her face, the result of falling against a cast-iron stove.

'She not so good,' Zafir replied. 'But she just one girl. She dies, no matter. My father have four other daughters. Only I his son. Mr Max, back home in the UK, you have a wife, a son?'

'I'm not married,' said Max. 'I have no children.'

When Zafir had gone away, Max unzipped the inside pocket of his battered rucksack.

Here he kept his papers: both forged and genuine documents, and ditto tourist visas, and his British passport – and a faded Polaroid of Harry and him with Lily in between them, the one that had been taken on the rugby pitch in Oxford when they were all students, long ago.

He looked at it and then he folded it so he and Lily were on one side of the photograph and Harry on the other: Harry, the false friend, the man who'd taken Lily from him. Slowly and deliberately, he tore off Harry's image and then he shredded it, ripping it in tiny little pieces and mashing them into the floor of beaten earth.

He slipped the photograph of him and Lily in the pocket of his dirty shirt, next to his heart. Then he lay down and tried to sleep.

Chapter Twenty-Seven

Lily was sleeping badly nowadays. She'd got into the habit of having a glass or two of wine with dinner, and this helped her relax a little, get her off to sleep. But, a couple of hours later, she'd find she was wide awake again. So, rather than stay in bed and fail to sleep, she often got up while it was dark and did some work.

She had an en suite shower room and so she seldom used the family bathroom, which was along the landing and next to Sarah's room. She sometimes liked to take a bath, however, and one Friday morning she decided a bath might be relaxing, comforting.

It was very early, she had lots of time to spare, so she would take the radio, a mug of coffee and she'd have a wallow.

She found the bath towels dumped in soggy piles on the floor and draped over the towel rail and scarlet with what had to be her daughter's blood. The bath itself was streaked bright red with gore and this had clumped and clotted in the plughole. A trail of scarlet droplets led to Sarah's bedroom door.

Lily and Sarah's child psychologist, whom Sarah still agreed to see from time to time, had spoken on the phone only the previous week. Elizabeth had seemed quite pleased with Sarah's progress but had used a range of terms like *adolescent angst* and *underlying trauma* and said that Sarah clearly found it hard to open up or ask for help or even to admit she needed help. But she hadn't mentioned any risk of suicide.

A cry for help …

As she gazed around this charnel house, Lily almost vomited. She was the child's mother. She should know her daughter best. Why had she not seen the signs? Why had she not realised?

Why am I staring like an idiot now?

Why am I doing nothing apart from hyperventilating?

'Sarah!' Lily hammered on her daughter's bedroom door, which she knew was likely to be locked. After she had read the riot act about clumping mud and worse all over everywhere and getting into bed still in her shoes and outdoor clothes, Sarah always locked her bedroom door.

Getting no response, she put her shoulder to it – rammed it hard – found it wasn't locked at all and fell into the bedroom. Sarah's huddled form was humped in bed. 'What have you been doing?' Lily dragged the duvet off, dreading what she might discover – slashed wrists, gushing arteries?

'It's Roman Red,' said Sarah, sleepily.

'Why didn't you ask me to help?' Lily was torn between relief and fury. 'Why did you leave the bathroom in that state? Oh my God, I thought—'

'I didn't ask because I knew you'd have a cow, just like you're having now.' Sarah pulled the duvet back over her scarlet head, over the profusion of crimson curls replacing the natural blue-black. 'Mum, it's only half past six,' she grumbled. 'So could you push off and let a person get some sleep?'

'You're going to be in trouble at school again, you know. There will be detentions or perhaps you'll even be excluded.'

'Yeah, yeah, yeah – I'm scared.'

'What will your father think of this – this travesty?'

'Dad will say it's cool.' Sarah met Lily's angry gaze and giggled wickedly. 'Fiona has done hers as well.'

'Oh?' Lily's breathing had returned to normal but she was still incensed. 'That isn't going to please her mother.'

'She'll probably have an elephant. The box said not to use the stuff on blondes. Fiona's hair went neon-pink, like bubblegum.' Sarah yawned extravagantly. 'When you leave – like now – please close the door?'

Lily went back to the bathroom, scooped up all the ruined towels to put them in the wash, and in the bin she found an empty bottle of hydrogen peroxide and two of Roman Red. She should have looked there first, she realised, not – as Sarah put it – had a cow.

It was far too early in the morning to start drinking, but Lily wondered if a little brandy might be medically useful? It would help to calm her shattered nerves.

Sarah might prefer to dress in tattered black and look as if she lived under a stone, but luckily a lot of other adolescents couldn't get enough of Lily's and Gina's pretty clothes.

'Most girls of your age love our corduroy pinafores,' Lily made the big mistake of saying at breakfast one December morning.

'Girls like that are retards,' retorted Sarah scathingly, rubbing her left earlobe. It was red and swollen and looked as if it might be going septic round the small black plastic skull which was embedded there.

Although Lily had forbidden it, Sarah must have gone down Cowley Road to some nasty unhygienic so-called studio in someone's garden shed, and got herself another piercing.

'You need to put some TCP on that,' said Lily.

'Yeah, and if I don't?'

'You'll lose your ear, then you'll look like Van Gogh but not as pretty.'

'Ha ha ha, Mum, you're so funny. I need thirty quid for Tuesday: school trip to Stratford.'

'Where's the form?'

'I lost it.'

'What's the play?'

'I can't remember.'

'Sarah, if you want me to give you thirty pounds, maybe you could do some jobs around the house and earn it? Tidy up your bedroom, for example? Do some vacuuming, perhaps?'

'Okay, I won't go to Stratford. I don't want to see some boring play in any case.'

'I'll save my thirty pounds, then. Who did that piercing, anyway? Some fly-by-night with needles and a cork? There are codes of practice for people who do body-piercing. Nobody of your age should have piercings unless their parents say they—'

'You'd have given me permission?' Sarah sniffed and tossed her scarlet curls. 'Fiona Fox got a tattoo last week,' she added, grinning. 'A little purple butterfly. It's on her shoulder like it landed there. When her mother saw it, she went mental.'

'Where did Fiona go to get her butterfly?'

'You think I'm telling you, Mum? Yeah, and then it's not as if you wouldn't be on the phone to the police, demanding that they raid the place or even close it down?'

Fiona Fox was even worse than Sarah, Lily thought. She'd been such a strength and a support while Sarah had been mute. But nowadays, according to her mother, the bastion of the Mother's Union and the PTA, she was practically ungovernable.

Lily could believe it, for Fiona was a fair-haired clone of Sarah and, if they hadn't both been clever, joint top of their class in everything, in spite of doing hardly any work, they'd have been excluded from their posh fee-paying school a long, long time ago.

'They look like apprentice hookers,' Lily said to Gina. 'Snow White and Rose Red as re-imagined by a paedophile.'

'My twins look like refugees,' said Gina. 'Their clothes are all from Oxfam. They wouldn't wear our designs to save their lives. Jessica's had her navel pierced. I know it's going septic.'

'It's enough to drive us both to drink,' said Lily, thinking she drank quite enough already. Those empty bottles of Chardonnay had quite a habit of mounting up. 'But I guess we'll laugh about it one day.'

'We'd better get some practice, then,' said Gina.

But it was often hard to laugh. Lily had tried everything to get through to her daughter, to make any connection: coercion, threats, we-are-both-adults-style discussion, cajolery, persuasion.

Nothing worked.

'Stop trying to pretend we're sisters, Mum,' said Sarah, after Lily asked if she would like to go to London for the weekend, this time with her mother for a change? Do some girly stuff like shopping in the big department stores? Or maybe they could see a musical? They'd both enjoy that, wouldn't they?

'I'm not trying to pretend we're sisters,' added Lily carefully. 'I know you're upset about your father going. But I'd like us to be friends, at least. Whatever differences your dad and I—'

'Just stop going on about it, will you?' Sarah cried. 'You can't blame Dad for leaving you. After all, you did commit adultery.'

'Did he tell you that?' asked Lily.

'No, but since I'm Max's child – yeah, I heard what you and Dad were saying when you were splitting up. You must have thought I couldn't hear as well as speak.'

'I did not commit adultery. I wasn't married to your father then. It was just the once, when Max and I met up in Delhi, and—'

'I don't want to know the gruesome details! I don't care if it was once or half a million times!'

'But it could help to talk about it, don't you think?'

'I'd rather eat my brains.'

Part 3

January 1985
–January 1998

Chapter Twenty-Eight

These days, Sarah looked so much like Max – she had his face, his eyes, his slightly crooked and sarcastic but disarming smile! Well, that was when she chose to smile at all – that Max had to be told, decided Lily.

So she resolved to tell him.

When she saw in the *Guardian* that he was back in London after his most recent expedition, this time to Namibia where he had been helping some biologists to count endangered monkeys, she wrote to him care of his publisher and said she had to see him.

'Why, what's up?' he asked, the three words scribbled on a tattered postcard.

'I'll tell you when I see you,' she wrote back. 'I'll come to London one afternoon next week. Where are you living now?'

'When do you think you might be back?' asked Lily as her daughter packed her CND be-sloganed rucksack for a weekend with her father.

'When you see me,' Sarah said. 'Mum, did you know that Molly Fox has run off with a fireman?'

'She's done what?'

'You heard me.'

'But – a fireman?'

'Yeah, you must have seen them? They wear yellow helmets. They ride in big red lorries. They rescue cats from trees.'

'I don't believe you. Molly runs the Christian Wives, the Brownies and the League of Purity. She takes Bible study classes.'

'Yeah, she does – and when this bloke went to her class

last summer it seems he lit her fire. Fiona says she used to go to meet him in a pub at Marston Ferry, but Mr Fox found out and hit the roof. Nowadays, she's living in a flat in Blackbird Leys.'

'What about Fiona?'

'She's staying with her father in Victoria Road.' Sarah grinned. 'Go on, Mum,' she prompted. 'You know you want to laugh. When Molly told Fiona what was happening, Fiona wet herself. Mrs God Squad Fox, the scarlet woman – you must admit it's funny.'

'It's not remotely funny,' Lily said.

Molly had always been a bossy-boots, a smug, self-righteous know-all. But when they'd had the fire she had been kind and helpful too. She'd offered Lily's family sanctuary. She had looked after them.

A family breakdown wasn't anything to laugh about; if anybody knew that, Lily did.

But – Molly Fox! The same Molly who encouraged teenage girls and boys to sign the Pledge of Purity! Lily snorted, then both she and Sarah were giggling together, and for about five minutes Lily felt a bond with Sarah she hadn't felt for years.

Molly Fox, a fireman's floozy. Well!

'I shouldn't laugh,' choked Lily, knuckling her eyes.

'Go on, laughing does you good,' said Sarah. 'I'm getting the five-thirty back from London, so could you pick me up?'

'Say please?'

'Please, Mum?' said Sarah. But not sarcastically, and for a fleeting moment Lily saw her little girl again.

'Of course I'll pick you up,' she said.

'Thanks, Mum.' Then Sarah looked away. 'Sometimes,' she added, almost shyly, 'when I get home from Dad's, I'm a bit hungry. I was wondering if we could have pizza on a Sunday evening now and then? I mean, could we get a takeaway?'

'We could eat it in the sitting room and maybe watch a bit of rubbish telly, couldn't we?' ventured Lily, delighted with this unexpected overture, but telling herself she must tread carefully.

'We could get some Coke and coleslaw, too?' Now, Sarah met her mother's gaze, but warily. 'I know it's junk food, but—'

'Once in a while, a bit of junk food is all right.' Lily risked a kiss on Sarah's cheek and was relieved to see her daughter didn't flinch. 'Off you go or else you're going to miss the train, and Sarah – enjoy yourself with Dad.'

Max glanced round his rented studio flat.

This was a disorganised but in-reality-precisely-ordered eagle's nest of books and papers, clothes and shoes. A desk and chair, a mattress on the floor, a typewriter, a personal computer and a dot matrix printer he had yet to learn to love, but which his new publisher had told him he had to learn to love, because computers were the coming thing – they were all he needed.

But was this cluttered burrow made for love? Other women didn't seem to mind rolling around on floorboards, tearing off their clothes and his and having sex on piles of books and magazines and papers, staples, paperclips and all.

But Lily wasn't other women. When he'd received her letter, he'd been dumbstruck for a moment. He had almost needed to remind himself to breathe. He should have written back to say of course they'd meet. He'd come to Oxford now. So why had he merely scribbled, *Why, what's up?*

Oh, come on, he told himself, perhaps it isn't anything to do with her and me? Maybe Harry or Sarah ...

Perhaps he ought to phone and say he'd meet her in a public place – a restaurant, a museum or a gallery? They could go to see an exhibition, couldn't they, and she could say whatever it was she had to tell him while they looked at art?

'No,' she insisted when he called. 'I'll meet you somewhere private. I'll see you on Tuesday afternoon. I'll be there by three.'

'I'll put the kettle on.'

Why was she coming? What did she want to tell him? Did she – was she – did he dare to hope?

When she arrived, Max realised straight away it couldn't be what he'd hoped. She wasn't all dressed up in one of her astonishing creations. She didn't have a suitcase. She didn't smell of roses. She was wearing a plain navy dress and navy tights and comfortable, flat shoes.

Of course it didn't matter what she wore. But it mattered what she did or didn't do, and she didn't fall into his arms. She didn't say that she was leaving Harry and had come to him, that they were going to make it work between them, whatever he might say. When he kissed her on the cheek she hardly seemed to notice.

'Why all the cloak and dagger stuff?' he asked, pouring boiling water into mugs then adding Nescafé and powdered milk. He tore open a packet of digestive biscuits, offered Lily one. 'What's going on?'

'I don't know how to tell you,' she began, her fingers twisting nervously. 'I thought it would be easy. But now I'm here, I don't know what to say.'

'You're scaring me.' Max put down his coffee mug and biscuits and took her by the shoulders. 'Come on – whatever it is you want to tell me, you need to tell me now.'

'It's Sarah,' Lily managed to choke out.

'What's wrong with Sarah, Lily – is she ill?'

'No, she's fine. It's just that you and she ...'

On the train to London, Lily had written half a dozen screenplays in which she led up to it, in which Max was gradually lulled and soothed into acceptance of the situation and he was fine with it.

But instead she shot the information at him like a bullet from a gun. 'Sarah's yours,' she said. 'She's your daughter, you're her father – biologically, I mean.'

'What?' Max stared at Lily as if she were insane. 'But how can she be?'

'You and I, that afternoon in Delhi, when we had – do you remember?'

'Yes, of course I do, even though I sometimes think I must have dreamed it and it didn't actually happen.'

'Oh, it happened all right, and Sarah's proof.'

'How do you know she isn't Harry's?'

'I ... I know because ...'

But Lily hesitated then. She didn't want to say that Harry couldn't be a father, that he had discovered he could never sire a child. It seemed so disloyal, somehow, salting the original wound, when the original wound was cruel enough.

'Lily?' prompted Max.

'Sarah had to have an operation,' she replied at last. 'It wasn't serious – please don't look so worried – it was just some slight corrective surgery on an arm she'd broken years ago. But they needed to have blood on standby. It seems they always do. What's your blood group?'

'I don't know offhand.' Max found his wallet, rummaged round inside it and then produced a donor card and handed it to Lily.

242

Since she had decided to see Max, she'd hoped – she'd almost prayed, although she never prayed – that by some fluke, some stroke of kindly providence, Harry was Sarah's father, after all. But now she must accept he couldn't be. The blood had spoken, hadn't it, and why would it lie?

'It's the same,' she whispered.

'Lily, love – are you all right?' asked Max. She could hear his voice, but now it seemed to come from far away or under water. 'You and Harry – Harry said you didn't want more children because you had a difficult time with Sarah.'

'Yes, I did,' said Lily. 'I hated being pregnant, giving birth and all that stuff.'

'He'd have liked more children?'

'Yes.'

'But as the years went by it didn't happen?'

'No.' Lily looked at Max. 'When he found out he wasn't Sarah's father, he took it very hard; so hard we're separated now. But Sarah's still his daughter, at least in every way that really matters. You must never try to take her from him. Max, you must promise me.'

'I'd never try to hurt any of you. But now I know that Sarah's mine, it changes things. You must see that?'

'I ought to leave and let you think about it,' Lily said.

'Okay – I'll be in touch.'

When she got home, Lily found a message on her phone from Max. He said he'd be in London for a while, finishing a book, and hoped they could meet up occasionally, just to talk.

But then, thought Lily, he would probably be off again, travelling to some unhygienic, inhospitable and ghastly place where running water, flushing lavatories and electricity were all as yet unknown.

It would never have worked between us, she repeated to herself time and time again, determined to believe it.

All the same, she still agreed to meet him now and then in London. She didn't see the harm, and in any case she found she couldn't – didn't want to – keep away. The sight of him, the sound of him, the smell of him, the touch of him – it was as if he drew her like a magnet, and she had no choice.

He said he wanted to see Sarah. Lily said she'd speak to Sarah, ask her if she wanted to see him. Sarah said she didn't. 'You shouldn't see him either, Mum,' she added.

'But we only talk,' said Lily. 'What's so wrong with that?'

'Dad wouldn't like it, that's what's wrong.'

'Dad won't know.'

'I'll tell him.'

'I'll tell him myself. Actually, I think they ought to meet. They used to be best friends. Maybe if we all four work together, we could make it right and be as happy as we used to be?'

'Yeah, yeah, Mum,' said Sarah, but not meanly or unkindly, 'in your dreams.'

Although he and Lily met occasionally for coffee or some lunch, Max didn't hang around in London. After he had written up his notes, he went off to Mexico to look at Mayan ruins with a five-strong team from Harvard who had need of an experienced, knowledgeable and English-speaking guide. A few days after she had said goodbye to him, Lily saw a feature about them in the *Sunday Times*.

Three of the group of five were women – bright, attractive, clever, adventurous young women. Max had his arms round two of them: a pretty, curvy blonde and a fierce-looking tall brunette, both obviously in their early twenties. He was smiling at the camera while the women smiled at him, and Lily felt her heart was going to break.

'What's the matter, Mum?' asked Sarah.

But she was too full of grief for words. Now at last she understood why Sarah had been silent for so long. Sometimes, words are useless.

It had been a great wrench to leave Lily, but Max supposed that Mexico was worth the ride.

The Harvard people seemed to think so, anyway. They saw their Mayan ruins. They took their measurements and photographs. They made their calculations then went home to write their no doubt very tedious academic papers while Max wrote half a dozen articles for British broadsheets.

'Where shall we send you next?' asked Max's publisher. 'You haven't done the Philippines or Borneo. Do you fancy going to look for undiscovered tribes? Maybe you could find some cannibals? I'm sure your readers would adore to hear about how cannibals conduct themselves in their domestic lives. *Canoodling with the Cannibals* – I can see it in the bookshops now, a hardback first edition for the Christmas market, colour photographs and marbled endpapers, a paperback to follow in the spring.'

'You probably wouldn't get a book at all if I found any cannibals.' Max was suddenly tired of travelling, tired of being chased and beaten up and eating grubs and getting shot and stabbed and jailed.

'What about going somewhere really dangerous, then?' his publisher suggested. 'I understand Siberia can be tricky. Or do you fancy Lebanon again?'

'I think I'll go to Scotland.'

'Scotland as in Scotland to the north of England, home of orange bulls with great long horns and cullen skink?'

'Yes, I fancy going on a walking holiday, striding through the heather in the rain. I fancy sleeping in a proper bed in a pleasant, comfortable hotel. I fancy acting like a normal person for a change.'

'You must be getting old.'

'You mean you want to try again?' asked Harry, when she spoke to him in London, when he had at last agreed to meet her in a coffee shop. He could spare her half an hour, he said.

'I don't think that would be possible. But we both love Sarah, don't we, and it can't be good for her to have her parents quarrelling or not speaking. I don't want us to be enemies.'

'I still want a divorce. But we could be civilised about it, I suppose. The three of us could meet for dinner sometimes. But if this is what you really want, there's one condition.'

'What?'

'You won't meet Max again. I heard about you seeing him in London.'

'Oh ... did Sarah—'

'No, she didn't tell me, so don't jump to conclusions. You were spotted here and there by mutual acquaintances, fawning over him in public places.'

Fawning over him in public places.

It was the sneer that did it. 'I'll see who I like!' she flared. 'Harry, you're determined to make me out to be an unfit mother, liar—'

'—adulteress,' said Harry.

'I am not an adulteress! When I went to bed with Max that time – the only time – you and I weren't married!'

'But we were engaged. You're married now – did you forget?'

'We're separated and I thought you wanted a divorce. You mean to have it all ways, don't you?'

Chapter Twenty-Nine

Max soon got tired of being normal and decided it was time that he did something more worthwhile than merely bumming round the world, doing his best to be arrested, thrown in jail or killed.

Maybe he could volunteer to work in leper colonies, get a job with Oxfam, Save the Children, train to be a paramedic? He researched the various possibilities, but in the end he got a job with Reuters, filing from the world's most dangerous and impoverished places. He also got involved with charities supporting feeding programmes in various famine zones.

'You should be on the telly,' said a colleague in Sudan. 'You've got that serious but ironic look about you all the viewers love. You've also got your hair. You have some sex appeal as well. You could be famous.'

'I don't want to be famous.'

'We all want to be famous,' said the colleague. 'You used to be a writer, didn't you?'

'I'm still a writer.'

'There you are, then. Why did you start writing? You wanted to be famous, right?'

'I wrote to earn some money.'

'I'm going to write a novel. Of course you need connections if you want your novel to be published. I know somebody at the BBC. Why don't you write a novel?'

Max glanced round the feeding station, at the sacks containing a mix of grains that would be used for porridge, at the drums of powdered milk, at the sacks of sugar and of peanuts, at the queues of ragged and malnourished people with their bowls and mugs, at their stoical, despairing or occasionally hopeful faces. 'Real life's enough for me,' he said.

Max got hold of the occasional British newspaper. He was in Uganda when he read about it in the New Year Honours, months after the announcement. Harry Gale was now Sir Henry Gale KBE. Did he and Lily get divorced, he wondered. Or did they decide to make a go of it? It would be very fitting, wouldn't it, if Lily was now Lady Gale? Signora Hurricane, Milady Storm, Doña Tornado?

Since he and Harry had met Lily in the Parks in Oxford that October afternoon, she had devastated both their lives. It was years, but he still dreamed about her almost every single night. He made love to Lily again, again, again.

He made a vow, a promise to himself. Of course he'd be in London now and then. One day, when he was very old, he might even settle down in the UK for good. But he must never see or speak to her again. Whatever happened, wherever he went next, he knew he had to stay away from Lily, because she'd drive him mad.

Daisy Designs had prospered – more than prospered. Who'd have thought a small-scale project like the one she'd dreamed up with a friend while chatting at a mother-and-toddler group would have become a global empire?

She and Gina made a lot of money, but ploughed back half their profits into charitable trusts supporting small-scale clothing industries in Africa and Asia, helping working women earn enough to feed their children, educate them, provide them with clean water and inoculations.

'I'll be off to Ghana in July,' said Lily. Sarah and she were checking proofs of a new catalogue, Sarah earning fifty pence for every glitch or typo she could find. 'It's just a business trip, of course,' she added. 'But I must admit I'm looking forward to my African adventure.'

At fifteen, Sarah wasn't quite as scathing as she used to be. These days she would even offer style tips and suggestions for new ranges, even though she was too old to wear the clothes herself and was still dressed from head to foot in black.

She'd be doing Cambridge Entrance soon, even though she wouldn't be sixteen until September. The school was optimistic she would pass. Or, thought Lily, possibly the school had had enough of Sarah Gale, the outspoken rebel with the piercings and pink hair, who set every other student such a bad example, apart from academically – in that sphere, she excelled.

'Ghana, eh?' said Sarah. 'What's in Ghana?'

'A village school that we supply with uniforms and desks and chairs and books. A women's workshop where they hand-block prints for us.'

'So it's a flying visit from Lady Bountiful. When are you going?'

'On the twenty-fourth. I'll be away two weeks.'

'Gosh, you're getting quite intrepid, aren't you, in your declining years?' said Sarah, grinning. 'My stay-at-home old mother, jetting off to places where they don't have power showers or Special K or Waitrose! However will you manage without bog roll and deodorant?'

'What will you do while I'm away? Stay here by yourself? You're not to have that Alan Flynn boy here overnight.'

'Alan's gay, we've known each other since we were in ankle socks and he and I are friends. Mum, you're like Fiona's gruesome mother. You both have dirty minds. I'll stay with Dad in London and commute.'

'But won't that be expensive?'

'Dad will pay.' Sarah glanced up from the catalogue and looked at Lily. 'Now you and Dad aren't married any more, why don't you both find someone else? Why doesn't he get himself a girlfriend? Why don't you get a boyfriend? After all, you must have some vestigial sexual urges, even though you're borderline decrepit? You've still got most of your own teeth. You're not incontinent. So you're not past it yet.'

'I don't have time for boyfriends, and I expect your father's busy, too.' Actually, he must be very busy, Lily thought, for Harry was a mandarin now, the head of a department. The minister was his former boss Sir Nicholas, who nowadays was Father of the House.

I don't have time for boyfriends.

But sometimes Lily wished she could find someone else. A nice, kind, clever man, perhaps with children of his own, a widower, divorced – Oxford must be full of men she'd like? She couldn't spend the rest of what remained of her whole adult life vainly and idiotically hankering after Max? Oh, God – why did it give her so much pain and pleasure just to think about him, say his name?

'Did you see that article by Max about Sudan?' she asked her daughter. 'It was in the *Sunday Times* last week.'

'I'm not interested in Max,' said Sarah. 'Mum, why don't I come to Africa? It will be the holidays so I won't need to go to school. All right, I'd miss a few days at the end of term, but that won't really matter. I'd like to go to Africa with you.'

'You mean it?'

'Yes. I'd like to see your project, meet your workers.' Sarah grinned. 'I could make sure you're not exploiting them.'

'Africa would be too hot for you. You'd boil in those black rags.'

'Perhaps,' said Sarah. 'Okay, here's the deal. You take me to Africa and while we're there I wear some of your hideous Daisy vests and shorts and whatnot.' Sarah's grey eyes twinkled. 'After all, you'll need someone to keep you out of mischief while you're in foreign parts.' She circled two more typos. 'This is costing you a mint, you know. We're up to twelve pounds fifty and we're only on page nine.'

After he had been at Reuters for a couple of years, Max met someone from the BBC who knew his publisher. 'What about presenting a television series?' he asked Max.

'What sort of series?'

'Oh, documentaries and in-depth investigations – serious-but-accessible kind of *Panorama* stuff.'

They made a pilot and it was successful. Max was a natural, said the BBC, which now commissioned a whole series about refugees and refugee camps all around the world.

Max thought he was accustomed to suffering, to poverty. But, as he made the series, he found he was profoundly moved by what he saw in Palestine, in Lebanon, in parts of Africa. How could people who'd done nothing wrong exist in such conditions and live with such injustice? How could they quietly accept that they were being punished for crimes that other people had committed, and stay sane?

At home in the UK for a few months to write a book about the series, Max decided it was time he made amends for all the crimes and misdemeanours of *his* life.

He would start with Harry. After all, they'd been best friends since childhood, and that must count for something, mustn't it?

'It's been years,' he said, when finally he managed to

speak to Harry on the phone. 'Surely we can let bygones be bygones?'

'I don't see why we should.'

'But what's past is past, don't you agree?'

'No, so if you've finished spouting clichés, maybe we could end this conversation? You might be a gentleman of leisure, but I'm very busy. I have nothing more to say to you.'

'Harry, listen, we were such good friends—'

'You destroyed our friendship.'

'I would like to try to make amends.'

'It's not possible to make amends.'

'Why isn't it?'

'Because you – you and Lily—'

Harry paused, so Max talked on, cajoling, begging, pleading, reminding Harry of the good times, ever mindful of the subject he must never mention, the one thing he must never say: if you could have fathered any children of your own, you would not hate me. 'I'd like to see Sarah, too,' he added hopefully.

'Okay,' said Harry finally. 'Come to Oxford one day in the Christmas holidays, when she'll be home from Cambridge. We'll have lunch.'

'Do you meet Lily when you go to Oxford?'

'Yes, occasionally. We could all have lunch at a new place in Little Clarendon Street.'

So much for never seeing Lily, Max thought ruefully, as Harry put the phone down. Lily and Harry and Sarah, he would see them all together, and he couldn't wait.

Lily was delighted with the new development.

Harry had been civil on the phone. So now she dared to hope old wounds might heal at last, and her only worry was the restaurant would not admit a lunch guest wearing hideous black rags. Maybe they'd end up in Burger King or KFC? Well, that would be all right. It might even be fun. But ...

'I'm not coming!' Sarah told Lily on the phone from Cambridge, where she was studying zoology. She added she'd decided to stop in Cambridge over Christmas, rather than come home to Oxford.

'What are you going to do for money?' Lily asked.

'I'm not angling for a sub, if that's what you're suggesting. I've got myself a part time job in Heffer's bookshop and, before you ask, I'm staying at my tutor's house in Trumpington, not with some weird boy.'

Lily hoped the tutor was safely married and had seven children. But of course that never stopped a man. So it probably wouldn't matter if this one was twenty-five and gorgeous, or sixty-five and hideous and wore a ginger wig.

'Maybe think about it, love?' she wheedled. 'I feel it might be good for all of us to have a pleasant lunch together at a quiet restaurant, to put the past behind us and move on.'

'Mum, I've thought about it and decided you're all mad and I would rather impale myself on railings. Why would I want to sit there with the three of you while you get drunk, then maudlin, then wander off down Memory bloody Lane?'

'I'd have thought you might want to see Max. Did you watch his documentaries on the BBC? I thought they were excellent.'

'I don't watch television.'

'What a shame,' said Lily. 'He's a natural presenter. I read in the *Guardian* he's up for some award.'

'What award ... the man by whom most menopausal

women would like to be knocked up?' demanded Sarah acidly. 'He's quite the favourite pin-up of the female middle-aged. Last week, I saw him gurning on the cover of the *Radio Times* – the home of ads for stairlifts and comfortable shoes.'

'Darling, he's your—'

'Mum, I've told you half a million times. I'm not interested in Max. I already have a father. I don't need another one.'

'Okay. I'll tell him you can't get away. I'll say you send your love.'

'You'd better not, because I don't and never will.'

Chapter Thirty

'You're looking very well,' said Max, while thinking privately his friend – or should that be his former friend, no doubt he'd be finding out today – looked every inch the pompous Whitehall mandarin: staid and middle-aged and tubby, smooth and pale and going bald.

'I can't say the same for you,' said Harry. 'You're so grey and weather-beaten I doubt if I'd have known you.'

'I should have used more moisturiser, shouldn't I?' Max said easily, determined not to rise to any taunts because he wanted this meeting to go well. 'Hello, Lily.'

'Hello, Max.'

Lily was aggressively dressed down – grey skirt, grey jacket, thick black tights and flat black shoes, hair scraped back into a ponytail, plain glasses and no make-up. Max tried not to think of sexy school headmistresses, who underneath their formal knee-length dresses wore wisps of fine lace knickers and—

'Let's get on,' said Harry. 'Some of us need to work today. I have a meeting in Whitehall at four.'

'We could have met in London,' Lily told him.

'I suggested Oxford because I was assuming I'd see Sarah. But today I got a postcard saying she isn't home.'

'No, she's staying in Cambridge over Christmas.'

Max didn't know if missing seeing Sarah was responsible for Harry's mood, but it very soon became apparent this lunch date looked like being a disaster from the start.

Harry spoke to him and Lily as if they were juvenile delinquents, as if they were teenagers who were going to be expelled from school for smoking pot or nicking stuff from Woolworth's, and he was their headmaster.

'You sit there,' he said to Lily, pointing to a chair facing the window. 'You sit opposite,' he told Max. 'Now listen to me, the pair of you. There's to be no fumbling, stroking underneath the table.'

'Of course not,' Lily said. 'Why would we?'

'You're the two most passionate lovers since the world began,' sneered Harry. 'So why wouldn't you?'

Max stared at Harry for a moment and wondered briefly about walking out right now. But then he remembered this meeting was supposed to build some bridges, not burn them down, and so he dropped his gaze.

But it was heavy going. When the waiter brought the menus, Harry didn't ask Max and Lily what they wanted. He just ordered for them all and told the waiter they were in a hurry.

As they ate their first course, Lily played the silent, chastened penitent, eyes downcast, and in his opinion she did this rather well. Max also did his best to play the chastened penitent. But, from the looks that Harry shot at him from time to time, he suspected he was failing miserably.

He drank no wine or other alcohol. He didn't even risk a beer. He didn't dare, and neither – rather obviously – did Lily. She'd asked for sparkling Pellegrino and he stuck to plain and boring water.

But Harry drank their share of wine and more, downing half a bottle of claret in the first ten minutes, finishing the bottle and ordering another one.

The waiter brought their second course.

'Madam, sirs – I hope everything is to your satisfaction?' he enquired a couple of minutes later.

'I'll let you know,' said Harry, briskly waving him away.

The food was fine. This was an expensive restaurant in the heart of Oxford, after all. But to Max, who could eat anything – and very often did – it tasted dry and ash-like.

'So tell us, how's your love life?' Harry asked Max suddenly, looking up and grinning, but it was a cold, sarcastic grin. 'Who are you shagging these days, while her unsuspecting husband's not around?'

'I understand this must be very difficult for you,' said Max. 'But please try to understand that Lily and I – we never intended it to happen. We—'

'You're a liar,' Harry said. 'But then, of course, you've always been a liar. The story that you spun me years ago, about when you went to find your mother, when you met her gangster lover in her dressing gown – I bet you made the whole thing up. I expect your mother lives in Surbiton and breeds exotic fish.'

'Max, I thought your mother was dead?' said Lily.

'She's dead to me,' said Max.

'She probably disowned him when she caught him at it with her sister, or a barmaid, or a nun.'

'Stop it, Harry,' Lily murmured.

'Stop what?' Harry asked wide-eyed, mock innocent. 'I was only asking sex god Farley here to bring us up to date. Bafta winner-in-waiting these days, aren't you? As we speak, a thousand stupid women are lusting after you?'

'I'm off to Ecuador next spring,' said Max, determinedly changing the conversation from the personal to the professional. 'I'm taking teams of botanists and lepidopterists to look for undiscovered species in the forest. Quito, that's the capital of Ecuador, is the best-preserved colonial city in the whole of South America, and it's full ...'

Max knew that he was rambling, but he didn't want to have an argument with Harry. Lily clearly wasn't going to make small talk. So he felt he had to fill the silence with something – anything.

The waiter took their main course plates away and asked if they would like to see a menu for dessert.

'No dessert for me,' said Max.

'May I have an Americano, black?' asked Lily.

'Oh, you're both on diets, are you?' Harry said, after ordering fig and walnut pudding with Cornish clotted cream. 'Of course, you'll need to stay all fit and nimble for the exercise you take together.'

'Harry, that's enough,' said Lily, getting up. 'Max, will you see Harry to the station? You can have my coffee.'

'You will drink your coffee, slut.' Harry grabbed Lily by the arm and pulled her down again. 'You ordered coffee. You will stay and drink it.'

'Stop this, Harry,' Max said quietly.

'Who are you to tell me to stop doing anything? Why should I defer to you?' Harry glowered at Max. 'I've met some selfish bastards in my time. But you eclipse them all. It's always about you. What you want and who you want and stuff the rest of us. You were the most disruptive child at school, you wasted all your time at Oxford, and then you wandered off around the world, accepting people's hospitality, but never doing anything to help them or improve their lives. You observe them, then write books about them and grow rich. You think that's a life well spent?'

Max said nothing.

'As for your mistress here, she dabbles in design, and nowadays she's earning more than me. So she thinks this makes her someone special. But she's a moral bankrupt. She's made herself a fortune selling overpriced designer clothes to children of the middle classes. She doesn't care if those in Africa and Asia dress in rags.'

Harry glared from Max to Lily. 'I've been in Whitehall for eighteen years,' he added. 'I've seen ministers come and go, a truly representative collection of rogues and vagabonds. But, in all that time, I've never seen a pair of shits like you.'

The waiter brought the fig and walnut pudding.

'Harry, please?' said Lily as he grabbed a spoon then started digging into it. 'Please don't talk so loudly. People are staring, looking at us.'

'Let them look!' Harry dropped his spoon and twisted round to glare at two old people who were sitting quietly, trying to enjoy their lunch. 'Let them stare and let them listen, too!'

He took a gulp of claret. 'Look, everyone!' he cried, slamming his glass back on the table and spilling most of what was left in it. 'Look at this woman, this adulteress and her lover! Butter wouldn't melt! I always thought so, anyway. But I was bloody well mistaken, wasn't I?'

Harry met the old man's puzzled and embarrassed gaze. 'Your wife, is that?' he asked him, glaring rudely at the woman. 'You have children, do you?'

But he didn't wait for a reply. He pushed his pudding to one side, stood up and fell against the table. 'Any man who thinks he is the father of the children he has raised and loved – that man's a fool,' he cried. 'Women – they're all harlots. As for women's lovers – they're all scum.'

'Harry, shut up now,' said Max and looked round for the waiter. 'May we have the bill?' he asked. The waiter brought it, hovered momentarily between the men then handed it to Max.

Harry snatched it from him.

'Let me – please?' said Max.

'No,' growled Harry as he scrabbled in his inside pocket

for his wallet, found it and got out his Amex Gold. 'You think you can pay for what you did by buying lunch? Lily, do you see? It's all you're worth to him – a bit of lunch.' He snapped his fingers at the waiter, an anxious-looking teenager. 'Get our coats, boy, and be quick about it.'

'Let him pay, Max,' whispered Lily.

'Shut up, slut,' said Harry. He signed the bill with an illegible, meandering scrawl, snatched up his overcoat and stumbled out.

'I'm sorry he was horrible to you,' said Lily to the waiter.

'He's not well,' added Max. The waiter shrugged and Max gave him a ten pound note.

They followed Harry out into the street. 'Let's get him to the station,' Max said wearily. 'He can sleep on the train and by the time he gets to Paddington he might have slept this whole thing off. I'll hope so, anyway.'

'What will you do?'

'Go to Paddington myself and put him in a taxi – make sure he gets to work.' Max shrugged. 'Somebody needs to keep an eye on him and, since I've upset him, I think it should be me.'

As they walked along St Giles, Harry lurched from side to side. But, when Max tried to steady him, he was roughly shaken off.

'Max, change of plan – could you help me get him back to my place?' whispered Lily. 'Then he can have a doze. It's obvious he won't be fit for work this afternoon. So there's no point in taking him to Paddington just yet.'

'I guess you're right,' said Max.

Lily took Harry by the arm. They crossed St Giles and then turned north towards the Banbury Road. Max had thought that Harry might resist, but he was docile now and followed Lily's lead as meekly as a little lamb.

'What about his meeting?' Max asked Lily.

'I'll phone and cancel it. I'll tell the minister he's ill.'

'Okay,' said Max. 'I'll call you soon,' he added as they walked along accompanied by an almost catatonic Harry.

'It will be better if you don't,' she said. 'I had high hopes, you know. But I was very stupid to think the three of us could meet as friends.'

'But surely it can't end like this?'

'So how else could it end? I'm sure I can manage Harry now. Max, the station's that way. Off you go.'

As Lily and Harry turned away from him, Max heard a muttering, intermittent growling. Then it became a louder and continuous rumble, then it was a roar.

The vehicle raced towards them, sounding more like a Ferrari than a transit van, the driver's face a blanched and ghastly mask from Halloween, his mouth agape in horror.

A power surge or something, Max supposed much later, as he did the only thing he could. One palm flat on each of their departing backs, he pushed Lily and Harry forward, catapulting them out of harm's way, only to be crushed beneath the white van's wheels himself. He was pinned helpless, squashed like some poor insect on a windscreen, against a high stone wall.

He watched blood flow and spread, a scarlet pool. So was it his? But if it was, why did he feel no pain? Why didn't he feel anything at all?

What had happened to his legs – could they still be attached to him? But he found he wasn't bothered one way or the other. Since he was dead or nearly dead, he would not be needing them again.

He heard screams, then shouts, then clanging bells. It was one of kismet's little jokes, he thought, as he observed what happened next with clinical detachment, as if from on high, as they almost literally scraped him off the pavement, leaving behind shreds of blood-soaked clothing and maybe shreds of blood-soaked Max as well.

He'd walked and hitched and ridden with thieves and lunatics and bandits through the world's most dangerous and barbaric countries. He'd been threatened, beaten up, mock-executed twenty, thirty times, but always saved by some kind fate, only to be mown down by a van in central Oxford.

He knew from long experience the pain was bound to come. As they strapped him to a stretcher, as they loaded him into the ambulance to take him to the nearby Radcliffe, as he drifted in and out of consciousness, he thought: perhaps it's better this way? It's tidier, more convenient for everyone concerned.

Chapter Thirty-One

Max had so many visions. Lily hovered over him, a pale-faced, hollow-eyed Madonna haloed by her blue-black hair. But when he tried to reach out, touch her features, his hand met empty space.

Ditto Sarah – or somebody he assumed was Sarah; she was also there occasionally, staring down at him with big grey eyes that were exactly like her mother's.

'Why are you here?' he'd asked or tried to ask, but found he couldn't form the words. She didn't speak and in the end she'd disappeared.

The nurses – he supposed they must be nurses from the way they touched him, as if they were authorised to do whatever suited them, as if he had no say in anything – swam like fishes in a great aquarium, a shoal of blue and green.

Doctors came to talk to him occasionally, to tell him he'd been lucky. What was their definition of unlucky, he had wondered cynically. One said he had needed so much blood he'd used up all supplies of his particular group in the UK, and they had had to get some airlifted from France and Germany.

Most of the time, he slept. But sometimes he woke up for half an hour, an hour, two hours by the wall clock that was opposite his bed, and one day when the sun was streaming through the window there was Lily's shadow on his bed, and when he looked up he saw that there was Lily, too.

'You're real this time, are you?' he enquired, for nowadays reality and unreality seemed very much the same.

'What do you mean?' She took his hand. 'Of course I'm real!'

'How long have you been sitting here?'

'About an hour, I think. I've come to see you every day, of course, but most of the time you've been unconscious. You're on so much morphine you've probably got a poppy field that's all your own out in Afghanistan.'

'Why do you come?'

'What a silly question, Max! I have to come. When I thought you were dying, I was beside myself. I didn't know how I'd manage to survive if you should die.'

'I nearly did. I tried to bleed to death at least three times. A doctor told me I've had thirty pints of blood. I had twenty in one single operation, so he said.'

'Yes, I believe you did.'

'How much longer will I be in here, do you know?'

'They're going to kick you out next week. They need your bed. You're going to a nursing home.'

'We'll work something out,' said Lily as they sat together in the nursing home surrounded by the clutter that came with Max's disabilities.

'We?' said Max. 'What you do next is up to you, of course. But you don't need to worry about me. After all, you must have other options.'

'I don't have other options, Max. I want to be with you. I've always wanted you.'

'But after what I said to you in Delhi – you do remember, don't you?'

'Yes, I do,' said Lily. 'But you were an idiot to say it and I was an even bigger idiot to believe you.'

'When you married Harry, were you in love with him?'

'I liked Harry lots – and yes, I loved him. But it was a

gentle, passive love. I never felt for Harry what I feel for you. Max, I've made my mind up. I'm going to make a home for you. It's time you had a home.'

'You want to be my nurse?'

'Of course – you'll need a nurse.'

'I'll need nurses, doctors, physiotherapists – the works. I shall need to learn to walk again, that's if it's even possible, and they've already told me it's looking quite unlikely. There's some damage to my spine, as well. I've lost a lot of feeling. So as for being – I mean I doubt if I'll be any good to anyone in bed.'

'You think that's all women care about?'

'I think it's quite important, isn't it? I'm sure no reasonable woman wants a cripple who is impotent as well?'

'You won't be impotent and you won't be a cripple. I won't let you be a cripple.'

'But my strolling-through-the-jungle days are over and the next few years will be quite difficult for me, and anyone around me. I shall hate to be confined. I shall be bad-tempered, surly, angry. When you're sad, upset or worried, I shall look at you and think you're sorry that you tied yourself to me. I'll worry that you'll leave me. I'll be paranoid and jealous. I won't like it even when you go to Waitrose. When you're not with me, I'll think that you're in bed with someone who can be a man with you.'

'I believe you love me and you'll trust me.'

'I would like to think so, but all this is so new to me I don't know what I'll do. Lily, being with me will be the opposite of glamorous and romantic.'

'Whatever you do, whatever you say, I'm going to stay with you.' Lily took his face between her hands and kissed him on the mouth. 'I need you in all sorts of ways and you need me. You know you do. I don't mean for sex. Yes, it was good that time, I don't deny. But it was never such a big, important issue for us – was it?'

'I don't know,' said Max. 'I don't understand why you want me. As you know, I'm selfish. I've spent most of my life sponging off people who have little enough already, instead of helping them.'

'Oh, don't be stupid, you're not selfish. What about your television work? Over the years, you've raised some very important issues, and I'm sure this has resulted in people giving more to charity. When that van came at us, why did you not jump out of harm's way? Why didn't you let it hit us? Or let it hit Harry, anyway? After what he said to you, I don't think I'd have blamed you. But your instinct was to save us, even though you must have thought – you must have known – you would be hit yourself.'

'I didn't know anything. I wasn't thinking, certainly. There was no time to think.'

'If you didn't think, that makes it even better – don't you see? It means you automatically put other people first. You saved us, not yourself. Whatever version of yourself you like to show the world, the bad boy who does anything, goes anywhere, does what the hell he likes, the real Max is naturally unselfish, altruistic.'

'You think so?'

'Max, I know so.'

'It's you and me at last, then?'

'Yes, Max – you and me.'

'We'll get married, shall we?'

'I don't think we need a piece of paper and, since everybody thinks we're sinners anyway, let's just live in sin.'

Lily had the house in Oxford redesigned to suit an invalid, and four months after he'd been injured Max moved into it.

It wasn't easy, looking after Max and working, too. He was an impatient cripple, as he called himself, always trying to push himself too far, and furious when he failed to make the progress he'd decided was essential.

Bad days outnumbered good days five to one. But the good days were amazing, wonderful, made up for all the bad days, made Lily's heart sing like a nightingale.

'I miss him very much, you know,' said Max.

'So do I,' said Lily, who didn't need to ask Max who he meant.

'I don't know how we can go forward.'

'I don't, either.' Lily shook her head. 'All we can do is give it time. You never know, he might come round. One day, he might forgive us.'

Max's disabilities were not an issue. Lily often told him so. When you loved somebody, she explained, it really didn't matter what they looked like, walked like, acted like, if you could have any kind of sex with them or none.

You saw past things like that.

But Sarah was an issue. She was so like Max in many ways. She looked like him, rebelled like him, dropped out of further education like him, leaving Cambridge halfway through her second year to travel in the Middle East, writing up her notes in volume form and a few years later getting published, just like him.

When Harry and Lily were divorced, Harry had been civilised and fairly reasonable about it, agreeing to divide their assets fifty-fifty, obviously determined not to fatten any lawyers by picking any fights, resigned to letting Lily keep the house in Oxford while he moved to London permanently.

Sarah had been furious when Lily set up home with

Max. She didn't speak to Lily for a year, and she refused to speak to Max at all.

'But he's your father,' Lily pointed out, when – temporarily back in the UK – Sarah agreed to meet her mother for a casual coffee in a big department store, the perfect neutral space, full of the muted buzzing of a hundred busy shoppers, one afternoon in Oxford.

'He is not my father,' Sarah said. 'Harry Gale's my father. Max is just someone my mother – well, you know.'

'I think you're old enough to stop this Harry-is-my-father-and-I-don't-need-another-father stuff.'

'When you went to bed with Max, I think you were old enough to know you were betraying your fiancé, were acting like a – Mum, don't make me say it.'

'Just wait until you fall in love yourself, my girl, until you meet somebody who gives meaning to your life.'

'So it wasn't just a one night stand, then, like you said before? When you were going on about it being only once?'

'Sarah, is it always going to be like this between us?'

'Be like what?'

'You know.'

'I know it's time I went,' said Sarah. 'I need to catch a plane.'

'Where are you off to this time?'

'Lima.'

'Where is Lima?'

'It's the capital of Peru.'

'Be careful, darling, won't you?'

'Yeah yeah yeah,' said Sarah. 'Mum, I'm always careful. I don't have a death wish, honestly, not like some people we could mention.' She scooped her coat up, shrugged it on. She pecked her mother on the cheek and gave her a quick hug. 'Off you go, Mum, home to Max – and don't give him my love.'

Lily watched her daughter stride out of the restaurant then did as she was told – went home to Max.

'It's okay,' he said when Lily told him what had happened, how the meeting had turned out to be abortive. 'Sarah can't help how she feels. Nobody can help their feelings. You and I know that.'

'But we can all decide how we behave.'

'How many times have you known very well you shouldn't say or do a thing, decided not to do it, but done it anyway?'

'Maybe once or twice,' admitted Lily. 'You're looking better these days. How's the walking?'

'I managed to get up and down the hall this afternoon. I went into the kitchen, filled the kettle and then I made a coffee. I didn't scald myself or spill a drop.'

'Jolly good – that's excellent,' said Lily. 'So no more lazing round the place, you hear? I think I ought to get you making three course dinners soon.'

'I'm a hopeless cook,' said Max. 'You need a wife.'

'I do.'

'I think we should get married. You said it didn't matter, we don't need a piece of paper, but I'd like to make it legal.'

'You want to be a househusband?'

'Yes,' said Max. 'I do.'

Chapter Thirty-Two

'Sarah says she's getting married,' Lily told him. 'It will be quite soon, as well. I wonder if she's pregnant? I didn't like to ask.'

Max remembered telling Harry many years ago he'd like a daughter. He'd long since realised he would never have one, or not in the fullest sense, or not with the only woman he'd have wanted one. But now it seemed he might one day have grandchildren.

After speaking on the phone to Sarah in the middle of the night – when Sarah was abroad she never bothered to check time zones – Lily made them both a mug of chocolate then got back into bed.

'Anyone we know?' asked Max as Lily stirred and sipped.

'A Colombian she met on a beach in the Galapagos. He's twenty-nine, writes poetry and loves to scuba-dive. She won't tell me any more about him. I don't know if she'll ask us to the wedding or where it will be.'

'She'll want to invite her mother, won't she? I'll pay for everything, of course, whether I'm asked or not. Did I ever say I made a will? I made it years ago, before I knew about her being mine. I've left Sarah everything.'

'Oh, Max – that's so kind of you! But you know she won't care about your will. Sarah is like you. She'll do exactly what she pleases, and damn the rest of us.'

'I still think she'll ask you to her wedding.'

Sarah asked them both and was quite cordial about it in her letter to the two of them.

A determined atheist, but also contradictory as always, she was marrying her Colombian – who turned out to be a biochemist with a degree from Harvard, not a beach bum, as Sarah had led Lily to believe, and whose parents looked like Spanish royalty – in a church in Oxfordshire.

Max decided he would give it one last try. So, as the guests were milling round the churchyard, telling each other that it was a lovely day, he escaped from Lily. She was talking to her parents, fussing round her father who had had some health scares recently, and he didn't think she'd see him go.

Sitting on a bench beside the lychgate, he waited for the wedding limousine. When it arrived and she got out, he saw Sarah was so beautiful and looked so much like Lily that it almost made him cry. She took Harry's arm and walked towards him, gliding like a swan.

But he was in deep shadow and they clearly hadn't seen him. 'Dad, it's nearly time,' Sarah was saying. 'You don't want to do it, but you have to hand me over to another man today.'

She kissed him on the cheek. 'Please don't look so sad,' she whispered softly. 'You know you'll always be the most important person in the world to me.'

'Your husband needs to be the most important person in your world,' said Harry gravely.

'Yes, but you're always going to be my dad.'

They walked on towards the church, a father and his daughter on her wedding day.

Lily tracked Max down at last. He was sitting on a tombstone in the furthest corner of the churchyard, head in hands. When he looked up, she saw his face was grey.

'What's the matter, love?' she asked him gently. 'Do you

need some pain relief? I have some of your tablets in my bag.'

'No, I'm fine,' said Max.

'You're not.'

'I saw them,' he told Lily. 'I watched them as he walked with Sarah up the path and now I know that Harry is her only father, always was and always will be.'

'She still cares about you.'

'Does she?'

'Yes!'

'She never wants to see me. I think she must hate me.'

'She doesn't hate you, Max.'

Then Lily knew she had to tell him something – something she had meant to tell him long ago, but now realised she had needed to keep in reserve for an occasion like today. 'Max, when you were hurt, you needed lots of blood.'

'I know.'

'Thirty pints, I think you said a doctor told you?'

'Yes.'

'Two of those were Sarah's.'

'What?' Max's head jerked up. He stared at Lily. 'I'd assumed they'd got the whole lot from the banks. But you're saying Sarah gave me blood?'

'She did.'

'While I was in hospital, I thought I saw her once or twice. But she didn't speak or touch me so I thought I was hallucinating.'

'She's confused,' said Lily. 'She and Harry fell in love the day that she was born. But about the blood for you – nobody forced her hand. She offered.'

'Why?'

'I think it was because she had no choice. She had to do

it. It was like when you saved me and Harry. You didn't have a choice. Sarah is a copy of you through and through, whatever she might say.'

'She loves Harry, Lily.'

'But she's still your daughter and she can't get out of that. Biology, you know?'

'It's scary stuff.'

'It is indeed.' Lily helped him stumble to his feet. 'Come on, they must be about to start.'

Lily and Max found Sarah and Harry in the porch, where they were presumably still waiting for the organ to strike up. Harry was fussing over Sarah's veil. 'Oh, Farley – there you are at last,' he said. 'Where've you been? Sarah mustn't keep her bridegroom waiting for all eternity. Sarah, love – Max should be on your right. Then he can use his stick.'

Sarah looked at Max. 'Dad and I decided my wedding day's a time for new beginnings.'

'Yes, for us all,' said Harry.

'So, Max,' said Sarah, 'if you like—'

She offered him her hand.

Lily glanced from one man to the other and saw the happiness on both their faces. 'I'll see you all inside,' she said.

Fifteen minutes later, as Sarah and her husband turned to walk back down the aisle, Harry glanced at Lily, smiled a proud, paternal smile.

'As parents, we did well, I think?' he asked.

Lily was astonished, almost dumbstruck. But, at last, she managed to find her voice. 'Yes,' she replied. 'I think we did.'

'Come on, I'll help you to get Farley up,' said Harry. 'He still looks unsteady on his feet. Some time,' he added, 'the three of us should try to get together. We could have a beer in The Lamb and Flag, perhaps? It would be like old times – when we were students – you and me and Farley in the Lamb.'

'You've missed Max, haven't you?'

'I suppose so,' he admitted sheepishly.

'He's missed you.' She smiled and took his arm. 'Let's fix a date to have that beer,' she said.

Thank You

Dear Reader

Thank you so much for coming on Lily's, Harry's and Max's journey with me.

I hope you enjoyed the rather turbulent ride and you felt that all three of them got what they desired and also deserved. I always wanted to give this story a happy ending but I hope it's also a believable one.

As writers, we all value feedback from readers and we are especially grateful when a reader finds the time to post a review online or to write to us. You can find my contact details in my author profile. I would love to hear from you.

Happy reading and – if you are a writer as well as a reader – happy writing, too. I know that when a story works well it's the best feeling in the world for both the reader and the writer!

Thank you once again for spending time with my characters and me.

My very best wishes

Margaret

About the Author

Margaret James was born and brought up in Hereford and now lives in Devon. She studied English at London University, and has written many short stories, articles and serials for magazines. She is the author of seventeen published novels.

Her debut novel for Choc Lit, *The Silver Locket*, received a glowing review from the *Daily Mail* and reached the Top 20 Small Publishers Fiction List in November 2010 and in the same year a Reviewers' Choice Award from Single Titles. *The Golden Chain* also hit the Top 20 Small Publishers Fiction List in May 2011.

Margaret is a long-standing contributor to *Writing Magazine* for which she writes the Fiction Focus column and an author interview for each issue. She's also a creative writing tutor for the London School of Journalism.

Girl in Red Velvet is Margaret's sixth book with Choc Lit. Her others include the historical 'Charton Minster' trilogy: *The Silver Locket*, *The Golden Chain* and *The Penny Bangle*. She has also published two contemporary novels: *The Wedding Diary* and *Magic Sometimes Happens*, which are linked to the Charton Minster Trilogy.

For more information on Margaret visit:
www.twitter.com/majanovelist
www.margaretjamesblog.blogspot.com

More Choc Lit

From Margaret James

The Silver Locket

Charton Minster series

*Winner of 2010 Reviewers'
Choice Award for Single Titles*

**If life is cheap, how
much is love worth?**

It's 1914 and young Rose
Courtenay has a decision
to make. Please her wealthy
parents by marrying the man
of their choice – or play her
part in the war effort?

The chance to escape proves irresistible and Rose becomes a
nurse. Working in France, she meets Lieutenant Alex Denham,
a dark figure from her past. He's the last man in the world
she'd get involved with – especially now he's married.

But in wartime nothing is as it seems. Alex's marriage is a
sham and Rose is the only woman he's ever wanted. As he
recovers from his wounds, he sets out to win her trust. His
gift of a silver locket is a far cry from the luxuries she's left
behind.

What value will she put on his love?

Available in paperback from all good
bookshops and online stores. Visit
www.choc-lit.com for details.

The Golden Chain

Charton Minster series

Can first love last forever?

1931 is the year that changes everything for Daisy Denham. Her family has not long swapped life in India for Dorset, England when she uncovers an old secret.

At the same time, she meets Ewan Fraser – a handsome dreamer who wants nothing more than to entertain the world and for Daisy to play his leading lady.

Ewan offers love and a chance to escape with a touring theatre company. As they grow closer, he gives her a golden chain and Daisy gives him a promise – that she will always keep him in her heart.

But life on tour is not as they'd hoped. Ewan is tempted away by his career and Daisy is dazzled by the older, charismatic figure of Jesse Trent. She breaks Ewan's heart and sets off for a life in London with Jesse.

Only time will tell whether some promises are easier to make than keep …

Available in paperback from all good bookshops and online stores. Visit www.choc-lit.com for details.

The Penny Bangle

Charton Minster series

When should you trust your heart?

It's 1942 when Cassie Taylor reluctantly leaves Birmingham to become a land girl on a farm in Dorset.

There she meets Robert and Stephen Denham, twins recovering from injuries sustained at Dunkirk. Cassie is instantly drawn to Stephen, but is wary of the more complex Robert – who doesn't seem to like Cassie one little bit.

At first, Robert wants to sack the inexperienced city girl. But Cassie soon learns, and Robert comes to admire her courage, finding himself deeply attracted to Cassie. Just as their romance blossoms, he's called back into active service.

Anxious to have adventures herself, Cassie joins the ATS. In Egypt, she meets up with Robert, and they become engaged. However, war separates them again as Robert is sent to Italy and Cassie back to the UK.

Robert is reported missing, presumed dead. Stephen wants to take Robert's place in Cassie's heart. But will Cassie stay true to the memory of her first love, and will Robert come home again?

Available in paperback from all good bookshops and online stores. Visit www.choc-lit.com for details.

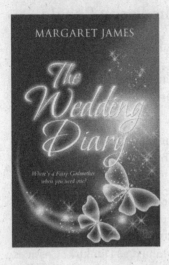

The Wedding Diary

Charton Minster series

Shortlisted for the 2014 Romantic Novel of the Year award

Where's a Fairy Godmother when you need one?

If you won a fairy-tale wedding in a luxury hotel, you'd be delighted – right? But what if you didn't have anyone to marry? Cat Aston did have a fiancé, but now it looks like her Prince Charming has done a runner.

Adam Lawley was left devastated when his girlfriend turned down his heartfelt proposal. He's made a vow never to fall in love again.

So – when Cat and Adam meet, they shouldn't even consider falling in love. After all, they're both broken hearted. But for some reason they can't stop thinking about each other. Is this their second chance for happiness, or are some things just too good to be true?

Available in paperback from all good bookshops and online stores. Visit www.choc-lit.com for details.